Mornings on Main

**Also available from
Jodi Thomas
and HQN Books**

The Ransom Canyon Series

JODI THOMAS

Mornings on Main

Jefferson Madison
Regional Library
Charlottesville, Virginia

Recycling programs
for this product may
not exist in your area.

ISBN-13: 978-0-373-80417-7

Mornings on Main

www.HQNBooks.com

Printed in U.S.A.

Mornings on Main

1

Laurel Springs, Texas, had the warm feel of a Southern town long forgotten by progress. A hundred years ago the main street had been built wide enough to turn a wagon around. Today, the only sign of change was marked at every intersection by swinging stoplights. They clanked in the wind like broken clocks beating out time in red and green.

A trickle of day visitors flowed down the uneven sidewalks in front of quaint little shops with catchy names like A Stitch in Time, Hidden Treasures and Mamma Bee's Pastries. Occasional sides of buildings and entrances to alleyways were painted with murals of cattle drives and oil fields, as if anyone needed reminding what built this state.

Jillian James drove through the heart of town, fighting back tears. This wasn't where she wanted to be. It was impossible to remain invisible in a small town. Strangers would be noticed. People would ask questions. Welcome her with smiles or glare at her like no one ever did in large cities.

She dropped her chin, letting her dark, straight hair curtain her face as she waited for the light to change.

Look at the bright side, she almost said out loud. Time slowed in a place like this, and she had to catch her breath. She had to plan her next move. A small town. A slower pace would give her time to think.

She'd been a traveler, a wanderer for as long as she could remember, and like it or not, this town offered her a place to rest and regroup.

In a strange way, this dot on the map reminded her of Budapest, Hungary. But a creek ran through the center of this town, not the Danube river. No hauntingly beautiful Chain Bridge joined the split cities as it did in Buda and Pest, but she sensed the beat of two separate towns between the city limit signs.

Two worlds divided by a ribbon of water.

One side of town was dark and industrial, with warehouses and grain elevators that blocked the sunset to the west. The other side was postcard cute, with gingerbread trim on brightly painted cottages and the Texas flag hanging from nineteenth-century streetlamps.

Here she was, stopped at a tolling light in the middle of town. Not belonging to either side. Not belonging anywhere. At first, her traveling had been an adventure she thought she was born for, but lately it felt like drifting. Just wandering with no more direction than the leaves dancing along the gutters.

Sniffing, she managed a smile, remembering what her father used to tell her every time they packed. *If you want to see the world, Jillie, you've got to rip off the rearview mirror and never look back.*

Somehow, she doubted he'd been talking about Laurel Springs, Texas, when he'd said *the world*. She'd grown up moving with him. Alaska in the summers, the oil rigs off the coast of Texas in winters. Norway when she was eight. Australia at ten. Washington State when she reached her teens, and a dozen other places. Never the same. Never staying long enough to grow roots.

When she was eighteen, he'd left her at a dorm on a small college campus in Oklahoma and disappeared without a trace. She'd made it two semesters before her money ran out. She hadn't bothered to look for him. Her father had spent her formative years teaching her how to live without leaving a footprint to follow.

Travel light, he'd once said. *Pack nothing from the past, not even memories.* And, finally, he'd left without packing her along. Deep down she'd known he would leave someday. Whenever he talked of her as grown, he never mentioned being in the picture.

Only now, a dozen years later, she longed for an anchor. One relative. One harbor. One place where she felt she might belong for a while.

The light changed. Jillian scrubbed her face with a napkin from McDonald's, where she'd had lunch, and followed a sign advertising the town's only historic bed-and-breakfast.

Papa's rule: *Never stay at a cheap motel. It marks you as a drifter.*

A small bed-and-breakfast was cheaper if you considered the one meal a day could stretch into two if you picked up fruit on the way out, and the friendly staff usually offered a wealth of information. Innkeepers almost made Jillian feel like she had a friend in town.

She parked her car in one of the four Special Guest of Inn reserved spots.

When she climbed the steps of what looked like a minia-ture Tara mansion from *Gone With the Wind*, a tiny woman, in her late fifties, rushed out with a welcoming smile. Her chocolate-colored apron was neatly embroidered and read *JOIN THE DARK SIDE. We have chocolate chips in our cookies.*

"You must be Jillian James. I'm Mrs. Kelly, the innkeeper, but the locals call me Mrs. K. I've got your room all ready, dear. Did you have a nice drive? The internet didn't give us a home address on you so I don't know how long your journey was, but I hope it wasn't too far. Don't you just love our town?"

Papa's rule: *Never give out too much information. It'll trip you up.*

"I had a great drive and I love your beautiful home. You'll have to tell me a bit of the history of this place." Jil-lian smiled, thinking of one of her own rules. *Never try to outtalk a talker.*

"Of course, dear. This house is old enough to have not only a history, but a ghost, as well, though he's quite shy." The innkeeper handed her the key, then they climbed all the way up to Jillian's room on the third floor. "I'll tell you about Willie Flancher over coffee some cloudy morning. It's the only time to talk about ghosts, you know. Folks in town talk about the house Flancher's Folly because he built it for his fifth wife and died on their wedding night."

Jillian didn't care about ghost stories. All she wanted was a quiet, clean place to stay for a while. Third floor, back of the house. Usually least expensive and quietest.

Once Jillian circled the tiny room, she gave an admiring smile. This room would be perfect. Just what she needed.

The chubby innkeeper, who was very spry for her fifties, moved to the door and made her official announcement, "Breakfast at eight, if that's all right. Soft drinks in the small fridge on the landing, and I put cookies out in the parlor after sunset for those who like a late snack."

"Thank you." Jillian pulled off her coat. "I think I'll rest before I explore the town."

"You do that, dear. There are maps in the foyer but you're only a half block from Main, so you can park your car around back and walk if you like." Mrs. Kelly's head rocked back and forth as if ticking off an invisible list of what she needed to say. "I'll see you in the morning. You're the only one booked up here tonight. Both my other guests are on the first floor. No one wants to climb two flights of stairs these days."

"I don't mind." Setting her suitcase and backpack down, Jillian grinned when she spotted the wide window. "It's worth the climb for the view alone."

Mrs. Kelly smiled as she backed out of the room. "I agree."

When the lock clicked, Jillian pulled out her ledger and curled up in a window seat that had three times more pillows than it needed. On a blank page she wrote the date and "Day 1" beside it, along with the cost of the night's lodging: "Winter rate: sixty-three dollars."

Papa's rule: *Always keep count or you might lose track of how long you stay and forget to leave.*

She had to be very careful. Thanks to car trouble a month ago and two crummy bosses in a row, she was less than a thousand dollars away from having to sleep in her car—or worse, a shelter. In her ten years on the road, she'd ended

up broke twice before. Once in California when someone
had stolen her purse, and again in New York City when
she'd been in a wreck. None of her belongings had made
it to the hospital with her. Both times she'd lost not only
her money, but also her identification.

Papa's rule: *Always keep copies of vital papers somewhere safe.
Birth certificate, driver's license, passport, social security card.*

In New York, without money and looking like she'd
been in a street fight, it had taken her three months to
collect enough cash to buy a bus ticket to Oklahoma City.
There, she'd found her stash, money, ID and the letter, still
unopened, that she'd left for her father just in case he ever
used the secret hiding place beneath a shelf in the basement
of the downtown library. Both times she'd come back to
the hiding place, her stash was still there and the letter was
unopened.

If he'd dropped by, he'd left no sign, and she doubted
when she circled past Oklahoma City again that anything
would be different. All her papers and the mailbox she
rarely checked showed her as from Oklahoma. When she'd
asked her father if that were true, he'd simply said, "Oklahoma City is the center of the country and as good a place
as any to be from."

Jillian took a shower and changed into dress pants and a
sweater. She was close enough to her stash now to relax. If
she had to, she could make the drive northwest for more
cash in a matter of hours, but somehow that would mean
she'd failed.

She wasn't running to or from anything. She wasn't hiding out. She just wanted to continue drifting. It was all she
knew. Maybe in a few more years, she'd come up with an-

other plan. Maybe she'd drift forever. To do that, she had
to get better—smarter—at managing.

As she always did, she unpacked her few belongings.
Clothes on hangers in the closet. Underwear in the top
drawer. Shoes and backpack in the bottom drawer. Her father's tiny journals on the nightstand beside the bed. Everything in order.

Her billfold and her laptop slid into her shoulder bag.
The laptop went everywhere with her. The backup drive
always remained with her clothes tucked away in the back
of a shelf or tucked into a pocket. Against her father's advice, she kept details of everywhere she stopped, be it for
one night or a few months. He might have jotted only zip
codes and number of days stayed, but she liked to log in
the history of each place, how it looked, how it might feel
to live there.

Walking out of her room, she studied the polished old
mahogany of the staircase. The faded wallpaper peeling
free in places, reminding her of fragile lace. The house was
beautiful and well cared for, like an aging queen, still standing on a street with abandoned and broken-down homes
huddled near, as if hoping the memory of great days gone
by might still live in reality's shadow.

Slipping past the foyer, Jillian rushed down the front steps
like an explorer hungry to begin digging. This town's zip
code, like dozens of others, had been listed in her father's
first journals. Maybe in his early years, he'd left a trace.

She told herself she'd feel it if he'd been here. If this was
the place where he'd stopped wandering just long enough
to care for someone.

But she felt only the cool winter wind whipping between buildings, whirling her around as if pushing her off any direct course.

A few blocks later, she was strolling down Main, her still-damp hair swinging in a ponytail. She blended in with the crowds, window-shopping, as if she had no direction. The smell of cinnamon and ginger drifted in the winter air, blending around pieces of conversations and laughter like icing melts into warm cake.

Jillian swore she could feel her heart slow. The very air in Laurel Springs seemed to welcome her.

Halfway down the block she found what she was looking for. A small help-wanted sign in the corner of a window.

Above hung a faded sign that read LAUREL SPRINGS DAILY.

She let out a breath through her smile. Newspaper work. She could handle that. Selling ads. Writing copy. No problem. Mentally, she made up her resume in her head. Nothing too fancy, nothing too bright. Nothing too easy to check.

As she pushed open the newspaper office door, she selected a new identity as easily as she might change a hat.

2

Connor Larady looked up from the copy machine he'd been trying to murder for an hour. "Morning," he said as he set down his latest weapon of destruction, a screwdriver. "May I help you, miss?"

The woman clamoring through his office door was tall and slim enough to be a model. With hair in a ponytail and little makeup, she could have still been in her teens, but the wisdom in her big, rainy-day-colored eyes marked her as a good ten years older.

He shoved his tools aside, walked over to the front desk and tried to find a scrap of paper to write on. No one ever came into a newspaper office without either wanting something written, or rewritten.

You'd think a writer would have a pen and pad handy. Only he wasn't much of a writer, and this wasn't much of an office. The *Laurel Springs Daily* had been whittled down to little more than a weekly flyer and a spotty blog of what was happening in town when he got around to it, but he kept up the office his father and grandfather had both run.

Considering himself a good judge of people, Connor had

a premonition he'd be filling out a free obit form or a lost dog report, also free.

There were some days he'd thought of combining the two columns in the weekly paper. The header could read LEFT TOWN FOR PARTS UNKNOWN. The byline could be Those Recently Departed or Run Over.

The woman moved one small step closer. Connor had no idea if she was just shy or half-afraid of him. Maybe his grandmother and daughter were right: he was starting to look like the mug shots on the Dallas nightly news. Hair too long, this was the third day he'd worn the same old wrinkled shirt, and he hadn't bothered to remove the raincoat his gram said only a vampire would wear.

He'd tried to tell them both that he didn't have time to commit a crime. He was too busy running the town and keeping up with them. His grandmother had taken to wandering off alone, and his daughter was worse. She preferred wandering off with any pimpled-faced, oversexed boy who had a driver's license. Between the two of them, his curly brown hair would be gray before he turned forty. That is, if it decided to stay around at all.

Connor shoved his worries aside and waited for the attractive stranger to say something. Anything. Or run back out the door. He didn't much care which. He had more than enough to deal with this morning, and he didn't want to hear a complaint. Everyone thought if you were the mayor, you loved listening in detail of what was wrong in town.

Maybe this stranger just wanted to talk, or ask directions?

Conversation wasn't his strong point. Plus, she was just the kind of woman who made him nervous—pretty, and near his age. With his luck, any second she'd decide there was more to him than people could see and would start trying to remake him into marriage material.

Maybe he should wear a sign. TO ALL WOMEN: I AM MADE OF MUD. NO MATTER WHAT YOU MOLD ME INTO, WHEN IT RAINS, I'M BACK TO MUD. *Save us both some time and move on to another project.*

Raising her head, she studied him a moment, then said, without smiling, "I'm here about the job."

"What job?" He hadn't had a secretary for two years. That had been a disaster. He could go slowly bankrupt by himself without a helper continually suggesting they buy supplies or turn up the heater, or paint the place.

The attractive woman before him tilted her head, and he noticed her eyes weren't quite blue or gray, but they were looking directly at him. "The help-wanted sign posted?"

She'd said the words slowly as if he might need time to absorb them. "I can write copy, proofread fairly fast, and I'm willing to try any type of reporting."

He lifted an eyebrow, thinking maybe he should recite his resume to her if that was how she wanted to introduce herself. One degree in English, one in history, a master's in anthropology. None of which had ever earned him a dime. Come to think of it, maybe he was slow? No one had bothered to tell him that he was wasting his time in school.

This stranger in town pointed at the faded note in the window and his brain clicked on. "Oh, that job's not here at the paper. It's across the street at the quilt shop." He pointed out the window to A Stitch in Time, the shop directly across Main.

"It's been so long since I put it there, I forgot about the sign."

"Sorry to have bothered you." She turned, obviously not a woman to waste time.

"Wait." He hadn't had a single bite for the job at the quilt shop in weeks. Everyone in town knew what it was and no one wanted it. But this outsider just might be dumb enough to take it. "It's only a short-term job. Three or four months at the most, but it pays fifteen dollars an hour if you have the right skills."

"What skills?"

She wasn't running at the thought of working in a quilt shop. That was a good sign. "My grandmother has owned the town's quilt shop for over fifty years. She's closing down, but what we need done has to be accomplished carefully. Every quilt in the place has to be cataloged for the county museum. She holds the history of this town in there."

Connor had no idea how to say what he needed to say, but he had to be honest. "Gram's slipping a little. Beginning to forget things. Over the years she's collected and made quilts that mean a great deal to the people of Laurel Springs. They'll have to be treated with care. The history of each one logged and photographed."

"Museum-quality preservation. I understand. I worked at the Southwest Collection on the Texas Tech campus while I was in college. My salary will be twenty an hour for that detailed kind of work."

She stood her ground and he had no doubt she knew what to do. Which was more than he knew about the process. The county curator had been excited about the collection but offered no time or advice.

Now Connor was sure he was the one afraid of her. "All right. I'll walk you over and let you meet my grandmother.

If you last an hour, you're on the payroll. She'll be the boss. Some days you'll be working at her pace."

Nodding, she passed through the front door he held open. When they started across the street, she hesitated. "Aren't you going to lock your office door?"

"What, and hamper anyone trying to steal my copier? No way."

The woman was giving him that look again. She'd obviously decided he was missing critical brain cells.

"I'm Jillian James." She held out her hand, palm up as if to say, *your turn next.*

"Connor Larady." He grinned. "I'm the town mayor."

She didn't look impressed. She'd probably heard he'd run unopposed.

Without another word, they stepped inside the quilt shop. He didn't miss her slight gasp as she looked up at the size of the place. It widened out from the small storefront windows in a pie-slice shape, with two stories opening to an antique tin ceiling. Massive fans turned slowly, so far above he couldn't feel the air move.

Every inch of the twenty-foot-high walls was covered in colorful quilts; a collage of fabric rainbows.

Deep shelves lined the wall behind the wide front counter. Folded quilts were stacked five deep for a dozen rows.

"This may take longer than three months," she whispered.

"I'll help," he offered. "But I should tell you, Gram is in charge here. This is her world, so whatever she wants goes. I don't want the cataloging to cause her any stress."

"I understand."

"I'm not sure you do." He looked at her closely, wondering how much to tell a stranger. "We're working against a ticking clock and it's in Gram's head. The cataloging, the inventory, may not always be her priority. You may have to gently guide her back to the task."

Her intelligent eyes looked straight at him, and he guessed she was one of those rare people who listened, really listened.

"I can put in overtime and will work Saturdays, but I can't promise you I'll stay in town more than three months. If you think I can complete the job by then, I'll give it my best shot."

"I understand," he said, even though he didn't. Why couldn't she stay longer? Who moves to a town for three months? Someone just killing time, he reasoned.

A mix of conversation and laughter came from the back of the shop where the ceiling lowered to eight feet, allowing room for a storage room above and a meeting room below.

Connor took the lead. Unlike the stranger, he knew exactly what he was walking into. The twice-a-week quilting bee. An old frame hung from the beams, allowing just enough room for chairs to circle the quilt being hand-stitched together. It might be a lost art in most places, but here, the women seemed to love not only the project, but the company.

The moment the ladies saw him their voices rose in greeting. All eight of them seemed to be talking to him at once. As soon as he greeted each one, he introduced Jillian James to them. "I've hired Jillian to help catalog my grandmother's collection. Gram's got a great treasure here in her shop."

The ladies agreed with his plan, but two reminded him that it would be a long time before his gram retired.

His grandmother, Eugenia Ann Freeman Larady, slowly stood and offered her hand to Jillian. Where Connor had been told his eyes were Mississippi River brown, his gram's had faded to the pale blue of shallow water. Every year she'd aged he'd grown more protective of her, but today he needed to take a step backward and see how she got along with a stranger brought in to work with her.

Gram winked at Jillian as if she already counted her as a friend. "Call me Gram if you like. All Connor's friends do."

"Gram," Jillian said with a genuine smile.

"I've decided." The willowy old dear cleared her throat before continuing. "I'll probably be working on a quilt when the good Lord calls me home and I'll have to say, 'Just give me time to finish the binding, then I'll come dancing through the Pearly Gates.'"

He'd heard her say those words a thousand times over the years. Now, most of what she said were old sayings like that. New ideas, new thoughts, were rare.

"Gram," he said gently. "Jillian wants to help you get these quilts all in order so someday they'll be on display in the county museum."

His grandmother nodded as she looked around the shop, every inch of its wall space covered in quilts. Gram smiled. "I'd like that. I'll even get out my pioneer quilts. The ones brought here in covered wagons. Some are worn. They were used, you know, but then, that's what quilts are made for, too. Plain or fancy, they wrap us in our families' warmth."

"She'll write down the details and take pictures so you

can show them all off at once to your friends," Connor pressed, hoping Gram understood.

Eugenia had lost interest in talking to him. She took Jillian's hand and tugged her to the only empty chair around the six-foot square of material pulled so tightly on the quilting frame it could almost have served as a table. "Before we start, we have to work on this quilt. Dixie pieced it for her niece, and the wedding is in two weeks. Hand quilting takes time."

Connor moved away as the ladies folded Jillian into the group. She glanced over at him, looking as if she hoped he'd toss her a life preserver.

He shook his head. "We'll go over the details later," he said, low enough for only Jillian to hear. "As of right now, you're on the clock. I'll return at a little after five."

At the door he looked back, wondering if the tall woman would still be there at closing time.

Once on the street, Connor walked left toward the natural park entrance near the bridge. He dodged traffic, three cars and a pickup, then headed down a trail to the creek. A stream meandered through Laurel Springs as wild as it had been when his people settled here. The tall grass, dry now, appeared bunched in thick clumps over the uneven land. Huge old cypress trees huddled by the water, hauntingly gray in their dusty winter coats. February. The one month he'd always thought of as void of color.

Connor could breathe here by the stream. He could think. He could relax.

The rambling acres running untamed through town were more swamp than park now, but next spring the city would have the money to clean it up. They'd fight back nature to

make running trails and small meadows spotted with picnic tables.

But Connor craved the wildness of this spot in winter.
The cold. The loneliness of it. As he strolled near the water,
the sounds of the town almost disappeared, and he could
believe for a few minutes that he was totally by himself.
That he was free. No responsibilities. No worries.

Duty would pull him back soon. It always did. But for
a while he could allow his mind to drift, to dream. There
were days in his organized, packed routine that all Connor
wanted to do was run away.

Only he never would.

Some people are meant to grow where they're planted.

Jillian's words echoed in his thoughts. *I can't promise you
I'll be here in three months,* she'd said, as if it were a possibility for everyone. Didn't she know that the people in this
town of Laurel Springs were like the residents of the mythi-
cal Brigadoon: they lived here forever, and she was simply
a visitor for a day?

A story danced in his head as he walked through the
dried buffalo grass of winter. The stiff stalks made a swish-
ing sound, like a brush lightly moving over a drum. His
imagination was all the escape he needed most days.

He was leaving his world, his reality, his home, if only
for an hour. If only in his mind.

3

Jillian closed her eyes for a moment and took a deep breath. She loved the smells of the quilt shop. Lavender soap left on the women's skin as they routinely washed their hands so no perspiration stained the quilt. Lemon wax on the eighty-year-old counter that had been left behind when a mercantile became the quilt shop. The smell of cotton, fresh and new, blended with the hint of dyes pressed into material. She even liked the scent of the oil on the hundred-year-old Singer Featherweight machines lining the back wall. Soldiers waiting to do their duty.

Eugenia served orange blossom tea and gingersnap cookies when the ladies took a break. Her hands were worn, with twisted bones covered over in paper-thin skin so fine not even fingerprints would show.

Jillian was surprised that they'd accepted her into their group without many questions. She'd never spent much time with women more than double her age and found it fascinating that they talked in stories, flowing from one to another. No hurry, no debates, no lectures. Just a gentle current that moved as easily as the sharp needles through the padded layers of material.

Paulina, with her funny tales of living in Dallas in the sixties.

The three Sanderson sisters, who finished each other's sentences and laughed at their own jokes.

The classy lady, dressed in a silk pantsuit, who didn't seem to mind a bit that everyone called her Toad.

Dixie didn't say much; she worked with her head down. Neither did a pixie of a woman named Stella, but she laughed at everyone's jokes as if she'd never heard them before.

Stories they'd all probably heard a hundred times circled around them like classical music, comforting and welcoming to their ears.

Eugenia Larady sat on Jillian's left, showing her how to make the stitches. Jillian tried her best but didn't miss the fact that Paulina, on her right, pulled each of her lines and redid them.

The afternoon passed with Eugenia and Jillian getting up each time a customer came in. The old woman Connor had lovingly called Gram treated each stranger as a special guest. Some only wanted to look, so she followed them about the shop offering them cotton gloves so they could examine the quilts. Some customers wanted to buy squares of fabric called fat quarters, or tools of the quilting trade.

The third time Eugenia stood in front of the cash register, Jillian noticed she seemed to have trouble remembering the order of making a sale.

"Let me, Gram," Jillian suggested. "I'll try not to mess up."

Eugenia moved to the side. "All right, dear, but I'll be watching you."

Jillian had worked a dozen jobs that had this standard cash register, but she glanced over to Eugenia for approval with each step. She'd rarely been around anyone in their eighties, but she assumed memory slips might be common.

The woman smiled and nodded each time.

Jillian almost wished she had a grandmother. Her father had told her from the beginning that she had no living relatives except him. Not one. She'd known it so young she hadn't thought to be sad. No sense missing someone you've never had around.

As the day ended, she took Gram's arm. They walked back to the now-silent quilting corner. No constant stream of voices echoing off the walls. No *ting* of the cash register drawer after each sale of the day.

Jillian thanked her for teaching her so much, and Gram patted her hand as if pleased she could be of help.

The shop was empty now, but the place still seemed alive in the late-afternoon light. Shadows slow dancing beneath the multicolored sky of quilts above.

"You're a fast learner. A great help." Eugenia patted her hand again. "You'd best be going. It will be dark soon."

Jillian didn't want to leave her alone. "I thought I'd help clean up. After all, I ate most of your cookies."

"Oh, no, you didn't. Paulina always eats a dozen." Eugenia covered her mouth as if she might hold back the words.

They both giggled as the front door chimed, and Connor walked in.

She found herself thinking more of this man now that she'd met his gram. A man who cared so dearly for his grandmother couldn't be as clueless as he appeared. She laughed suddenly as she noticed a pencil sticking out of his shaggy head of hair. Or maybe it was a small tree branch. She didn't plan to get close enough to see.

"Did you have a good day, Gram?" Connor passed Jillian as if he hadn't noticed her.

"A grand one, as always. I taught your friend many things about the shop today." Gram grinned. "Now, what did you say her name was again?"

"Jillian," he said, smiling over Gram's head at her. "She's Jillian James."

Gram nodded. "She's a keeper."

Connor looked away. "Good. I'm glad everything went well."

Jillian saw a shyness in the mayor she hadn't noticed before. He might be comfortable around the quilting circle ladies and Gram, but he was nervous around her.

Two short beeps sounded from the street.

Connor lifted Gram's sweater from behind the counter. "Time to go, Gram."

"But I don't want to go home. I don't like it there. Benjamin won't be there. He's gone and the boys went off to college and never came back. They grew up, I know. But Benjamin just doesn't come home anymore."

Jillian felt anger rise. She didn't care if Connor was Eugenia's grandson; he shouldn't try to make her go home to an empty house.

Connor put his arm around Gram and walked her to the door. "You're not going home. The girls have supper waiting for you. Don't you remember? Tonight you're having dinner with your friends at Autumn Acres. Then all of you are going to watch a movie." He stuffed a bag of popcorn into her knitting bag. "I got you caramel corn tonight, but you have to share it."

Gram smiled. "Oh, yes. I remember. It's my turn to bring a snack. Tell Benjamin I might even sleep over."

Jillian watched Connor walk his grandmother out to a little bus that had steps that lowered almost to the street. He helped her all the way to her seat, then stood on the curb waving as she waved back.

The side of the bus read Autumn Acres: Senior Living in Style.

When the bus was gone, he turned back to the quilt shop. His face was cold now, sad, tired. "I need to lock up."

"I'll get my bag." They bumped shoulders as they neared the door. She tried not to notice and asked, "What's Autumn Acres?"

"It's a new living center being built for the aging. They've got the independent apartments finished and one wing of the added care where they check on residents, give them their meds, etcetera, but the final wing, the nursing care, isn't finished."

"Gram just visits?"

His gaze met hers. "No," he said in almost a whisper. "She's lived there for a while, but she thinks she's just visiting."

Connor vanished into the back room to turn off the last of the lights.

When she collected her things and stepped back outside, he was waiting. All the little stores on Main were closing, and the sun's glow seemed to be pulling any warmth with it. Now the smell of coffee drifted from the bakery as low clouds hugged the horizon and the few people left on the street seemed to be in a hurry.

He fell into step with her as she turned toward the bed-and-breakfast. Her long strides seemed to match his in an easy gait. "How'd it go today?" he asked without looking at her.

"Fine. She thinks you and I are friends."

"That's all right. Just log your hours. Give me the report at the end of the week, and I'll write you a check. She can think you're just helping out, if it doesn't bother you and it makes her happy."

"I will." They walked in silence for a few minutes before she added, "You don't have to walk me home."

"I'm not. This is my way home." Without any hint of a smile, he added, "I thought you were trying to walk me home. I was starting to get a bit freaked out about it. Thought you might be after the other bag of popcorn." He patted the stuffed pocket of his raincoat.

Jillian smiled. He was as hard to read as his grandmother. Shy one minute, funny the next. In an odd way she found it cute. She usually had to fend off at least a few advances from men she worked with. Even the married, do-it-by-the-book bosses sometimes took casual flirting too far.

Somehow, this good-looking man who carried a book under one arm didn't frighten her.

Trying to kid him into smiling, she said, "I don't like caramel, but if it had been cheesy flavored, you might have needed to worry. I could easily mug you for nacho-cheesy popcorn."

He didn't respond. Just nodded as if logging her comment

to think about later. No jokes. No flirting. She wasn't sure Connor Larady even knew how.

Jillian matched his steps and his mood. "Your grandmother doesn't have a home to go to besides Autumn Acres, does she?"

"No. She moved to the Acres last spring right after it opened the first wing. My grandfather, Benjamin, died when I was a kid. She lived as a widow for years, ran the shop, walked home, and claimed she enjoyed her quiet time. Then one day she just decided Benjamin wasn't dead—he simply forgot to come home." Connor grinned suddenly, but there was no humor reflected in his eyes. "She's been mad at him ever since. I used to think it was just a game she played with herself, but lately I think she forgets that she moved to the Acres and just thinks she's spending a night out with the girls. Strange thing is, she's never asked to go back to her house, not once. So, I'm thinking somewhere in the back of her mind she knows she's where she needs to be."

"What about your parents?" Maybe because she had no family, Jillian felt a need to know about other families.

"My folks died in a car crash my last year of college. My dad was Gram's only living son. I came home and finished my studies online while I took over his newspaper business. My brother went the other direction. We hear from him now and then. The conversation is usually about how busy he is, but he hasn't been home since our folks died."

"Gram mentioned her boys were grown?" Jillian was trying to make the pieces fit.

"She did have two sons. My uncle died before he started school."

He offered no more explanation and she didn't want to ask. She knew the story would be sad.

They walked in silence for a few minutes. The streetlights blinked on, making the shabby old homes on the block with the bed-and-breakfast look quaint, charming. The lights on an old refinery across the creek morphed the ugly pipes into the towers of a castle.

"On the days I can't come get Gram for lunch, I'll have something for you and her delivered from Mamma Bee's Pastries." He looked straight ahead, not seeming to see the beauty around them. "I just don't want Gram left alone. She knows not to leave until I come, but I'd feel better if you were with her."

"I'm not a nurse." Jillian wondered exactly what she was getting into. There was far more to this job than she thought. She could handle museum-quality logging, but she wasn't prepared for taking care of anyone.

"I'm not asking you to be. Just sit down and eat with her." His voice was still low, but frozen now.

"Fair enough." Jillian stopped at the gate of Flancher's Folly Bed-and-Breakfast. "I eat a big breakfast. If you order her a meal, just make it soup for me. I'll eat with her, but if you take her out as she said you do when it's not a quilting day, I'll stay and work. I can take care of myself. Feeding me is not your problem, and those days I can log another hour."

He nodded. "Understood. Just a job, right? Don't want to get too involved."

"Right." She answered without looking up at him. He might read her lie in her eyes. She needed the job, but she was in town hoping to find a tiny piece of her dad's life. She hadn't been surprised when he first vanished, but as the years passed she wished for one thing, one thread, to hang on to.

Part of her still looked for him in a crowd. Still thought about what she would have said, or asked, if she'd known he'd be disappearing the last time he'd walked away so casually.

For the first few years she'd thought he'd appear just to check on her. The fact he didn't told her more than she wanted to admit about the man who raised her.

She knew so little about Jefferson James. Nothing about her mother. It was like she'd found a hole in her mind and had nothing to fill it with. His journal had noted this zip code in one of the margins. Maybe there was something or someone he'd cared about here.

Connor nodded a silent goodbye and she did the same. But she turned when she reached the shadows of the porch and watched him until he disappeared into the night.

An interesting man, this Connor Larady. Cold at times, like he had a heavy load to carry. Formal, almost, at other times. Yet Gram loved him dearly. Jillian suspected he was a man with a great deal on his mind, and she didn't plan to know him well enough to ever find out what that entailed.

They were polite strangers. Nothing more. Maybe he was too shy to get closer. Maybe she was too afraid of being hurt. It didn't matter. She'd be on her way in three months.

His wrinkled raincoat had flapped in the wind, almost like wings. Then, as he'd turned the corner, he'd vanished. Or flew away. She grinned, letting her imagination run. For as long as she could remember, she'd longed to see a real hero, or even a villain, but people were just people. Interesting, but not worth getting too close to.

Strange, she thought. She had no one who'd claim her body if she died tonight. Yet she'd just met a man who probably knew the whole town, and she had a feeling he was more alone than she was.

The next morning, when Jillian ventured into the sunroom that doubled as guest dining, Mrs. Kelly had Jillian's place set. In summer this room, with floor-to-ceiling windows on three sides, would be an oven, but on this cloudy, winter day, it seemed to draw bits of light without bringing any warmth along.

Dozens of crystals hung in circles like wind chimes. Now and then, one caught a ray that escaped from the clouds and splashed rainbows along the one pale yellow wall.

A dusty old piano stood in the corner of the room, out of place and looking abandoned. Mrs. Kelly must have tried to camouflage the eyesore with a huge arrangement of plastic sunflowers.

Jillian almost giggled aloud. Staying in the bed-and-breakfast was almost like being in a real house. Of course it was just a business, but she could pretend. Even the banging coming from the kitchen added atmosphere.

For her father, old trailers or two-bedroom apartments furnished with the bare bones for living had been enough. But she liked having pictures on the walls, rugs on the floors and curtains on the windows. The two semesters she'd lived in a dorm she'd spent more than she should have at the dollar store buying all kinds of decorations for her room. Then, she realized she couldn't take any of them.

Only necessities travel.

As she sat down, she winked at the old upright piano in the far corner. If she could take anything extra packed away in the trunk of her car, it would be a piano. Impractical. Far too big. Impossible.

"Oh, my goodness!" Mrs. Kelly's words came so fast as she stepped into the room, they almost sounded like a hiccup. "Look at the beams of light coming in. If a crystal beam shines on your face, you're blessed by the angels today. I just saw two on your cheek, dear."

Jillian rubbed her face. "I don't believe in crystals or angels, but it's a nice thought."

"Don't worry, they believe in you."

Papa's rule: *Stay away from the crazies. Insanity spreads like the plague.*

Mrs. Kelly laughed as if she'd only been kidding, and Jillian relaxed as breakfast was delivered on a silver tray.

A Dallas Cowboys football player couldn't have finished all the meal. Pecan pancakes, sage sausage, fresh fruit, and a cinnamon roll for dessert. Who has dessert for breakfast?

While Jillian ate, the tiny woman circled the room, talking as if even one guest needed a floor show to go along with her meal. "I heard from Stella, one of the quilters at the shop yesterday, that you're working in Miss Eugenia's shop. It's been there forever, and I've never known her to hire help."

"I'm logging and photographing all the quilts for the county museum. Miss Eugenia is telling me the history of each one."

"That's a very brave and honorable thing you're doing," the little lady said as if Jillian had joined Special Forces. "Are you planning on staying with me while you're in town?"

"I'd hoped to. The job will only last a few months, then I'll be moving on."

Mrs. Kelly rocked her head back and forth as if sloshing an idea around in her mind. Finally, she said, "If you don't mind cleaning your own room, you can have the two rooms up there for a hundred a week, breakfast included. Those rooms are never rented in the winter anyway, and you could use the small one as a living area or study. It only has a half bed in it, so I'll toss pillows along the wall side and make it look like a couch. There's also a desk if you're one of those 'work into the night' people."

"That's a very fair price."

Mrs. K grinned. "Oh, I forget to add that I sometimes have to leave town for a night now and then. You would have to fend for yourself and watch over the house and the ghost while I'm gone."

"I could manage that." Jillian hoped Mrs. K's wink meant that she was only kidding about keeping up with the ghost.

Jillian frowned, fearing this setup might be too good to be true. People usually weren't so nice. Most folks only trusted family and longtime friends. Strangers they kept at arm's length. She knew this because she was always the stranger. Even in grade school she was usually still being called the *new girl* when her father pulled her out to move. After a while she quit even trying to make friends. It hurt too much to leave them.

"That's very kind of you, Mrs. K. I'll try to be quiet. The other guests won't even know I'm upstairs."

Mrs. Kelly laughed that fully rounded laugh that shook her whole body. "Oh, don't be that, dear. I'll enjoy the company. Being alone in this old place always makes me a little sad."

Jillian looked up from her breakfast. Mrs. Kelly's apron read *I'm not short. I'm just compacted.*

Jillian couldn't hide her grin. Crazy and kind, she could live with. "You've got yourself a deal. A hundred a week. I clean my own rooms and house-sit when you need me. But when I'm the only guest for breakfast, we go light. Toast, one egg and coffee."

Mrs. Kelly widened her stance as if preparing for a fight. "All right, with one exception. We add a muffin and sausage to the light breakfast. I feed that crow, who thinks he lives on my back fence, more than one egg and toast every morning."

"Deal." Jillian glanced out the window and was surprised to see a huge old crow propped on the dog-eared fence that had been painted red. He reminded her of the black ravens around the Tower of London. Rumor was, six ravens had to guard the tower at all times or the monarchy would fall. Maybe one crow was all that was needed to stand guard here.

Mrs. Kelly had disappeared when Jillian turned back to the table. She finished her grand meal, thinking this must be her lucky day. Maybe there was something to that crystal thing.

As she walked the block to the quilt shop, she planned. If she worked eight hours a day, five days a week, she'd bring in over seven hundred a week after taxes. A hundred a week for the room, maybe twenty for the car, fifty or sixty for meals on weekends and essentials. If she watched her money she could pocket five hundred a week easily. Two thousand a month. Even allowing for emergencies during the three months in Laurel Springs, she'd walk away with five thousand dollars.

Enough money to move to a big city, rent a nice apartment, find a real job. Disappear into the crowds.

Her good mood lasted until she opened the shop door and saw trouble perched on the old mahogany counter like a six-foot-tall buzzard.

4

A long slice of light shone into the dark shadows of the quilt shop. For a moment, Jillian thought she was in the wrong place. No soft ribbons of fluorescent bulbs twenty feet above. No laughter from the quilter's corner. No smell of coffee drifting from the tiny kitchen.

Only a long-legged girl dressed in black, staring at her as if Jillian had just interrupted a demonic ritual.

The backward lettering of A Stitch in Time circled across the front window. Right place. Jillian was in the quilt shop. Squaring her shoulders, she moved forward.

"Hi," Jillian managed as she widened the opening of the door. She wasn't sure if she was trying to see the invader better or simply wanted to enlarge her escape route.

The strange girl swung one leg so it bumped against the side of the counter in a heartbeat rhythm. Her hair was so light it appeared white, and hung straight past her shoulders. A dozen bracelets, all appearing to be made out of rusty bolts, clanked on her arms as she turned toward the back of the store.

"Dad!" the intruder yelled. "Someone's drifted in."

Rows of lights began to click on, starting from the back and finally reaching the front. All the beautiful colors of the store returned, but the escapee from the Addams Family remained. Her black peacoat, with batwing shoulder pads, was ripped in several places. Black eyeliner extended almost to her ears and charcoal, lace gloves covered her hands.

Jillian studied the girl carefully. On the bright side, the coat and leggings matched. Both black and ragged. She appeared to be wearing three blouses, the last one a lace nightgown. Silk, holey as if moth-eaten, and spotted with what looked like bloodstains. Her skirt, with several chains hanging off it, reminded Jillian of a midnight plaid kilt.

They both turned as footsteps stormed from the back. "Sorry," Connor Larady shouted. "I usually have the place all opened up by this time."

He didn't seem to notice the girl still perched on the counter. "I'll have a key made for you so you won't have to wait for me if I'm running late."

When Jillian turned her gaze to the girl, Connor finally acknowledged the goth in the room. "Oh, I'm sorry, Jillian, this is my daughter. Sunnie, this is the lady who is helping Gram organize the shop."

Jillian offered her hand, hoping the strange girl wouldn't try to suck her blood. She was so thin and pale she probably hadn't eaten in days.

The girl reluctantly took Jillian's offered hand, but her handshake was limp.

If there was a prize for someone born with the wrong name, Sunnie Larady would win. Stormy might be better. Or Scary.

She slid off the counter. Six feet of pure adolescent rebellion. "I need to get to school, Connor." She said her father's name louder than the rest of the sentence.

"Right." Connor turned to Jillian. "Will you be all right here? Gram should be dropped off any minute."

"I'm fine. I'll watch for her." Jillian smiled at Sunnie. "Nice to meet you."

The girl shrugged and walked out.

"I'm sorry about that." Connor sounded as if he'd said the same thing often lately. "She's just going through a stage. The doctor says it's normal for kids who lose a parent in their teens. He claims Sunnie is mad her mom died, and I'm the only one left to take it out on. Hating me keeps her mind off death."

"When did your wife die?"

"Three years ago. Sunnie was thirteen." He shoved his hands in the pockets of his baggy pants and rounded his shoulders forward as if trying to seem smaller, or maybe hold his grief inside. "Sunnie wanted to meet you. I don't think she'd ever admit it, but she's protective of Gram. I told her she could maybe help out after school now and then. But don't look for her until she's at the door."

Jillian thought of screaming *No!*, but she simply smiled and said, "I'd appreciate the help."

He nodded, then hurried out.

Jillian stood by the front window, watching the town come alive. This street reminded her of a beehive. Everyone seemed to have their job and all were working frantically to get the day started. She almost wanted to tell them all that it didn't matter how many flags or sandwich boards the shops put out—this one street would never draw much of a crowd.

The old warehouse buildings across the creek hung over the cute main street like death's shadow. The stillness just across the water was a constant reminder that a few blocks away, half of the town had been abandoned. Jillian wondered if the people who lived here even saw the crumbling buildings anymore.

When the Autumn Acres bus pulled up, she went outside and waited for Gram to come down the steps.

The lady, still tall for her age even though her shoulders had rounded, was dressed in a very proper wool suit with lace on her white collar. Her shoes might be rounded and rubber, but she hadn't forgotten her pearls.

"Hello, dear," Gram shouted. "How nice of you to come help me again."

"I had so much fun I just had to return. You don't mind me hanging around?"

"Oh, no. I love the company and there is always plenty to do."

They walked in with arms locked. Jillian wasn't sure Eugenia remembered her name, but the Southern lady seemed to assume she knew everyone, and she treated all, old friends or strangers, the same.

"Let's make a cup of tea first this morning," Gram suggested. "That will start the day right. I do love tea in the spring."

Jillian followed her back to a small kitchen, without mentioning it was still winter. They talked about the tea and the day as if they were old friends.

The morning passed like a peaceful river. Customers came in, mostly to talk. Jillian made note of the ones who had lived their entire lives in this town. A long-retired teacher named Joe Dunaway, most of the quilters she'd met yesterday, the mailman named Tap. As she settled in, she did what she often did in little towns: she'd ask if they knew a Jefferson James who might have lived around here thirty years ago. The answer was always no, a dead end. She'd found a few Jameses over the years, but none knew a Jefferson. Her father never allowed anyone to shorten his name.

Joe Dunaway said he thought the name might be familiar, but after forty years of teaching, all names sounded familiar.

While Joe watched the store, Gram took the time to show her around the tiny office after Jillian explained for the third time that she was there to make a record of all the quilts.

"Someday, your quilts will hang in a gallery at the county museum, and you'll want all the facts to be right. I'll compile that record for you, Gram."

"Oh, of course you will," Eugenia agreed as she sugared her tea for the second time.

When their cups were half-empty, they began to stroll through the colorful garden of quilts. Jillian kept her questions light. Never too many. Never too fast.

She noticed how Gram stroked each quilt she straightened as if it were precious. The kitchen and the office might be a cluttered mess, but all the quilts had to be in perfect order.

"You touch them as if they're priceless. Like they're your treasures, your babies," Jillian said.

"Oh, they're not mine. But in a way they are alive. Each one holds memories. I just put them together in the final step of quilting." She pulled one from the shelf and spread it out on a wide table designed for cutting fabric. "This one belongs to Helen Harmon, who made it as a gift to give the man she loved on their wedding day. They'd known each other since grade school." Gram pointed to one square. "See, that's them as kids on the playground. He's pulling her pigtail. I swear, Helen's hair was stoplight red when she was little."

Jillian saw thick red threads braided together and sewn onto the quilt.

Gram's wrinkled fingers passed over another quilt square. A UT logo stood out in burnt orange. "That's for their college days, and she made this one when he went into the army. When he came home a few years later and started work, his first job was in construction. Turned out he had a real knack for it."

Jillian saw the square with tools crossing, almost like a crest.

"And here we have vacations they took camping, hiking, riding across the country on what Helen called hogs." One square ran like a road map. "When they finally got engaged, both were thirty-four." One square held nothing but sparkling material in the pattern of a diamond ring.

Jillian touched the square of a house. "When they bought their first house, right?"

Gram shook her head. "When he built what was to be their first house, she made that square. They both agreed neither would move in until after the wedding."

"What happened?" Jillian realized she was holding her breath.

"I'd worked late into the night the evening before their rehearsal dinner. I wanted to have the quilt ready for her to give to him. She was not a natural seamstress, and was years away from being a skilled quilter. Each piece came hard for her. She'd laugh and say she really made ten quilts because she had to do each square over and over to get it just right."

"What happened?" Jillian asked again.

"She didn't come pick up the quilt the day of their rehearsal. When she woke that morning before her wedding, she found a note on his pillow. He'd had an offer for a new job up north and hadn't known how to tell her. The note said he'd tried a hundred times to break off the engagement, but she was too busy planning the wedding to listen."

"So he just left her?"

Gram nodded. "And she left this quilt. She told me I could sell it, but who buys another's memories? She'd even embroidered the wedding date in the middle."

Jillian looked at the quilt. June 19, 1971.

"You've kept this for almost fifty years?"

Gram nodded. "How do you throw away memories? It's a beautiful quilt made with love. Helen eventually married a man named Green and moved to Houston, but she didn't make anything for her next groom, and she never dropped by the shop to even look at this."

Jillian helped her fold it up and gently lay it back on the shelf. This would be the first quilt she logged.

The story had been fascinating, but Gram's memory of the details surprised Jillian. A woman who couldn't remember if she'd sugared her tea had told every detail of something that had happened nearly fifty years ago.

As soon as Connor picked up his gram for lunch, Jillian put the be-back-soon sign on the door and spread Helen Harmon's quilt back out. With care she took pictures and wrote down details. Then, the last thing she did before folding it back into place was to stitch a two-inch blue square of fabric in one corner of the quilt's back.

No. 1
Helen Harmon Green's memory quilt. Made as a wedding gift to her future husband. Completed 1971. Never delivered.

As Jillian ate the apple she'd brought from the bed-and-breakfast, she walked around the shop. She'd have to do two or three handmade treasures a day to get them all logged. And she'd have to hear every story. Some might be short, but she'd bet they'd all be interesting. If only Gram's memory would hold up just a little longer, she'd get them all down.

When Connor brought Gram back from lunch, Jillian showed him what she'd done and he approved of her system. "You know," he added as an afterthought. "If you want to write up a few of the stories, they might make nice human interest pieces for the Laurel Springs online paper I put out. It's mostly just a blog, a bulletin of what's happening, but something like this might interest people."

"I'll give it a try after work. See what you think."

He handed her a key to the shop. "If you want to work after hours when the shop is closed, that's fine with me."

"Thanks. I might do that."

To her surprise, he smiled. "I'm not trying to run you off early or keep you longer than you want to stay. I get a feeling you have somewhere else to be."

She thought of denying it. No matter what she said, she'd be giving away too much information, so she simply smiled back.

That evening, they walked home together, each talking about their day. When she turned into the gate at the bed-and-breakfast, he didn't say goodbye. But this time he did smile as he waved.

She stood on the porch, watching him vanish. A paper man who would disappear from her mind as fast as a match fired. Maybe she'd describe him on her "Laurel Springs" journal page.

Yes, she could mention how normal it had felt to just walk and talk about nothing really. Her father had called it *passing time* like it was a waste of energy, but he was wrong. Invisible threads were binding people who took the time to talk, helping them to care about each other even in a small way, to know each other. Making them almost friends.

She'd seen it happen with doormen in big cities or clerks in stores she'd frequented in towns. Not friends exactly, but no longer strangers.

This was something rare for Jillian, but she realized Eugenia Larady had been doing it all her life. With Joe Dunaway, with customers, and with the quilters. Talking, caring, relating with everyone she met.

Invisible threads. Invisible bonds. Not strong enough to hold her down, but nice to feel.

5

Connor Larady's world of routine shifted as the days passed. After a week, Jillian James had become part of his life as easily as if a piece had always been missing and she simply fit into the void.

He liked the easy way she greeted him every morning, not too formal, not too friendly. He looked forward to the few minutes they'd talk before the bus chauffeured his grandmother to the door of the quilt shop. He liked collecting little things he learned about Jillian, the pretty lady who never talked about herself.

Some mornings he'd studied the way Jillian dressed, casual yet professional, as if every detail about her mattered somehow. She might be tall, but she wasn't too thin. Her eyes often caught his attention, stormy-day gray one moment and calm blue the next. She watched the clock, always aware of time, and she seemed to study people as if looking for something familiar in their faces. And she listened, really listened.

All the women he knew in town seemed shallow water, babbling brooks. But Jillian was deep current and he had a feeling it would take years to really know her. She never started a conversation, but if she disagreed with him she didn't mind debating.

Who knew, maybe they'd become friends. But no more. The one thing Connor had figured out about himself a long time ago was that he was a watcher, not a participant, where women were concerned. If life were a banquet, he was the beggar outside the window looking in. He'd rather put up with the loneliness than take another chance.

He'd stepped out of his place once. He'd married Sunnie's mother, Melissa, a few months after they slept together on their first date. He'd been home from school for the summer the year he turned twenty-one and she'd been nineteen. He'd used protection, but she'd told him it hadn't worked.

Marriage had seemed the only answer. She went back to school with him. He took a part-time job and rented a bigger apartment. He'd known the marriage was a mistake before Christmas that year, but Connor wasn't a quitter. He carried on.

Funny, he thought, he'd been caught in her net like a blind fish, but he hadn't minded. It was just the way of life, and Sunnie made it all bearable.

Melissa loved that he was from one of the oldest families in East Texas. *Almost royalty*, she used to say. He was educated, a path she had no interest in following. His family might be cash poor at times, but they were land rich, she claimed, though none of them seemed inclined to sell even one of their properties.

Sunnie was eight months old when his parents were killed in a wreck. Afterward, Connor, Melissa and Sunnie had moved back to his childhood home, where he finished his degrees online. The house was roomy, but Melissa hated it from the day they moved in. She went back to her high school friends for entertainment, and he spent most of his days learning to handle the family business and his nights in his study with Sunnie's bassinet by his desk.

He wanted to write children's stories, blending Greek myths with today's world. Though he rarely left Laurel Springs, his character, a Roman soldier, traveled through time visiting battlefields that changed the world. In his novels, Connor's hero collected knowledge in hopes of ending all conflict.

But in reality, Connor simply fought to survive. To keep going when there never seemed enough time for his little dream; reality's voice was always outshouting creativity's whisper.

When Sunnie started school, he moved his stories to the newspaper office and set up a writing desk. As the newspaper dwindled to a one-man job, he set up a business desk across from his editor's desk to handle his rental properties in town and his leasing property outside the city limits. Next came the mayor's desk, with all the city business stacked high. Of all the desks in his office, the writing desk was the most neglected.

It had been that way from the beginning of his marriage. There was always too much to do. Too little time for dreams of writing.

Even when Melissa had started needing her nights out after Sunnie was born, he never thought to complain. But after they moved back to Laurel Springs, the nights turned into long weekends. She needed to feel alive, she'd say. She needed to get away.

About the time Sunnie started school, the weekends grew into weeks at a time.

When Melissa would return, she'd bring gifts for Sunnie, and her only daughter would forgive her for not calling. They'd go back to being best friends, not mother and daughter, and Connor would prepare for the next time she'd leave with only a note on the counter.

Even before she could read, Sunnie would see the note and cry before he read it.

He learned to cook. Kept track of Sunnie's schedule. He was there for the everyday of her life. Melissa was there for the party.

Until three years ago, when she didn't come back at all. A private plane crash outside of Reno. Both passengers died. Connor hadn't even known the man she'd been with.

That day, he became a full-time widower, not just a weekend one. No great change. But Sunnie's world had shifted on its axis. That one day, she changed.

Connor lost himself in the order of his repetitive days. He ran the paper his grandfather had started, even if it was little more than a blog, except on holidays. He looked after his daughter and his grandmother. Ruled over the monthly meetings of the city council. Paid the bills. Showed up.

And, now and then, late at night, he wrote his stories. The dream of being a writer slipped further and further away on a tide of daily to-do lists.

He told himself that hiring Jillian hadn't changed anything. She was simply someone passing through, no more. Gram's time in the shop would soon be ending, and somehow he had to preserve an ounce of what she'd meant to the town.

The short articles about the quilts Jillian penned were smart and well written, and they were drawing attention. The number of hits was up at the free *Laurel Springs Daily*, and more people were dropping in to see the quilts she'd described so beautifully.

Which slowed her cataloging work for the museum, leaving him with hope that she'd stay longer. He hadn't thought about how much it meant, talking to an intelligent woman his age for the first time. Now, he was spending time trying to say something, anything, interesting on their walks home. All at once he didn't have to just show up in his life; he had to talk, as well.

Tonight he'd ask Jillian all about the tiny houses quilt she had logged. She'd said a lady quilted a two-inch square of a house every day for a year, then put them all together. Every one unique. The discipline would be something to talk about.

"Dad, did you get a haircut?" Sunnie interrupted his thoughts as he pulled into the high school parking lot.

Connor glanced at his daughter sitting in the passenger seat. "I did. What do you think?"

She shrugged. "Not much change. Better, I guess. I'm glad I got Mom's straight hair and not your wavy curls. After you scratch your head it's usually going every which way."

"You have a suggestion?"

"Yeah, wear a hat." Sunnie glared at him, her substitute for smiling. "Derrick says you should slick it down a little, then you'd look like one of those newscasters. He said his mother thinks you're handsome in a nutty professor kind of way."

"Tell Derrick's mother thanks for the compliment, I think." Connor tired to remember what Derrick's mother looked like, but all he remembered were the tats covering her arms like black vines.

He studied his beautiful daughter beneath her mask of makeup. The last thing he ever planned to do was take advice from Derrick or his mother. "You know, women thought I was good-looking when I was in college."

"Dinosaur days." She rolled her eyes.

He nodded. Without reaching his fortieth birthday, he'd already become old to someone. Maybe he'd talk to Jillian about that on the walk home. She had to be in her early thirties, so surely she wouldn't think of him as old.

No, he decided. People who don't have children don't want to hear what other people's children say. Correction, what their children's pimpled-faced, oversexed boyfriends say.

Sunnie was always texting Derrick, even when he sat a few feet away. If she ever glanced up and really looked at him, she'd drop the reject from *The Walking Dead*. Ten years from now Derrick would still be wearing his leather jacket while he worked at the bowling alley.

As soon as Connor pulled up to the curb, Sunnie bolted from the old pickup. He remembered a time when she'd lean over and kiss his cheek before she headed to school. Those days were long gone.

A few minutes later he parked behind the quilt shop, walked through the place turning on lights, and unlocked the front door. He was early. It made sense to go across the street to his office and at least go through the mail, but he liked the silence of the shop. He'd known every corner of this place for as long as he could remember. In grade school he'd run, not home, but to Gram's after school, where she'd have warm cookies from the bakery and little milk bottles in her tiny fridge waiting. He'd do his homework on one of the cutting tables until his mother came over from the paper and picked him up.

He knew his parents were just across the street, working on what was then a daily paper filled with local ads, but they were busy. Gram always had time to talk, even when her fingers were busy sewing. She'd ask about his day, and she'd tell him who came by the shop. Only, she'd never told him the stories about the quilts that Jillian was writing. To him, each one was a treasure and he wished he'd thought to ask about them when he was a kid. It would have been nice to have the stories woven into his childhood.

The door chimed and Jillian rushed in with the winter wind. She stopped the moment she saw him and hesitated, as if unsure how he might react to her.

"Morning," he said, as he did every morning.

"Morning." She relaxed. "I know I'm a little early, but I wrote another three articles last night and couldn't wait to give them to you."

"I'll take them with me and let you know if I can use them. Everyone is talking about the last one I put on the blog."

"Good." She smiled and he took a moment to study her mouth before looking away.

Not something he should notice. They weren't even friends. Might never be, but it might be worth a try. He could handle *friends* with a woman. For a short time anyway.

"You're welcome to come with Gram and me for lunch."

He always asked. "We're headed a few miles out of town to a Mexican place she loves, though all she ever eats is quesadillas."

"Thanks, but I'll work through lunch."

He tried not to look disappointed. The Autumn Acres bus pulled up out front and their conversation ended.

After lunch, any chance to talk was quickly forgotten. By the time Connor had Gram back in the shop and helped her strip off a few layers of coats, Joe Dunaway had slipped through the unlocked shop door. He stopped long enough to turn the closed sign over to open, as if he thought of himself as the designated flipper.

Connor greeted the retired teacher. He had the feeling the old guy thought the quilt store was really a Starbucks in disguise. He rarely went a day without Gram's coffee. He even had his own mug in her tiny kitchen.

"Got any coffee, Jeanie?" he asked Gram as he leaned on the counter like it was a bar.

"Of course, Joe." She made no move for the cups in the kitchen. "Did you tell my Connor about your new invention?"

Joe lowered his voice. "No. Haven't had a chance. Have to be careful, Jeanie. Make sure no one is around to steal it. Loose lips sink ships, you know."

"What invention?" Connor doubted it could be any dumber than the last twenty inventions Joe had come up with since he retired. A few months ago he'd invented a birdfeeder that attached to a telephone pole. Said since everyone was using cell phones they wouldn't be needing phone lines so he'd thought of a use for them. Only hitch was getting seed that high.

"You're going to like this one, boy." Joe had known Eugenia long enough to call her Jeanie. And Connor, no matter how old he was, would always be "boy."

Gram lost interest in Joe's great invention and followed Jillian as she disappeared into the tiny kitchen to put coffee on.

Connor waited. If he was going to listen to details of one of Joe's inventions, he'd need caffeine to stay awake.

The little man was developing a kind of hobbit look. Hair seemed to be growing in every direction from every exposed square of skin. Everything he wore was at least two decades out of style but intelligence, or maybe mischief, still sparkled in his eyes.

Joe cleared his throat and straightened. "I've been thinking. You know how hard it is to sleep on your back with your feet sticking up?"

"No. I sleep on my side." Connor held little hope that his answer would earn him a get-out-of-one-invention-lecture free pass.

"Well, if you did, you'd know how the blankets cramp your toes when you've got them pointed straight up. Colder it gets, more blankets and more cramped toes. So I got this idea. Doesn't take much in materials or time. Just canvas and some eight-inch poles, maybe longer for those with big feet."

Connor nodded as if following a logic that long ago had gone rogue.

Joe lowered his voice. "I'm calling them Toe Tents. You put them under the covers at the bottom of the bed. Slip your feet in and your toes can wiggle all night without being cramped."

"Brilliant!" Connor shouted. Joe had finally come up with an invention dumber than Tele-Birdfeeders.

Joe smiled, scratching his beard. "I knew you'd like it. I figured I'd cut you in for a share, son, if you'd let me set up in one of those old barns on the other side of the creek. If I remember right, your family owns them and a few are still solid enough to be of use."

"No one ever goes over there." Connor's family did own the worthless piece of town. From the thirties to the early sixties there had been several small businesses. A barrel shop. A furniture store that made rockers and coffins. A repair shop that could fix anything from toasters to TVs and a small winery that shipped as far as a hundred miles away. One small storage shed had even been used to weave Angora rabbit fur into yarn. But that was long ago, before Connor was born.

His dad had told him the businesses died one by one when the chain stores came in. Folks could buy another radio or toaster cheaper than having one repaired. If Joe wanted to use one of the buildings, he'd be the one man in town who'd know if it was safe. Joe Dunaway knew everything about the building industry. He'd spent his summers in manual labor. Said it kept his mind sharp to work with his hands. He could have been a big-time contractor, but he'd chosen to teach.

On the bright side, Connor had gone from being called *boy* to *son*, so he was moving up. Maybe he could listen at least until the coffee arrived.

Joe didn't seem to notice Connor was only half listening. "People will go over there when the big orders start coming in for my Toe Tents. You might want to tell the city to repair the roads. I'll put a big sign out so the locals don't have to pay postage. Once it takes off, I thought I'd reopen one of the factories and hire some of my friends who've been sitting around for years."

Connor patted the old man on the back. "When the orders start, I want in. Tell you what. You pick what place you want, and I'll lease it to you free for six months."

"I'm not asking for anything free. I got this niece who's got a houseful of kids, and she buys everything online. She says she'll help me get set up with a website next week. I'll cut you and her in for ten percent right from the start." Joe thumped his fist on the counter letting Connor know he wouldn't budge on the deal.

Connor agreed. Ten percent of nothing was still nothing.

Jillian brought out two cups of coffee and seemed interested in Joe's idea. She'd probably heard every word from the kitchen. She also called the old guy by name, so this must not be Joe's first time to stop by.

When she started asking if the Toe Tents came in different colors, Connor slipped out the door and carried his coffee and her short articles across the street. If he was lucky, he'd have a few hours to work on a short story explaining history through a time-traveling warrior's eyes. Kids would probably like that.

Since Sunnie was a baby, he'd been compiling a collection of stories about famous battles that changed history. His main characters were the Roman warrior and his dog. They saw the fighting and how each battle changed the world. They were searching for the secret to end all wars.

Of course, it occurred to Connor that if they found it in

the series, it would end his series. Then he'd have to come up with another idea.

His stories were about as likely to get published as Joe's Toe Tents were to be stocked on the shelf at Walmart, but his writing gave him direction. A mission. A small doorway he could step through and out of his life, if only for a few hours a day.

After lunch he always dropped Gram back at the shop, then drove to his house already thinking about the walk with Jillian that evening. On the days Gram didn't leave for lunch, he'd walk to work or drive the pickup. She'd finally reached the age that she had trouble climbing into the old Ford. If Connor had his choice, he'd walk everywhere, but the pickup was for hauling and the Audi was for Gram, so he owned two vehicles he didn't really want.

When he wandered back to Main, he took the creek route. He liked stomping through tall grass. Getting his boots muddy. Enjoying the escape. The World War II battle he'd been writing about danced in his mind as he worked off a few calories from the three-enchilada plate he'd finished off at Lennie's Tacos and More.

He thought of telling Jillian about how much he loved the wild nature park that ran though town, but he figured she'd just lump him in with Joe—another crazy person in the stop-off town for her. So he went back to his office and tried to concentrate on work.

After four hours of struggling with paperwork on several small farms the family business leased out, he closed the office. If he increased the rent, the farmers would suffer. If he didn't, taxes would eat him alive. Somehow in the past fifteen years since he took over the Larady family books,

he'd managed to keep the balance relatively even, but that
wouldn't be possible in the future.

At five, he ignored the chill in the air and darted across
the street with a biography of Patton under his arm and an
empty coffee cup in hand.

Jillian laughed when he walked in. "It's too late for a re-
fill; I've washed the pot."

"Too bad. I could use another cup." He walked past her,
set the cup in the kitchen sink and returned. "Is Gram about
ready? The Autumn Acres bus will be here soon."

"Of course I'm ready, Danny, it's closing time." Gram
stepped from the office.

He met Jillian's glance and shook his head slightly, silently telling her not to mention that Gram had called him
by his father's name. "She does that sometimes," he whispered when Gram was busy turning the sign over for the
night. "It doesn't matter."

Connor didn't miss the understanding in those blue-gray
eyes. There was a wisdom there, as well. A knowledge of
living many lives, maybe, or simply the loneliness of living one.

Jillian helped Gram with her coat. "Paulina came in for
a few more purple fat quarters for that new quilt. She told
us that tonight, after dinner, the high school choir is putting on a '50s songs concert at the Acres. She wanted to
make sure Gram would be there."

Gram nodded. "And we've got good seats. I told Joe that
if he wanted a seat in the front row with us, he'd better
manage to show up on time."

"Whose date is he for the night, yours or Paulina's?"

She huffed. "Mine, I guess. Paulina has been swearing

since she was twelve that she'd never date. How she ever managed to marry three times is beyond me. Come to think of it, I'd best sit between them just in case lightning strikes again. Joe's old heart probably couldn't take it."

Connor smiled as he walked Gram to the bus. He loved the way her mind always wandered into a story. Bending, he kissed her check. "I love you, Gram."

"I love you, too, Connor."

She'd remembered his name. It was a good day.

When he turned back to the store, he noticed Jillian was locking the door.

"Ready?" she asked as she turned to face him.

"Ready," he answered, thinking he'd been waiting all day for these few minutes they shared. He offered his arm as if they were in an old black-and-white movie.

Hesitantly, Jillian placed her hand around his elbow and began to tell him all the details of Joe's dream of being a Toe Tent king. The old guy swore his ideas came to him while he was daydreaming about camping.

Connor listened, but mostly he just enjoyed the walk. He liked the easy way their steps matched and how her words never seemed in a hurry, like some folks talk as if rushing the clock. In a few more days it would be March and almost time for spring. Then, maybe, if she was still around, they'd slow their pace.

The air had stilled and the evening glowed in sunset's last light. The smells of winter drifted near: wood fireplaces, the last scent of dying sagebrush. This was his favorite time of year. Spring might be for dreaming, but winter was for reflecting.

"I was afraid you'd be staying late tonight," he said as

they walked through leaves rushing nowhere in the wake of each passing car.

"Why? Did you think I needed to? The work still seems overwhelming."

"No. I'm glad you didn't put in longer hours tonight. Too great a time to walk. But if you'd like to come in on a Saturday morning or Sunday afternoon, I could offer to help."

"That would be great. I could move twice as fast with photographing if I had help with the layout."

"You've got a nice camera."

She nodded. "I bought it a few years back when I was a Realtor's assistant, and I found I couldn't leave it behind when I moved on. I never seem to get pictures developed though, just store them on my laptop and keep on taking more."

He grinned. She'd finally told him something personal.

When they reached the gate of the bed-and-breakfast, she broke the comfortable silence that had drifted between them for a few minutes. "I've been talking too much." She hesitated. "If you want to come in, Mrs. Kelly always leaves cookies out in the parlor."

Connor was too surprised by the invitation to answer.

Her words quickly filled the silence. "I've been waiting all day to hear how you like my latest articles. It might just be for the community blog, but I'm thrilled about writing something others will read."

"Oh, of course." He felt like a fool for even thinking she'd invite him in for some other reason. She hadn't even hinted at flirting with him. "I'd love to talk about them, and cookies are one thing I never say no to. But you'll have to promise to cut me off after two."

He followed her to the parlor. He'd been in the old home a dozen times, but it never seemed as inviting as it did tonight. Low flames in the fireplace. The smell of gingerbread drifting from the kitchen. Jillian removing her coat as if settling in for a chat.

She made him a cup of hot cocoa to go with the cookies and they talked about her writing.

"I'd like to submit a few to one of the big papers in the state." Connor was comfortable talking business. "Who knows, someone might pick them up. If they did, they'd pay far more than the twenty dollars I can afford."

"You really think someone would want them?"

"Sure. I loved the story of the Orlando quilt I read this afternoon. A girl driving cross-country every year to visit her grandparents and seeing all the sights through a child's eyes. Then, as an adult, she quilted from her memory. I loved the picture of her Yellowstone block with the bear as tall as Old Faithful.

"And, Jillian, you've got the pictures to go with each story. I'd think that would be a real selling point in a human interest piece."

She laughed with excitement, and the sound made him smile.

When he reached for his fifth cookie, her hand covered his. "I have to cut you off, Connor, I promised. You still have to walk home. Any more cookies and you'll have to roll."

He turned his hand over and held her fingers. "Thanks. I have no restraint."

Standing, he drew her up with him. "Okay if I send the articles? I think you've got a chance of making some money.

Plus, if one of the big papers does pick it up, the articles might draw people to the county museum to see the quilts."

"You think I might make as much as Toe Tents?"

He liked that she was so tall. He could look into her eyes. "Probably not," he teased.

A thump came from just above their heads.

"The ghost?" he whispered.

"Probably. Mrs. K is in the kitchen. I hear old Willie now and then. He likes to move around about the time the clock strikes midnight."

They both laughed.

Reluctantly, he let go of her hand and walked to the door. "There are always strange sounds in a house this old. See you tomorrow."

"See you tomorrow," she answered.

To his surprise, she followed him to the porch, and he didn't have to turn around to know that she watched him as he walked away. She had been standing in the same spot every night as he glanced back, just before he turned the corner.

He closed his hand tightly as if trying to hold the warmth of her fingers for one more moment.

In his thirty-seven years, he'd never learned to weigh his feelings. The important ones, the unimportant ones. Not for women anyway. He could be polite, even funny some-times. He could pretend to notice they were flirting, but he was never sure how to react.

But with Jillian, it was different. If she stayed around long enough, he might start to feel something for her, and it was his experience anytime his heart got involved, even slightly, it was bad news.

6

Sunnie Larady glared at the woman who had invaded Gram's shop for the past few weeks. Jillian James looked nice enough, but she had to be up to something. No one under forty spends all day in a quilt shop. Jillian was almost as old as her father. She was tall, a few inches less than six feet, and she looked intelligent.

So if she wasn't crazy, she must be up to something.

Sunnie knew her height because she measured everyone by her own height, hoping one day that all the people in the world would all grow half a dozen inches, then she'd be normal. The school counselor said she reached her elevation early, but how did she know? At sixteen, she might still be heading up.

Forget that worry. Right now Sunnie saw her mission clearly. She needed to keep an eye on the stranger.

Why had Dad hired someone to go through the dusty old inventory anyway? Maybe Gram was forgetting things. All old people do. That didn't mean Gram needed a keeper.

The woman couldn't be planning to rob the place. No one in their right mind would steal from a quilt shop.

Jillian looked up from her notes and smiled at Sunnie. "Shall we begin?" she asked, as if they were going on a great adventure and not simply counting quilts.

"I want to help, but I don't want to bother any of Gram's things." She was Eugenia Larady's only great-grandchild. It was her duty to protect Gram's stuff. "This place is like the cemetery. It's okay to clean up, but I don't think we should be moving the quilts around, or Gram might think she's lost something." It was ten after nine and Sunnie was already bored.

Jumping up onto the counter, she decided she'd wait until Jillian told her what to do. No sense giving her ideas. After all, she was just the assistant. Her dad had made that clear. If Jillian told her to do something she didn't like, she'd just call Dad. Until then, she'd follow orders.

Jillian smiled at her again and leaned against the counter, too. She must be working by the hour also. "Your comment reminds me of a graveyard outside of Hamm, Luxembourg. General Patton is buried there. He died in a car crash in 1945 just after the war was over, but he wanted to be buried with his men who died in the Battle of the Bulge. It's a peaceful place in the countryside now, but once, they say the spot ran red with blood."

"Any reason you're giving me this history lesson?" Sunnie picked at the hole in her jeans, making it bigger. "I've had enough history. My dad writes books about tribes in Texas who died off before the Pilgrims landed. He writes mysteries too, but none of them get published, and he wrote a time-travel series he doesn't even try to sell to anyone. To me, all those people are dead and might as well be forgotten. He also writes children's stories about battles. You two should have a long talk."

"I have no reason for bringing Patton up, except I just remembered that when Patton's wife came to visit her husband's grave, she had him moved in front of the other graves. Like he was still leading his men. Some said maybe he would have been happier being *with* them."

"I get it. Moving things in a cemetery." Sunnie rolled her eyes. She hated people who thought conversation was a connect-the-dots hunt. Doze off for two sentences and you're lost.

While she was on the hating things subject, she hated Jillian's straight black hair. It was too shiny and seemed to flow down her back when she moved. Witches, if there really were any, probably had hair like that.

As if Jillian could read her thoughts, she picked up a rubber band and tied her hair into a messy bun. Even that looked good.

Jillian got very professional all at once. "I'm here to log your Gram's things, not relocate them. I promise I'll be very careful with the quilts and I'm very happy to have your help."

Sunnie was glad when Gram came back from the kitchen. This new lady didn't make much more sense than her dad, always spouting facts of no use in the real world. Between Gram repeating herself and Jillian talking about cemeteries, Saturdays were going to be double boring.

But if Sunnie was being honest, at least Jillian James tried to talk to her, and that was more than most people over twenty bothered to do. Sunnie had thought of claiming to be sick this morning, but then Dad might not let her go out with Derrick and she'd been counting the hours since Wednesday when he'd ask her to hang out with him Saturday night. It didn't matter what they did tonight; just being with him was all she'd been thinking about for a month. He was so perfect.

Dad didn't seem to understand how lucky she was. Just turned sixteen and already dating the most talked-about boy in school. She was a sophomore and he was a senior. Even when she told Dad that Derrick had the best baby blue eyes in the world, he wasn't impressed.

Of course, it was Derrick's second senior year. He had missed some school because of a few car wrecks, but he was the hottest guy at Laurel Springs High. He'd played football last year, had the letter jacket to prove it. But he didn't wear it much. Claimed this year was strictly for partying. He'd said his new leather jacket was much cooler.

"I thought we'd start by taking down a few of the wall quilts." Jillian interrupted Sunnie's R-rated prediction of what might happen tonight. They'd been together during school several times, lunch, assemblies, but never for a date. But tonight, something was going to happen. They'd have time to talk, to be alone.

"Can't you just take pictures of them on the wall?" Sunnie hoped to rest at work; after all, she didn't want to be tired tonight.

"I could," Jillian seemed to be considering the alternate plan, "but the shadows of the fans and the angles from window light would not reflect each block to its best advantage."

Sunnie gave in. No point in arguing. She had to do something while she was here or her dad wouldn't pay her eight bucks an hour. He was such a pain. He thought she should earn money. Didn't he understand most of her friends didn't have to work; passing grades should be enough work? Besides, everyone knew the Laradys owned land in town and out. She shouldn't have to work.

Plus, this job wasn't turning out to be as simple as she'd thought. They had to carefully remove each tack, or brace, or cotton rope strapped to the back of the quilt. Once they got it down, it had to be dusted and spread out exactly right before Jillian took about a dozen shots. Then they did it all in reverse.

Sunnie decided she'd die of boredom before noon.

The only break she got was when Jillian asked Gram questions about the quilt she'd just photographed. Most of what Gram talked about wasn't worth writing down, but she did mention that one Texas Star pattern had been pieced by Sunnie's great-great-grandmother.

While Gram talked and Jillian took notes, Sunnie ran her hand slowly over the quilt, realizing that she was touching something that five generations had touched.

When they started on the next quilt hanging high on the wall, Gram said she had to clean the office this morning and couldn't help them, but she spent most of her time visiting with the customers and Mr. Dunaway. If it hadn't been impossible, Sunnie would swear the two were flirting with each other. Sunnie couldn't bear to watch. Even if they were flirting, Mr. Dunaway wouldn't remember what to do after hand patting and winking. Every time he called her grandmother Jeanie, Gram smiled.

Three hours. Four quilts. A dozen visitors, and every time the door chimed Gram popped out of the office like a jack-in-the-box. This was going to take forever. Sunnie tried to stay awake by trying to calculate how many hours it would take for her to earn enough to buy a car.

When Derrick came in, Sunnie almost ran to him and yelled, "Save me. I'm dying in this place."

Only, he didn't like that kind of thing. Derrick said he liked things "real." The first afternoon they'd hung out he'd told her what he expected from her if they were going to be together. No holding hands. No touching in public. No junior high stuff like boyfriend and girlfriend.

He said she was lucky a nineteen-year-old guy like him ever agreed to be seen with a sixteen-year-old, so she needed to understand how things were before it got out that they were together. He picked the time and place. Then, he'd texted her Wednesday that they'd get together Saturday night.

When she texted back that she had to work, so needed to know the exact time, he just answered, I'll find you.

That sounded so exciting. And now, here he was.

Sunnie grinned and almost said aloud, "Isn't he wonderful?"

But she realized Jillian and Gram thought Mr. Dunaway was cute, so she'd be wasting her time.

"How you doing, Shorty?" Derrick winked at her. "I can't wait for tonight."

Sunnie nodded, trying to not look too excited.

He'd said he'd teach her a few things when they were alone. She'd bet it wouldn't be Texas history or where Patton was buried.

When she'd asked for a hint, he laughed. "Don't worry,

we can't go too far. You're jailbait, but we can still have fun."

Sunnie wasn't sure what all that fun might be, but she planned to be a quick learner. Most girls her age had had several boyfriends, but when you were a head taller than every boy in your class all the way through middle school, there's not much interest. Only now, Derrick was two inches taller than her. He'd nicknamed her Shorty the first time he'd talked to her.

He was the first boy who ever flirted with her. She'd been leaning over the railing at a football game a few months ago, and he'd walked right up to her and run his hand along her spine as if he couldn't wait to touch her.

When she straightened, he'd smiled. Most boys backed away. The others didn't realize that the way she dressed was "in" everywhere but this small town. Hadn't they ever walked Sixth Street in Austin? She dressed like the kids from the university did on weekends. She'd seen them once. She wasn't clueless.

Derrick said he liked her light blond hair and her dark makeup. He swore it made her look wickedly sexy.

"You about ready to quit work?" he asked as he moved behind the counter with her.

"No. I have to work until five." She kept folding squares of material. She loved how he moved closer and didn't seem to care he was breaking Gram's rule about no one behind the counter that didn't work in the shop.

He moved a little closer and glanced around, making sure no one was near. Then he slid his hand over her hip and leaned close to whisper, "You got a nice butt, Shorty. You wear any underwear beneath those holey pants?"

She didn't move. His hands, still on her, were below the counter. No one could see what he was doing. If she didn't react, no one would know.

His hand moved again, patting her bottom this time like she was some kind of pet. "I can't feel any. Maybe you're one of those girls who wears a thong."

She didn't like the way he was talking, but this was Derrick. He must know what he was doing. She was just being skittish, like a girl who'd never had a boyfriend.

When he gripped her hip in his hand so hard she knew he was bruising her, she stepped away, banging her side into the cash register.

"Sorry," he said. "But it's not my fault you're so damn touchable."

When she let out a nervous giggle, he leaned close and said, "Tonight we'll go somewhere really alone. I plan to examine a few more parts of your body. Play along, Shorty, and I wouldn't be surprised if you're not wearing my senior ring by Monday morning."

It wasn't exactly romantic, but she didn't need romantic. She wanted real. Life was hard and cruel. Why should love be any different? Besides, Derrick was just a *now* guy. She didn't see them as a couple forever. She never wanted anyone to matter to her as much as her mother had when she died.

"Where are we going?" she asked as she moved a few inches away. She had no doubt her father would ask.

"I thought we'd drive over to Tyler and catch a show. We could warm up a little in the back row."

"What are we seeing?"

"Who cares? Something rated R."

Sunnie nodded as if she agreed with the plan.

"Any chance you get a break from this prison? We could sit in my car and look up what's showing." Derrick bumped her shoulder with his fist.

"Yeah," she said as Jillian stepped from the office. "Oh," Sunnie said louder than necessary, "Derrick, this is Jillian. She works here with Gram."

Derrick nodded. "Nice camera."

Sunnie had the feeling he was looking more at Jillian's breasts than the camera hanging just below them.

Jillian lifted the camera and sat it on the counter, but Derrick's gaze continued to stare at her chest.

To Sunnie's surprise, Jillian's smile seemed to say that she thought of Derrick as a boy, not a man. "Take off for lunch if you like, Sunnie. You did a good job this morning. You need a break."

The woman had obviously heard Derrick's question, but she couldn't have seen him touch her. She'd turned her attention back to her camera, totally dismissing them both.

Derrick didn't seem in any hurry to leave. "You from around here, Jillian?" He said her name slow and low as he turned away from Sunnie.

"It is Jillian, isn't it? I know I would have remembered seeing you."

"No. Just passing through." She didn't look up.

"It's a shame. I like your name, among other things."

Sunnie watched as Derrick's gaze rolled over Jillian like thin paint.

She had heard the phrase *undressing someone with his eyes* but she'd never seen it happen before. Derrick's look was pure predator, like he'd just tossed aside a rabbit for a deer in the trap. Only Sunnie was the rabbit, and she had a feel-ing Jillian was the deer in his sights.

Sunnie didn't hear Jillian's answer. She was too furious to breathe as she grabbed Derrick's arm and almost dragged him out of the store.

"What?" he yelled. The door chime sounded more like a clank.

7

Jillian had been accused of looking younger than her age, but nineteen? The guy must be brain-dead. Or more likely his eyes never made it to her chin. She'd seen his type in every town she'd ever been in. They never change. They simply zip their brains up in their jeans every morning and go hunting.

A few had thought to take advantage of a woman alone. She'd learned to correct that thought swiftly. Trying to go easy on a guy like that only led to more trouble. Only this time, she'd hesitated because of Sunnie. This boy was obviously her friend.

Boys like Derrick were dying off though, or disguising themselves at first. Women no longer put up with them.

Obviously, Derrick wasn't even good at playing grownup. Maybe that was why he was dating sixteen-year-olds. A few weeks from now Sunnie would be smarter, and he'd be looking for his next puppet to manipulate. Jillian was glad Gram was a wall away in the office and hadn't witnessed the scene.

Moving to the side of the front window, Jillian watched

them arguing in the street. Sunnie was mad, jealous, or maybe just embarrassed, and Derrick was an idiot. An interesting pair to square off.

He reached to touch her and she slapped his hand away.

Jillian's glance caught Connor's outline in the newspaper office window directly across Main. He was staring at them, arms folded, feet wide apart. She could see the anger in his stance, but if he stepped outside, his daughter would turn on him and Connor was smart enough to know it. If he broke up the fight, Sunnie would hate him for treating her like a child. If he didn't, she wouldn't speak to him for allowing her to make a fool of herself to the whole town. Sometimes, no matter what a dad does, he can't win.

But Jillian saw something else going on. Sunnie was growing up in the middle of the argument, in the middle of the street. She was winning. Derrick was backing down, feeling cornered—and, like a wild animal, he might attack.

A memory of the first guy she'd dated flashed in Jillian's mind. He'd knocked her to the floor the first time they'd argued. When she'd cried to her pop, he'd told her one black eye was a cheap lesson. Step away. Don't get involved.

Jillian didn't want Sunnie to have to learn that lesson.

Neither of the kids seemed to notice people stopping to watch. If this fight escalated, Sunnie would be the one talked about. The one hurt.

A sound came from the kitchen as Jillian reached the door.

Gram must have dropped something.

For a second, Jillian froze, not sure which way to run. "Gram?"

"I'm fine, dear. Just dropped this old teapot and splashed hot water everywhere."

Jillian chose her crisis. She rushed outside and did something she never did. She stepped in and got involved.

"Glad I caught you, Sunnie," she yelled as if she hadn't noticed Derrick was spitting out swear words.

"What?" Sunnie's question was sharp, but she didn't turn back to Derrick.

"I need help. Gram is in trouble. I think she's hurt." It was only a small lie. Gram hadn't sounded hurt, just flustered, but it was all Jillian could think of in one second.

"Come on, Derrick," Sunnie ordered and took off running for the shop.

"Yes, come," Jillian encouraged in a lower voice. "Someone's got to clean up the vomit while we rush her to the clinic."

Derrick held up one hand and backed away. "I'm not good with old people. Or sick people. Or helping. I got to go." He wasn't smart enough to think of an excuse, so he just ran.

Jillian grinned and caught a glimpse of Connor's smile in the newspaper office window. He might not have heard the words exchanged, but he was aware that she'd broken up the argument.

She ran back into the store and found Sunnie kneeling at Gram's chair near the office door. "Now, Gram, you have to tell me where you hurt." Tears wiped away some of the girl's black makeup. "Maybe I can help."

Gram brushed her wrinkled hand over her great-granddaughter's light blond hair. "I'm just getting old, sweetie. We all do. Sometimes my grip isn't as good as it used to be." When she saw she had all Sunnie's attention, she added, "I feel a little faint. I scalded my hand with the boiling water I'd warmed for tea. It's nothing. It'll stop burning soon."

Jillian looked at Gram's hand. It was red. She'd been so busy with Sunnie, trying to get as much done as possible this morning, that she hadn't even noticed Gram hadn't had her morning tea.

"How can I help?" Sunnie lifted Gram's hand.

"Stay with her," Jillian ordered, acting as if she were the head nurse in the ER. "I'll get the first aid kit. If we get to the burn fast, it might not blister." She'd seen a kit in the restroom and prayed it wasn't fifty years old.

A minute later she was back with the kit and paper towels she'd wet with cold water. Sunnie gently placed them over Gram's hand as Jillian lined up the supplies. She had little knowledge of any kind of first aid. Her only hope was that Sunnie had less and Gram had forgotten.

Antiseptic cream, gauze, and tape. "The wet towels will take the heat out. I'll hand you another one as soon as that feels warm."

Sunnie nodded.

Gram played her part like a pro. She loved the attention. Her hand was now trembling, but her great-granddaughter held it gently in place.

"As soon as her skin feels cool, dry it off and spread the antiseptic out very carefully, then wrap it with gauze. I'll cut the tape strips for you."

"Good plan." Sunnie set to work like a pro. "I've seen this done on TV. I've got this." With each step she asked if she was hurting Gram, and the old lady kept saying that Sunnie was so gentle she didn't feel a thing.

Sunnie stayed on her knees in front of her gram after her nursing was finished. "What else can I do, Gram?"

"I think my stomach might settle if I had one of those crescent rolls from Mamma Bee's with chicken salad inside."

Sunnie laughed. "You got it. I'll bring back cookies, too." She kissed her gram and stood. "Three sandwiches and cookies?" Sunnie looked at Jillian, silently making sure of the number.

"Three. I'll watch over her till you get back." Jillian nodded. "You did a great job."

"She's got the gift," Gram bragged. "They used to say my mother had the gift of healing. Seems it passed down to Sunnie. My hand doesn't hurt at all."

"Maybe she should think about becoming a doctor," Jillian agreed. "I haven't known many people your age so calm in an emergency."

The girl shrugged as if she didn't care what they thought, but Jillian swore she saw the twitch of a smile.

Gram pushed very gently. "You'd have to give up boys for a while, if you're bound for med school."

"No problem there." Sunnie rolled her eyes.

How is it possible you can see someone grow up in a moment? Jillian thought. Only she knew it was true because she'd just witnessed it. The attitude might still be there, but a new intelligence was peeking through all the black makeup.

Sunnie vanished on her mission for lunch, while Jillian marveled at the change in the girl. Connor was right; his daughter did love Gram. She could think of nothing that would have brought her back into the shop except her great-grandmother.

"She's always been a sweetie." Gram looked up at Jillian. "You saved her out there. I was watching from the office window. I couldn't hear what you said, but when she hit that door with worry in her eyes, I figured I'd better think fast."

"Your hand was red. You did scald it."

"I did and it hurts, but if I complained every time I spilled the tea water or bloodied my finger with a needle, I'd be in *The Guinness Book of World Records*." She patted Jillian's hand with her bandaged one. "But you did a good job of letting Sunnie doctor me up."

"You think you could need Sunnie a little longer? I wouldn't be surprised if Derrick came looking for her. Having a sixteen-year-old break up with him must be a blow to his ego."

Gram giggled. "Let him come. He'll face me this time. I'll hit him so hard between his eyes the only thing he'll be seeing is his nose. He'll turn twenty-one before those baby blue eyes uncross." Gram rolled her eyes back, obviously imitating Sunnie. "I can play puny till Gabriel blows his horn if it'll keep that young man away from Sunnie. He's too old, too stupid, and too homely to even be on the same continent as her."

"I agree. Whatever you're plotting, Gram, I'm in." Jillian had the sense to know she was standing before a master. Gram might have forgotten whether she ate breakfast this morning and had already lost her scissors twice, but at this moment, she was fully on her game.

Twenty minutes later the three women were circled

around the tiny kitchen table eating lunch when Connor walked in. "Everything all right?"

They all smiled that closed-mouthed smile all men understand means women know something they're not talking about. Finally, Sunnie broke. "We're just fine, Dad. Just taking a lunch break."

The two others nodded as if they'd just sworn to a vow of silence.

8

Connor wasn't surprised when Sunnie climbed onto the Autumn Acres bus with Gram that evening. Everyone knew grandchildren were always welcome at the Acres, and tonight his daughter didn't seem to have anywhere else she'd rather be. Like Gram had been to Connor, she was always there, always loving, never judgmental.

"I'll call you, Dad, when the movie's over," Sunnie yelled out the window. "Gram says we're watching *Grease* tonight, and they're serving banana splits at intermission."

Connor nodded. "The Acres's movies always have at least one intermission for restroom breaks and snacks."

He noticed most of his daughter's black makeup was missing from around her eyes. "You know, Gram's seen *Grease* a dozen times."

"I know. We both sing along with all the songs. Pretty lame, I know. I'm trying to talk the event planners into doing a *Grease*-style dance one night. Mr. Dunaway said he and Gram used to dance together when they were young." Sunnie smiled as she hadn't smiled in weeks. "Later, Dad."

Connor backed away, watching them go. It seemed only

a few days had passed since he'd watched her leave for first grade on a yellow bus. He'd offered to drive her, but she shook her head. "I've been waiting years to ride the bus, Daddy." So she danced with excitement up the steps, and he stood in the driveway watching until the bus disappeared.

"She's a good kid." Jillian locked the shop door with the key he'd given her. "You should have seen the way she took care of Gram."

Connor crammed his hands into his pockets. "I know she's got a good heart, but sometimes I wonder where her brain goes. Point one being that jerk of a boy she planned to go out with tonight. His senior picture is probably a mug shot. Why would she pick that walking train wreck to be seen with?"

"I know." Connor couldn't have missed the anger in her voice as Jillian added, "For a while he had his eyes stuck to my chest. I think that may have been what started the fight they had."

"The one in the street for half the town to see?"

"Yes." Jillian laughed. "Both of them looked so livid I wasn't sure which one might throw the first punch. If it had turned physical, my money would have been on Sunnie."

"You don't know how hard it was for me to keep from storming out and decking the guy. Thanks for saving her."

"I just gave her a choice. A way out. As to why she picked him, I'm guessing it was simply because he is tall."

Connor shook his head. "She's got to have more requirements than that. Like potential, or manners, or at least a dozen functioning brain cells."

"She'll have a longer list, next time."

"There's going to be a next time? I was hoping she'd give

my inevitable heart attack a reprieve and not date again until college."

Jillian turned toward the bed-and-breakfast, pulling the collar of her jacket up against the cool breeze from the north. After a few steps, she glanced back at Connor. "Aren't you walking home?"

He swore he heard a hint of disappointment in her voice and wondered if she enjoyed the walks, too.

"My Audi and my truck are both behind the shop. Since I didn't take Gram to lunch, I didn't bother to take it back to the house. I was thinking I should take you out tonight to celebrate. Maybe someplace other than Mamma Bee's Pastries."

"If you celebrate every time your daughter turns down a jerk, you may be eating out a lot." She glanced up at the cloudy sky. "Looks like rain. I might catch a ride since you're heading that way."

He didn't move as he watched her closely. "I'm not celebrating losing Derrick for a son-in-law. The party is for you. Two hours after I emailed in your articles this afternoon, the *Fort Worth Star-Telegram* picked one up."

"Really?" She covered her mouth as though holding back a cry of joy. "Tell me all about it."

"Over dinner," he insisted. "I didn't have lunch today so I'm starving. When I came over to pick up Gram, she was already eating a sandwich. So, lady, you owe me a dinner partner for an hour."

"Fair enough, but you're right, not Mamma Bee's. Every time I eat one of her great sandwiches I can feel the pounds layering on my backside."

He opened his mouth to comment about the nature of

her backside but quickly reconsidered. After a moment he said, very formally, "Where would you like to go, Miss James? It's your party, after all."

"Lennie's Tacos and More."

"I had no idea you loved Mexican food."

"I don't. I plan to eat the More."

Thirty minutes later they were crowded shoulder to shoulder at the restaurant's bar. He ordered a taco plate, and she ordered a steak with fried eggs and hot sauce on top. Huevos rancheros, with eight ounces of steak as the bottom layer, pure Texas style.

It was so noisy they had to yell unless their heads were close. Once, her hair touched his cheek. A slight brush, nothing more, but his senses came alive. He could hear her, but had to fight the impulse to close the distance between them. Connor couldn't remember being so attracted to a woman.

She was excited about being paid for her writing and kept swiveling on her stool, bumping his leg now and then. It was accidental, a casual touch, but so rare in his world that he had to keep reminding himself it meant nothing.

Once he knew her better, they'd settle into being friends. That's how it always happened. He was too steady, too boring, too nailed down with baggage to be spontaneous. He had a wealth of worthless information to talk about—books, politics, ancient history—but he suspected women didn't want that these days. Maybe they never did. They wanted excitement.

He wouldn't even know where to start.

But Jillian didn't flirt with him, didn't even try. If she was waiting for him to make the first move, good luck with that. He was attracted to her, but that didn't mean he planned to do anything about it.

This dinner, one-on-one, alone with a woman near his age, was so unusual he wasn't sure how to react. He'd dated a few girls in college before he met his wife, and he'd gone out a few times after she died, but he'd never felt like he did now. Jillian was a friend, almost. An employee, almost. A stranger still, for sure.

After arguing over who paid, they ran back to his truck, dodging huge raindrops. He put his arm around her shoulders lightly, protecting her as much as he could and wondering if she felt the pull, too. If she didn't? If he guessed wrong? One mistake, stepping too far, could ruin the fragile alliance between them.

She was kind to Gram. She'd helped his daughter. They talked. They laughed. He'd helped her sell her article. None of that added up to anything more than friendship.

Better he keep things the way they were now. Venturing out into feelings had never done him much good.

He drove back to the bed-and-breakfast, staying on safe topics.

"You could build on this one article, maybe even do several? I'd be happy to help with the editing. I've published a few dozen articles in research journals and a few in travel magazines."

He'd even done three books on early Texas—*way* early, before Columbus. They'd sold to a university press and the royalty check usually paid for a nice dinner out every six months. But he wasn't about to mention those. One chapter on the Clovis culture a thousand years ago would work better than the Queen's apple did in *Snow White*.

She asked questions about what the newspaper in Fort Worth paid and how often they might buy one of her articles, but didn't say if she planned to do more.

When he pulled in front of her lodging, she didn't move to get out of the truck. Both just watched rain running down the windows for a few minutes. The streetlights were fuzzy and the town looked like a fresh watercolor painting left out in the rain.

Finally she broke the silence. "I forgot to tell you about a quilt Gram showed me today."

He turned off the truck and shifted to face her, enjoying the stillness of the inside of his Ford compared to the noise in the restaurant. The sound of the rain was almost background music, and he liked being able to hear her sigh.

"It was a friendship quilt a group of women made. All done in Laurel Springs High School colors, purple and white. The women who put it together had been cheerleaders back in the early eighties. Most only kept in touch by Christmas cards and eventually emails, but they considered themselves a sisterhood. After twenty-five years they decided to have a reunion weekend. No husbands or family, lots of wine and laughing."

"I get the picture," he said, almost wanting to interrupt her story just to tell Jillian how much he loved all the stories she told. Gram never talked to him the way she did this stranger. Jillian was accomplishing exactly what he wanted her to. She was collecting the town's stories.

Maybe Jillian simply had the time to listen, or maybe Gram thought everyone else had already heard the stories. But Jillian was sharing them with him, as if letting him in on a treasure hunt.

She leaned back, relaxing, as she continued, "Each ex-cheerleader was to bring a quilt square picturing a memory of their high school glory. A football game won. The night they dropped Kandy and she broke her leg. The slumber party they had out at a scary cabin. The night it snowed on the way home from the state competition. The all-night party after graduation, when their last cheer routine stopped the dance with the crowd roaring."

He hadn't been popular in high school, but in small towns the cheerleaders are kind of like the local celebrity gossip channel. Everyone kept up with what they were doing, who they dated.

Jillian stretched her leg and bumped his knee.

Neither one commented. An accidental touch. Nothing more.

"So the story goes, according to Gram. They all spent two days drinking, singing old songs, trying to do all the old cheers, then on Sunday morning they each wrote their name with disappearing ink on the big square one of the girls had quilted in the school colors.

"By this time most were hungover from wine and several rounds of shots. They wanted to get home. They'd talked the high school year through. All except for the all-night party. The last night they were all together. Gram said they'd made a pact at the party when they were all eighteen. They promised in twenty-five years, if they all came together, they'd tell any secrets kept from the others."

"This is getting interesting." Connor leaned closer, wishing he could see her face clearer in the darkness. "Let me guess. Any murders? Secret babies? Wild affairs?"

"No. Only one real secret. Seven of them had kept it

from one girl. It seemed this one, a cheerleader they called Mag, was engaged and planned to marry at the end of summer after graduation. She was still a virgin and so was the shy boy she was marrying."

Connor didn't miss the tear that slid unchecked down Jillian's cheek and knew her story wouldn't have a happy ending.

"The women took the quilt to Gram's shop that last morning. Then each embroidered her signature on the quilt before the ink vanished. Little by little, they told what they'd all kept silent about. What all seven had tried to forget.

"The secret came out in pieces while they finished sewing. Several of the girls got the shy boy off by himself and, as Gram put it, 'tried to teach him a few things.' At first he must have thought it a harmless joke, but a few of the girls went too far. He fought them off and finally broke away, embarrassed by what they did, what he'd seen. It made the girls mad that he got so upset, and they told everyone he was gay."

"Was he?"

"I don't know. Gram said she thought he and Mag were planning to be missionaries. She thinks he was just naive. But he left town that night. Engagement broken. He'd changed his mind."

Connor followed the logic. "If he had played along, the story would have gotten out and Mag would have probably broken up with him anyway. The boy couldn't win with seven-to-one odds, plus groups tend to push each other. The girls probably went further than they'd planned."

She nodded, agreeing with his logic. "As the girls confessed their secret, Mag grew angry. It seemed she'd never loved another like him, and she'd spent years looking for him. Mag picked up the quilt and stuffed it in the trash. She swore they'd all be sorry."

Jillian jumped when she heard thunder roll. She bumped his knee again, and this time she didn't try to pull away. Connor didn't move his knee either. The coming storm was making her on edge. Maybe touching him, even slightly, was calming. But it was having the opposite effect on him.

"Folks heard about the fight at the quilt shop. A few said the women were running out the front door like the devil had come to town."

"I guess that broke up the weekend."

"It did. Gram said, as far as she knew, none of the girls kept in touch with each other after that. Gram found the quilt that Monday morning after they'd used her shop machine to put the names on as a final touch. She finished the border on it. She said she noticed all eight names were on the school colors square."

Connor could guess the rest. "Gram finished it off and no one ever came to pick up the quilt. She called a few of the girls and heard the story, but none wanted to claim the quilt."

"Right, but that's not all the story. Every now and then Gram takes the quilt from the shelf and refolds it. She says that's what everyone knows to do with quilts."

"Makes sense." He shrugged, guessing Jillian hadn't heard of that rule either.

She lowered her voice to a whisper and added, "One by one over the years, all the names have disappeared. The block where they'd been put is empty."

"You think Mag killed them, then came back to town, snuck into the shop and ripped out each dead cheerleader's name?"

Jillian laughed. "Sunnie told me you write mystery stories sometimes, but that's a little too much for a town named Laurel Springs, don't you think? Besides, if they'd died, Gram would have heard about it. Most still have family here. She says she asks about them now and then, like folks do with people that were high school stars. One had cancer, but lived. One's been married three times, but she's made a good income from it. None of the seven seemed to have any more heartache than anyone else their age."

"But the names on the quilt disappeared."

She smiled. "But the names disappeared."

He grinned at her. "Great story for a stormy night. You mind if I do some digging for a few facts?"

"No..."

Lightning crackled across the sky and he swore he saw sudden panic in her stormy blue-gray eyes.

Before he could react, the next flash lit up the sky and she was gone. She'd opened the truck door and was halfway to the porch before he thought to move.

9

Maybe it was telling the story of the cheerleader quilt, or maybe it was the stormy night full of dark shadows and eerie sounds, but Jillian felt a haunting in the air. As if something unseen walked the earth tonight.

Something far more real than Mrs. Kelly's shy ghost.

She ran from Connor's truck to the porch, not giving him time to open his door or reach for an umbrella to shelter her.

Stick-armed trees swiped at her from the bushes, and she swore she could hear a hungry animal howling in the wind.

She had heard Connor call, "Wait." But she didn't stop. Panic blended with memories of childhood nightmares, dark and thick in her mind.

Her dad used to leave her in the trailer on weekend nights, when his oil field work was done. He'd told her bad things run around after dark so she'd best stay inside. She had no phone, no one to turn to if she got scared.

On those nights when she was alone in a town where she had no neighbor to trust, she'd curl up trying to get warm and cry as the wind rocked the trailer and what sounded like wild animals cried in the blackness beyond the flimsy windows that rattled like paper. Sometimes she swore the trees scratched at the roof, but she'd been too frightened to even pull back the covers and look.

Shivering, Jillian opened the unlocked bed-and-breakfast door. Only tiny desk-lamp lights welcomed her. One in the foyer, one on each landing of the stairs, one on a table just outside her bedroom door.

Mrs. Kelly had left early for a wedding in Dallas and wouldn't be back until very late. "There are no other guests tonight," she'd said. "Make yourself comfortable in the place."

The old house creaked. Wooden arthritis accompanied by the *ting* on crystal chandeliers calling out to the slightest movement. No cookies waited for her on the parlor table tonight. No low warm fire in the old Rookwood tiled fireplace.

Trying to shake the feeling of being totally alone, Jillian ran up the stairs to her room and curled under the covers. She wouldn't cry. She'd made that mistake a few times before when she was afraid as a child. When her father caught her, he'd sworn and said, "If I hear one more sound out of you, I'll give you something to cry about. You're born alone and you'll die alone, kid, so you might as well get used to it."

He was rarely cruel, but one night he'd been drinking when he returned home and found her afraid. He'd slapped her hard and told her to stop being a fool like her mother had been. Then he'd walked out, mumbling something about a promise he'd keep if it killed him.

She'd cried in the shower after that night, or in the school restrooms, or sometimes when she walked home. But she never cried where he could hear her again.

Once she grew up, she always picked busy apartment houses to rent. She might still be alone, but she was among the herd. Safety in numbers.

Jillian heard the hard tap of half-frozen raindrops on the bay windows of her little room. She tried to slow her breathing and calm the child inside her who had never quite gotten over stormy nights. Reason never worked when fear climbed into her heart. She'd simply hide, and wait until exhaustion let her sleep. In the morning, like her father had, she'd call herself a fool, a coward. But for now, all she could do was withdraw into her covers.

"Jillian," the storm seemed to call.

She pulled a pillow tightly over her head.

"Jillian?" The voice was gentle, but growing louder.

She stilled. It wasn't the wind. And she knew it wasn't her father. Tentatively, she pulled the pillow away.

Connor Larady stood at her open door. Slowly, he walked closer until he reached her bed and looked down at her with worry in his eyes. "Are you all right?" His hair was wet and his jacket shiny from rain. "I'm sorry to barge in, but you looked terrified when I saw you in a flash of lightning, then you ran so fast I couldn't catch up to you."

Part of her wanted to sit up straight and act like the woman she was, confident, brave, used to being alone. But tonight wasn't her bravest hour. All the nights of fear piled up, making her unable to move. "No," she said simply as she glared at him, knowing there was nothing he could do about it. "I'm not all right."

Shakespeare was right. *A coward dies a thousand times before his death.*

He'd think less of her now. Maybe he wouldn't and be her friend; after all, she wasn't being rational.

To her surprise, Connor knelt beside her bed and his big cold hands cupped her face. "Are you ill?"

She shook her head without answer. She wasn't about to tell him she was afraid.

Lightning rattled the windows and she jerked as if bracing for thunder's blow. Maybe he wouldn't look so calm now if he'd lived through Alaskan winters in a tin box on wheels. If he'd been left alone with no one to run to. If he'd been slapped when he'd cried out in fear.

He seemed to study her a moment, then said calmly, "I think I understand." Without another word he bundled her into the blankets and lifted her up. He carried her to the third-floor hallway. There wasn't much room, but he set her down on the top step, then turned and closed the door leading to her room that now seemed to showcase the storm in the wide windows.

When he sat down beside her, he leaned his back against the stairs' sturdy mahogany balusters and pulled her against his chest.

Jillian had no idea what was going on, but suddenly the world calmed. The storm seemed far away and the blasts of lightning had been replaced by the low glow of a Tiffany-style lamp on the tiny table near her room's door.

Her breathing slowed; she warmed in the cocoon he'd made her.

"Better?" he whispered.

"Better," she answered.

As the storm pounded on the roof above, he simply held her. He asked no more questions. He didn't try to explain away her fear. His arm sheltered her, keeping the terror at bay, until finally the storm played out like a misbehaving child going from manic to exhausted.

When she straightened and pushed away on his chest, Connor didn't try to stop her. "You okay?" he asked.

"I am. Thank you." Standing, she felt like she carried ten pounds of royal robes about her. "I should put these back on the bed," she said, just to have something to say other than she was sorry for being a basket case.

Only, he didn't look like he thought her a fool.

He stood but made no attempt to follow as she walked back into her bedroom. A few stars were breaking through the brooding sky. The rain had turned to tiny patters on the windows.

Covers back on the bed, she turned and faced him. For a few heartbeats neither said a word. They just stood staring at each other in the low glow of the hallway light.

She couldn't simply say good-night and close the door. Not after what he'd done. He'd followed her through the rain to make sure she was all right, and when she wasn't, he'd known how to help.

For the first time in her life, someone had ridden out the storm with her. Not telling her she was silly or giving a lecture on weather, but simply holding her.

"You want some coffee? Mrs. Kelly said I could have the use of the kitchen if I clean up after myself."

"No, thanks. I…"

She watched as he stared at her as if he had no idea how to finish the sentence.

Finally his brain kick-started again. "I'd rather have that cocoa you made the night I came in for cookies."

He smiled slightly and she swore he looked ten years younger.

She removed her wet jacket and looped it over the banister. Her shirt was damp and clung to her, but it would dry quickly.

As she passed him she whispered, "Let's break into Mrs. Kelly's cookie jar."

"I'm right behind you, Sundance, but I'm telling you right now, I'm not wearing one of her aprons."

A few minutes later they were laughing at the apron lying out on the counter, ready for tomorrow morning. It read *I'm fully aware your advice isn't in my recipe, but keep talking if it makes you happy.*

Jillian made the cocoa while he ripped off paper towels to serve as plates. Then they slowly opened the huge cookie jar made in the shape of an apple.

Connor looked in and announced, "We can probably steal three each before she notices. No more or we'll be caught. They hang cookie thieves in these parts, Sundance."

"I'm willing to risk it, Butch." She giggled, glad that she remembered the old movie with Robert Redford and Paul Newman. *Butch Cassidy and the Sundance Kid.* A classic.

They sat across from each other at the tiny kitchen bar, arguing over which cookie was the best. Tiny tea cookies, thin lemon-sugar bars, double-dipped chocolate fudge, oatmeal cookies with applesauce mixed in.

He kept wanting to taste hers, just to be sure his was the winner.

"If Mrs. Kelly corners us," Jillian whispered, as if forming a plot to escape, "we claim the ghost did it."

Connor nodded. "So she's still swearing this place is haunted. I'm surprised she doesn't put it up on the internet. I can see the headline: Share a Bed with Long-Dead Willie Flancher."

Jillian pointed her cookie at him. "You don't believe in ghosts?"

"No, I've got enough things haunting me. Bad grades. Bad decisions. Half my weekends in college and pretty much all the ones in high school. How about you? What haunts you from the past?"

"I have no regrets." She lied and knew from the slight rise of his eyebrow that he didn't believe her.

"Someday," he said as if they had all the time in the world, "maybe you'll think of one and tell me."

"Maybe," she answered, relieved he didn't push. "But now's a nice time to tell me about old Willie."

"I don't know much. My dad did a feature on him once for the paper. Willie fought for Texas independence in 1836. Outlived four wives and died at eighty-three on his fifth wedding night."

"Just proves sex will kill you."

They both laughed and she decided she liked Connor. He'd be a steady friend to have for a few months.

"Strange thing about Willie," Connor added. "He didn't show up at the bed-and-breakfast until about ten years ago. Mrs. Kelly started mentioning Willie to folks about a year after Mr. Kelly ran off with the young organist at the Methodist church. I always thought the ghost arrival might be her way of having a man in the old house."

"Maybe Mrs. Kelly killed Mr. Kelly and just made up the ghost?"

Connor shook his head. "She may have made up the ghost, but she didn't kill Mr. Kelly. He married the organist and they live in Tyler. Have four kids, which must be hard on him since he's a few years older than Mrs. Kelly. He'll be well into his sixties before they all get out of grade school."

Jillian leaned her head sideways. "And you know all this how?"

Connor laughed. "Mrs. K keeps up with them, even sends them Christmas gifts. She has no hard feelings. Says she'd rather live with a ghost than old snoring Sam Kelly."

Jillian laughed so hard her sides hurt.

The rain was now only a dribble off the roof, almost forgotten, as she talked to this kind man trying so hard to make her smile. In a big city, with a tailored suit on and his hair styled, Connor Larady would have a powerful presence. But here in his wrinkled, damp, elbow-patched jacket, with his hair looking windblown even on a calm day, Jillian thought he was irresistible.

A dozen cookies and two mugs of cocoa later, when he stood to leave, he seemed to be studying her. "Strange that you're afraid of storms when your eyes are the color of rainy nights."

"I'm not normally so easy to upset. I'm usually more prepared for them. Watching the weather is part of my everyday routine, and this one wasn't predicted to come in before midnight." She was rattled and realized she didn't want him to leave just yet. "I like to be around people when any kind of storm hits. I've waited out many blustery nights in hotel bars or in rooms with blackout curtains so I couldn't see lightning. Once I spent the night in an airport before driving home so the bad weather couldn't get to me."

"You all right now?"

"I'm fine." She shrugged. "Storms are my Achilles' heel. The raging winds always make me think of wolves the size of horses fighting at the door to get in." She turned away, not wanting him to think less of her but knowing she had to thank him. "You helped me tonight. No one's ever done that before."

"I'm glad I was here. Call on me anytime to fight your storms."

She couldn't look up. How could she say that the next time he wouldn't be around? He was grounded, bolted to this land, and she was a tumbleweed blowing across ever-changing terrain. When she was caught by a storm again, she'd hide as always. She'd be alone.

"Are *we* all right?" He finally broke the silence. "I didn't step out of line, did I?"

She didn't pretend to misunderstand what he meant. "We're better than all right. I think we've become friends."

Now, he looked away, reaching for his jacket, all at once in a hurry as if she'd said something wrong.

"What is it?"

"Nothing," he said too quickly.

She'd never known one word could sound so hollow. "What?" Somehow she'd offended him.

"It's nothing, really. I just wish for once…" He moved to the kitchen door. "Never mind. Friends is fine. Friends is good. Friends is probably predictable."

She crossed to block the doorway, guessing how he felt. He wasn't the kind of man to make a pass or ever suggest something between them, but his thoughts were pounding in the silence so loud she swore she could hear the beat.

All the times she'd seen him standing at the big window looking out at Main. Always alone. The days she'd noticed him walking down by the creek all by himself. One of the quilters had even asked Gram once why he never dated after his wife died.

She took a guess at reading his thoughts now. "You wish for one moment, one hour maybe, we could be more than just casual friends without all the complications that come with stepping into a relationship?"

He met her eyes and she knew she was right. She grew bolder. "Maybe both our lives are rolling in a storm, and we just need someone to hold on to for a moment."

"Yeah. I'd settle for six minutes," he admitted as his body seemed to relax a bit. "I don't know if I could handle much more, not all at once. My life is far too confusing to invite someone in to stay longer. But it would be nice to shelter in one place for a few minutes."

"I feel the same." She studied him, this complicated man who took the entire town's problems on his shoulders. She stepped closer and smiled. "We're already criminals, Butch, so why don't we steal a little time? Six minutes, ten, and then never speak of it again. It'll be like we saw the trailer, but never watched the movie."

Taking his hand, Jillian tugged him into the old parlor with its turn-of-the-century Victorian furniture and pattern rugs.

Sitting on the small couch, she pulled him down beside her. She'd been so brave with this crazy suggestion, but where should they start? Maybe she was all talk and no action. Maybe he was, too. If so, there would never be even a spark of fire between them.

Neither relaxed. They seemed as stiff as the furniture. Finally, he stood and turned on a ribbon of gas in the fireplace. When he placed a few logs on the rack, the fire came alive.

Returning, he gently pulled her to her feet. She was only a few inches shorter than him. Five foot ten to his six foot one.

The night outside was silent now, and the fire offered warmth. He laced his fingers in hers and shrugged. "I think you've got a great idea, but I don't know where to start."

She leaned closer. "We're just sharing a hug, nothing more. No promises. Just two people holding on to one another after the storm. We're just passing a moment in time."

He put his hand on her waist and studied her face. "You're very beautiful, you know. I almost didn't hire you for Gram's shop because I figured I'd walk across the street just to stare at you. When I first looked up and saw you, I wasn't sure you were real."

"Then touch me. I'm real, Connor."

"Where?"

"Anywhere you like, but the talking is over. I just want to feel you closer, even if it only lasts six minutes." For once in her life she wanted to keep a memory, nothing more, just one pure memory. Then she'd leave the rest of Laurel Springs behind.

"I think I'd like that."

Like a bothersome bee, his cell phone buzzed. Once. Twice. Three times before either had the sense to move apart. He grabbed his cell as she closed her eyes, knowing their one moment was slipping away.

"Hello," he said, his voice sounding almost normal.

"Wake up, Dad." Jillian heard Sunnie's voice shouting from the phone. "The movie's over and I'm ready for you to come get me."

Connor stepped farther away from Jillian, but it seemed as wide a gap as the Grand Canyon.

"I'll be right there." He clicked the phone off and reached for his coat. "I have to go."

He froze, staring at her in the firelight. "I…"

Jillian could see his struggle and tried to help. "No strings. No promises. No worries. What almost happened, never happened. There is nothing to say."

"Right." He kept staring.

"Your daughter's waiting."

"Right," he said again and jerked as if he'd been poked with a cattle prod.

He was gone before Jillian could ask if she should forget what almost happened or wait for another chance. He didn't seem like a man who found himself alone with any woman, and the chances he'd be with her totally alone again were slight.

She couldn't save an almost-memory. What almost happened, never happened.

She turned off the gas flames beneath the logs and walked back to the kitchen. She could still feel him near her as she cleaned up. They'd been outlaws stealing cookies for only a blink in time, but it made her smile.

"It's Saturday," she whispered to herself. She'd have a whole day tomorrow to think about what had almost happened. Then she'd put it away and try her best to forget him holding her during the storm.

The logs were glowing when she passed back through the parlor.

"Six minutes more might have been more than I could handle." Her words echoed through the empty rooms. "If I allowed myself any more, one of us, maybe both, would walk away hurt."

Only she hadn't even gotten a chance to find out. Her words drifted in the still air, but no answer came.

"No regrets, though," she called to the empty house, then waited to see if an answer echoed back.

When the ghost didn't answer, she said, "I don't want to know what you're thinking, Mr. Willie Flancher. I don't even have time for a ghost to haunt me."

Laughing at herself, she wondered if crazy people settle in small towns or normal folks move there and are driven mad. In her case it appeared to be a fifty-fifty split.

As she climbed the stairs to her room, she decided it was time to make the drive to Oklahoma City. She was getting too involved with the people in this town. She needed to know that she could leave. She had to make sure she'd have everything in order.

The trip to Oklahoma City would put her mind to rest. The drive would give her time to think, to plan.

She'd deposit money in her account at the bank, then check her mailbox she'd paid rent on for years. She also needed to visit her secret stash and make sure her dad's letter was still in the stacks at the library.

Surely someday he'd wonder how she was. Maybe he'd check his old hiding place. It had been the first place she'd looked at the end of her freshman year. Her papers were still there, along with five hundred dollars. Nothing of his remained.

But now, after ten years, maybe he'd checked on her. Maybe he'd left a note for her. One thread was all she wanted, all she needed.

Tomorrow she'd go check, then she'd take the rest of the day to think about how the moments she'd shared with Connor had felt before she put them away in the back of her mind.

Papa's rule: *Don't pack memories. They'll weigh you down.*

She knew he was right. Tonight she'd almost collected a memory that would have been hard to leave behind. Now it was just a thought of what might have been. That was enough.

10

Sunnie sat beside Gram's bed, watching her sleep. The day had been endless, but being here close to her great-grandmother made everything seem right with the world. Gram was always there for her. She'd been the only one Sunnie could talk to when her mother died. If some people are solid as rocks in your life, Gram was a boulder.

She had stood beside her when Dad took the call from the Reno Police Department saying her mother's body had been pulled from the wreckage of a small plane. Sunnie had a thousand questions but was afraid to ask. She was old enough to realize she might not want to hear the answers.

Gram stayed close in those first few dark days, and she took her hand as they walked away after the funeral.

"It's going to be all right, Sunnie," Gram had whispered. "One thing I've learned is life goes on."

Even though Sunnie didn't believe her at the time, she felt better just hearing the words.

Finally, when the nightmare settled to a dull ache inside and all the company had gone home, Gram just held her tight and whispered, "We all walk close to death until the end, when death comes one last time and walks beside us."

A part of Sunnie thought maybe if she held Gram's hand real tight, death would never come for her gram. Discovering someone worth loving wasn't easy, and she'd been lucky enough to be born with Gram's love already waiting for her.

She had a feeling love would never come that easy again. Of course, her dad would always love her, but probably no one else. She wasn't pretty, or smart, or funny, or talented. And too tall, she added to the list. Look at Jillian; she was shorter than her and wasn't married.

Maybe she should forget about looking for what the songs call true love. Forget about even making friends. Better to make it through life alone than to constantly lose people. Jillian James obviously had the right idea.

Speaking of losing people. Sunnie had no doubt Derrick would never speak to her again. Not after she'd left him steaming mad on the sidewalk. His face was red, and his nostrils flared like a bull about to charge.

The visual made her smile. Serves him right. Flirting with a woman almost twice her age, like Jillian might go out with a guy in high school. Dumb Derrick probably didn't even consider that.

Mr. Irresistible turned creepy fast. Handsome must be a thin coat of paint that can wash off in rain. She might consider looking a little deeper next time. She'd thought Derrick was the whole package. Turns out he was just the wrapping.

But then, Sunnie hadn't really considered what would happen when she walked away from him either. The coolest guy in school. The bad boy everyone wanted to talk to or hang out with. A few other sophomores had seen her with him and acted like they were jealous. She was suddenly cool by association.

But no more. She'd be an outcast tomorrow. Not that the label was anything new. Sunnie didn't play sports, wasn't a cheerleader or in drama. She wasn't in any stupid club that wore matching shirts or had lunch together on Wednesdays. No band or orchestra. No talent for anything. At the rate she was going, she'd have nothing next to her name in the yearbook.

Or, maybe they'd print Held the Record for Doing Nothing, Including Dating, for Four Years.

Sunnie tucked her gram's hand beneath the covers and kissed her goodbye lightly, with what Gram always called "angel kisses."

"Good night, Gram. Sleep tight." She grinned. At least one person, her gram, thought she was perfect.

Her great-grandmother didn't open her eyes but answered, "Don't let the bedbugs bite, Chloe."

Sunnie slowly moved away. Chloe was Gram's sister, and she'd been dead twenty years. Maybe she came back to visit in Gram's dreams.

When Sunnie walked down the hall, it seemed more like midnight than nine o'clock. Her friends would be climbing into cars and driving around. Looking for something to do was the main activity on weekends in a small town.

The thought that she might have been somewhere with Derrick about now bothered her more than she wanted to admit. Weird how he'd gone sour so fast.

She'd fallen madly in love with him when he called her

Shorty, and just as quickly fell out of love with him when he stared at Jillian's boobs like he was in a library and her chest was something he could check out.

Being Derrick's girlfriend had the shelf life of warm ice cream.

The greeter at the Acres's reception desk waved as Sunnie passed. "Good night, Sunshine. Come back anytime."

"Night, Sharon." Sunnie kept walking, even if she did want to stop and tell the woman no one called her Sunshine anymore.

How could her mother have ever thought Sunshine was a great name? When she complained to Dad, he'd told her he wanted to name her Moonbeam. Then she could go by Moo.

After that, she shortened her name to Sunnie and swore she'd never get pregnant without having a name picked out and already inked in on the birth certificate. The drugs they give you during childbirth must really mess with your brain.

Dad was waiting for her when she walked out of the Autumn Acres Senior Living Home. For a change, he was smiling, despite the dribble of rain slowly washing the dirt off his old pickup. She thought of asking him if he got laid, but the last time she did that he cut off cable for a year.

"Did you enjoy the movie?" he asked.

"Yes. I helped take ice cream orders and made deliveries to the people in wheelchairs. One old man tried to tip me a quarter when I delivered his banana split, hold the banana, cherries, and whip cream. He said I was the first person who ever got his banana split made just like he wanted it."

Dad, as usual, missed the whole point of what she'd said.

"Working there isn't a bad idea. You could save your money for something special."

"Dad! I'm already working at the quilt shop. I was just pointing out how a banana split isn't a banana split without the banana, the cherries, or the whipped cream." She shoved her wet hair back. "Oh, never mind."

"Right, but the job at the quilt shop doesn't offer tips."

"What did you do without me tonight, Dad?" It occurred to her that once she left home, he'd probably binge-watch *CSI* reruns for the rest of his life.

"I went to dinner with Jillian."

"That was nice of you. She seems so alone. Gram says Jillian told her that she doesn't have one living relative. Imagine that." Sunnie thought for a minute. "You think we could give her Mom's whole side of the family? There's not one I'd pull out of quicksand."

Dad laughed, as she knew he would. "Surely there's one worth saving?"

"Uncle Rob is the best looking, but he licks the snot off his upper lip."

"Surely not."

"He does. I saw him do it when he thought no one was looking. You'd think he'd use one of the million tissues in his pockets. If his side of the family tree evolves, they'll all have pouches so they can steal more funeral tissues off the pews at church. Last summer at Great-Aunt Whoever's funeral, I saw Uncle Rob just pick up the whole box when he walked out, like he thought it was a party favor."

"That's not fair, Sunnie—he has allergies. His nose is always running." They'd played this game before, and both loved it. Dad picked another. "What about your mother's aunt Dot. She's a great cook."

Sunnie shook her head. "She's a better eater. If one of her six sons doesn't finish his food, she cleans the plate between the dinner table and the kitchen sink. By the time the potato salad bowl made it inside from the last family picnic, it had been licked so clean she probably just put it back on the shelf."

"Now I know you're exaggerating."

It crossed Sunnie's mind that maybe they should talk about what happened today with Derrick in the middle of Main, or he could give her a lecture about boys in general, but that wasn't her dad's way.

She watched streetlights reflecting off rain-soaked sidewalks as he drove through the streets, splashing through puddles.

Laurel Springs seemed to sparkle on stormy nights. Autumn Acres was on the far side of town, and her father always took the winding road through the dead neighborhood that the kids called "the district" like it was something out of a sci-fi movie and not just a vacant, crumbling part of yesterday. Maybe he crossed through the abandoned warehouses and workshops because he owned them. Or maybe he just didn't like traffic on the highway road. Even her dad wasn't old enough to remember the district being alive, but still it seemed to draw him.

"You ever going to do anything with this area, Dad?"

"Someday, maybe. The good thing about owning land is it'll wait until the time is right."

Like never, Sunnie thought as she looked around. A few of the buildings were leaning like old soldiers trying to stand their post one more year. One brick building had lost the roof. The walls were crumbling like a decaying skeleton.

"There's a light over in that green building." She pointed left. "Strange." The sudden sign of life reminded her of a heartbeat from a corpse.

She stared at a barn of a building that had probably been painted bright green years ago but had aged into olive. A low light shone from the second-story windows, giving the place foggy yellow eyes shining out onto the black street.

Dad glanced at it with little interest. "That's probably Joe Dunaway. I told him a few weeks ago he could use any building he liked for a workshop. Joe is inventing Toe Tents. Tiny little tents that fit under the covers so your feet won't feel cramped. He's really excited about the project. Jillian tells me he stops by almost every day to tell Gram about the progress."

"Did you have him sign a lease, Dad?"

"Nope."

"What if he doesn't pay his rent?"

"I'm not charging him any. The building is just sitting there. He might as well be using it."

"So, he pays no rent and he can stay forever."

"Sunnie, he's in his eighties. Forever isn't that long."

She gave up. Her father had no business sense, and until she grew up, he was in charge of the Larady family businesses. When she made it to twenty-one and got her inheritance from her grandfather, it would probably be handed out in change.

Dad didn't even charge for the paper he put out, and if someone did want to buy an ad, he usually offered them one free. He could charge for ads on the daily blog he did, and the real paper about the town he actually printed every season should cost a dollar at least.

His job of mayor paid a dollar a year for some odd reason, and he used his truck, older than her, to haul stuff for the town. As soon as she was old enough, she planned to ask a few questions. He was either the poorest rich man in town, or the richest poor man.

But he was her dad, Sunnie reasoned, and somehow he made everything work. People depended on him, respected him. She guessed that was worth something.

"You want to stop for dessert at the Pancake Barn, Dad? It's probably the only place still open." The banana split she'd had for supper was long gone. Gram had offered her tiny cucumber sandwiches to snack on. Sunnie swore she'd never be that close to starving but about now, they didn't sound all that bad.

He slowed the truck. "I'm not really that hungry, but I could use a cup of coffee."

"It'll keep you up."

He shook his head. "I have a feeling I'll be up thinking for a while anyway. Might as well enjoy the coffee."

After driving over the bridge he turned into the Barn's parking lot. This was the one place you could eat any meal from the menu anytime.

"You remember when I was little, you'd let me order whatever I wanted?"

"How could I forget? You ate pancakes every night and hamburgers with fries for breakfast. That strange habit probably stunted your growth." He cut the engine. "You can still have whatever you want, Sunshine."

"I know," she answered and knew he wasn't talking about the menu.

He'd never put a brick on her head, or on her goals. Dad just let her know he was there to help when needed. If she wanted to stay in college for ten years, he was behind her. If she wanted to pack up after high school graduation and take off to see the world, he'd hand her the credit card along with a lecture to be careful.

That kind of freedom sometimes terrified her. More than anything, Sunnie wanted to not to be ordinary. She wanted to explore the world, and she guessed he wanted that for her, too.

Maybe he felt that way because he never went anywhere. His only adventures were in the mysteries he wrote and never sold. The closest he ever got to a wild love affair was probably watching one by accident on PBS.

"Dad," she whispered as they walked into the almost-empty Pancake Barn. "Have you ever thought of taking a woman out to eat on a date? A real date."

"Sunnie, Jillian and I were just both hungry. It wasn't…"

"I know. But she's a nice lady. You could ask her out. I wouldn't mind."

"I've invited her to join Gram and me at lunch a few times."

"We're not talking about lunch here, Dad. We're talking about a date. Ask her out. Comb your hair. Pay for the meal. Kiss her good night if you remember how."

He shook his head. "So that's how dating is?"

Sunnie almost said no. It's only like that in the movies. In the real world you just agree to meet up. There is no meal, just parking outside the city limits or going over to a house where parents weren't home.

She knew how it worked, all right. She'd heard girls talk. Make sure you have your phone so you can call someone to come get you if it doesn't go well. Don't get drunker or higher than him. Make sure he has protection. Don't let him take pictures. Don't ever tell your parents anything.

It all sounded so ugly. So ordinary. Maybe she should forget about boys for a while. She didn't want ugly or ordinary.

If she planned to live an extraordinary life, she might as well start now. Her first goal was never, ever stick her tongue in a mouth that wasn't connected to a brain because if she did, she'd probably end up with children who looked like her mother's side of the family.

"Dad," she said as she sat down and the waitress handed her a menu. "I think I'll have pancakes tonight with a side of fries and tomatoes."

"Whatever you want. However you want it." He nodded to the waitress jotting down the order. "And I'll have coffee."

11

Sunday morning Jillian drove north on Interstate 35 toward Oklahoma City. She'd made a list of everything she needed to do, and as always, she planned to do it all in exact order.

By the time she crossed the Red River, she'd calculated in her mind how long it would be before she was heading back to Laurel Springs. Two hours tops.

Papa's rule: *Never stay in town any longer than you need to.*

Just like he had done when he'd passed through the capital of Oklahoma a dozen times when she was growing up. He'd stop at three places, each time pulling out an old briefcase he'd picked up in a yard sale somewhere. He'd also insisted she walk beside him. Her bag might now be a backpack, but the routine was the same.

"Why Oklahoma?" she once asked him.

He'd stopped just outside the bank, knelt low, and said simply, "Because it's the center of the world, baby doll."

She'd asked if her mother was from what Oklahomans call "The City," and he'd said no. Apparently her mother walked into Mercy Hospital in labor and alone. She delivered Jillian, filled out parts of the birth certificate, then left

the next morning with no address on file. No way for anyone to find her. Her father told her the facts once, ending
the story with, "Your mother just vanished after she made
one midnight call to me."

Once, when Jefferson James was far from sober, he'd
told Jillian that he'd driven most of the night to get to the
hospital before dawn so he could pick her mother up, but
when he'd gotten there, she'd already disappeared. "Since
my name was on the birth certificate, I got to take you
home as the consolation prize."

Jillian was too young to understand when he'd made
the confession, but she remembered his words. Years later,
after he'd vanished, when she was a freshman in college,
she'd drawn a circle around Oklahoma City, mapping out
in all directions how far he could have driven in one night.

She might not know where her mother lived, but she
had a clue as to where her father had been living when she
was born.

Laurel Springs, Texas, was inside that circle. The zip code
was in his first ledger book. Back then he'd logged the days
he stayed in one place, but he'd identified the towns only
by zip code.

Her father had tossed the tiny books out when he'd found
them in the glove compartment. He'd laughed and said, "I
have no idea why I kept these old things. No one, including me, cares where I've been."

She'd collected them from the trash and slid them under
the lining in her suitcase. She'd only been eight then, but
she'd known the little books were part of the past, her past.

A little after noon, Oklahoma City welcomed her with
a line of hotels and fast-food restaurants. Even in the state

capital, there was a Sunday-morning laziness about the flow of traffic.

Finding a branch of her bank was no problem. She dropped her deposit in the safe-drop box and drove on.

Next stop, Bethany Post Office. The small town seemed to have been gobbled up by Oklahoma City. All the mail in her box was junk mail addressed to occupant except a forwarded notice to renew her California driver's license. The years when she didn't make it back to check this mailbox, she'd have the contents forwarded, not to where she was living, but to another box.

When she walked out of the post office, the wind had grown colder. One more stop, then she'd be heading back south. To Texas. To her job at the quilt shop. To Connor.

The Metropolitan Library on Park Avenue sounded like it should be in New York City, not Oklahoma City.

Pulling into the parking lot, Jillian turned off the car and waited. Twenty-three minutes before the doors opened. She didn't want to look too anxious or the librarians might watch her. She'd wait awhile, then slip in with a crowd.

Leaning back in the warm car, she closed her eyes and remembered what had happened, or *almost* happened, with Connor last night. She'd had a few short affairs, usually with coworkers. Always careful not to get too involved. She never wanted to leave a broken heart behind.

But if she wasn't careful she'd be taking that broken heart with her when she left Laurel Springs. Connor would be a hard man to walk away from. He seemed to care about everyone but himself.

"Six minutes," she whispered, smiling. That was all

they'd wanted to steal from time and they hadn't even gotten that.

She thought about what might have happened if she'd had more time with Connor in the shadowy parlor. An hour maybe. A night.

When someone walked by her window, Jillian jumped and called herself nuts for daydreaming about something that would never happen.

She climbed out of the car, ignoring the wind, and walked into the library she'd remembered since she was a kid. As far as she knew her father had never had a library card, but he did drop by and check his stash when she was growing up.

If he'd traveled by here in the past few years. He knew where the hiding place was. He might check on her. If he cared.

Last row, basement shelves.

Jillian pulled a book from the shelf and waited half an hour before making her move. No one else was downstairs and, thanks to the steps, she'd hear them coming if anyone did venture down.

Her father had explained that he'd worked here for several months when she was little and had to have constant care. During that time, he'd cleaned the place after midnight. No one ever checked on him, so he brought her to work.

When she'd started crawling, he'd had to find another job, one that paid more so he could afford childcare while he worked.

But during those nights they were alone in the library, he'd built a hiding place no one would ever find. Beneath a concrete shelf that held a statue of a buffalo too heavy to ever be moved was one small shelf and a box that pulled out, opening like a drawer.

Jillian had learned the exact spot to kneel down and slide her hand into the darkness beneath the thick stone shelf. There on a ledge almost out of her reach, was a box measuring ten by four by two. Just big enough to hold a few documents. Papers she'd need. Her birth certificate her father had finished filling out with lies. Three state driver's licenses she'd kept renewing. An extra social security card. Several hundred-dollar bills, emergency money. A one-page letter to her father. And one tiny picture of her at about ten. A free school picture her teacher had cut out when Jillian didn't buy the pack.

She opened the box. The documents were still here. The letter didn't look like it had been touched.

Jillian added three hundred-dollar bills to the stash. *Rainy Day Money* her father always called it. He'd made a great income on the oil rigs, but when times were lean, they stopped here several times to collect enough to live on until the next job.

She moved her fingers across the bottom of the box, looking for the one picture of her childhood. Her father had forgotten that pictures were going to be taken that day. Her hair was short and poorly cut. Her shirt was clean, but too small. She hadn't smiled for the camera.

She moved her fingers around the small box again. Time was running out. She needed to put the box back in its hiding place before someone accidentally saw her.

Her hand spread out across the bottom of the box.

The picture wasn't there. She held a tight rein on any emotion as she closed the box and put it back in place.

With her head low, she moved slowly out of the library, not taking a deep breath until she reached her car.

Someone had found her stash. Someone had taken the picture.

Nothing but the picture.

Her father had been there. No other explanation fit.

12

Sunnie sat in the windowsill of her father's office on Main, picking at her black nail polish. Usually she found some reason not to come watch him work on Sundays. Since he was already here six days a week, making it seven made no sense. But it was his habit, and her father was a man of habits.

He got up at six fifteen every morning. Drank coffee like it was the fuel that ran him. Never forgot anything on his schedule, or hers, or Gram's or the town's. He always fell asleep watching the news at ten. When she woke him, he'd swear he was simply listening with his eyes closed, and then Dad would wander off to bed. He might be only thirty-seven, but she had the feeling he'd be doing everything exactly the same when he was eighty.

If Sunnie didn't know it was impossible, she'd swear her father was a robot.

He claimed Sunday afternoon was the only time he had to work on his books without being interrupted. She'd never thought to ask him how long he'd been writing. It was just something he did. He rarely talked about his work and never offered to let anyone read what he wrote. Which was fine with her. She couldn't imagine it being interesting.

When she'd been thirteen, just after her mother died, she insisted on coming with him on Sunday afternoons. It was like she was afraid to let him out of her sight. She'd curl up in the window and do her homework or read. Then, when it was almost dark, he'd yell from his office in the back of the big empty room, *Time to go!*

"Already?" she'd say like she hadn't been watching the clock for an hour. It occurred to her that when she grew old, she'd turn this place into a nursing home because time passed slower here in Dad's office than it did anywhere in the world. She might not live forever, but it would feel like it.

Glancing at the huge clock beside the desk he called the mayor's corner, Sunnie frowned, realizing it would be at least another hour, maybe more, before Dad would be ready to leave.

She could walk home. Only the clouds outside were dark, full of rain. Plus, there was nothing to do back at the house.

Staring out at the empty main street made her sad. She was in the center of town, the prettiest part of Laurel Springs some say, but today it looked barren, deserted, hollow.

Even Gram's shop across the street was dark, uninviting now. On summer Sundays, the shops would open, but in winter the visitors were at the winery outside of town. Business on Main was so slow even Mamma Bee's Pastries was closed.

It took her a few seconds to realize someone was standing in front of Gram's shop staring right at her. He was so still she hadn't even noticed him.

Derrick.

Sunnie leaned closer, putting her hand on the cold window, making sure. Tall, good-looking, worn leather jacket that looked like it came from a sci-fi movie, killer smile. Yep, it was him.

He straightened. Those blue eyes stared right at her.

Then, with a nod of his head, he turned and walked toward the end of the street where a path led down to the neglected park by a stream. Just before he stepped on the path, he glanced back as if to make sure she saw where he was going.

"I'm off for a walk," Sunnie yelled toward her father.

He didn't even look up from his work.

Pulling on her coat, she stepped outside.

Derrick had disappeared somewhere in the tall grass and cypress trees that were scattered along the creek. Reddish-brown leaves still hung on to branches as if refusing to admit that winter had arrived. The leaves were heavy, twisted, droopy, and making that sound only oak leaves seem to make.

Mourner's cloth draped over the death of summer, she thought, moaning in a throaty rattle. She had a feeling the dead leaves wouldn't fall until new ones pushed them off the branches.

Pulling her charcoal jacket closed over her black T-shirt and jeans, she decided she must look the same. The comparison bothered her so she ran. Ever since her mother died, she'd felt death stalking her and today it seemed closer than usual.

She couldn't see Derrick, but she guessed he was waiting. He probably wanted to tell her off someplace where no one would hear.

Maybe they needed to settle things before tomorrow when rumors of their very public fight would spread. If they both agreed to claim they were just kidding around, maybe everyone would buy the story. After all, making a public scene for laughs sounded better then arguing with a guy you really hadn't gone out with.

Turning her collar up, she walked down to the water. It always amazed her how the town seemed to disappear so quickly, as if stepping back and letting nature have this place.

The settlement of Laurel Springs had started here by the water. A campsite for Apache. A stopover for travelers when the wagon trains came. An early fort for a short time. All started because of the stream that ran year-round.

Almost at the water, she saw Derrick leaning against a pine whose branches started a few feet above his head and offered little shelter. In the dull light, he could have been a man from any time. A buffalo hunter. A soldier. An outlaw.

She walked closer and saw him more clearly. Nope. He wasn't any of them. He was just the boy she almost dated. Nothing more.

"Hi," she said as she tiptoed near the winding creek's edge and stared at the stream, not him.

"Hi." He was silent for a few minutes, then added, "I went by your house. When you weren't home, I figured you'd either be at your dad's office or at the quilt shop."

"Good guess." She wanted to ask why he'd come, but she knew he'd get around to telling her eventually.

They listened to the stream splashing over rocks for a

while. When raindrops started plopping in the water like tiny bombs, she was tired of waiting. "Did you come to apologize? If so, it's not necessary."

He looked up and she saw surprise on his face. "No. I thought I'd give you the chance to. You're the one who went ballistic on me."

The possibility of "going ballistic" again seemed an option, but she thought it might be overkill. He wasn't worth the effort. "Why'd you ask me out this weekend?"

He smiled that sexy smile he had. "I figured I'd give you a chance. Thought we'd have some fun. I don't usually even talk to sophomores. But, Shorty, you've got something. Long legs and hair so light it almost glows. I even like the quirky way you dress. Not to mention your old man is the mayor. I'm thinking that makes you almost royalty in this town."

Sunnie straightened. "I'm sorry I yelled at you, Derrick." She caught his grin, then continued, "I'm even sorry I said I'd go out with you. In fact, I'm sorry I even spoke to you that night at the game." She turned and started back. Three apologies should do it.

"Wait. We're not finished. It's not over between you and me. Not by a long shot."

She kept walking. "Yes, we are over. You're right. Age does matter. You're too young for me."

She barely heard his words above the wind. "You'll be sorry."

"I already said that," she called back. "Weren't you listening?" It appeared her love affairs were destined to have the stability of tissues.

When she made it up the path to the sidewalk, he was

still standing by the creek. Rain had made his hair flat and hanging in his eyes like a bowl cut. He no longer looked irresistible.

Silently she slipped back into her father's offices and smiled. The place with its overabundance of mahogany bookshelves and mission desks with matching swivel chairs all seemed to welcome her back. If a stranger came in they'd think several people worked here, but it wasn't that way. All the desks were her father's. One for the news blog he still called a paper. One for official mayor's work. One where he handled what he called the Larady accounts. And one where he wrote on Sundays for no reason at all.

"You all right?" Dad asked when she shook the rain off her coat.

She guessed he'd watched her follow Derrick. "Yeah. I count my wild encounters in minutes."

He shrugged as if he understood. "So do I, Sunshine."

13

The weekend fog hung over the town as thick as Southern gravy. Jillian walked the few blocks to work on her third Monday in town. The old, run-down homes were becoming familiar in a way that surprised her. She saw the beauty in their unique structures and one-of-a-kind craftsmanship. Each day she looked to see if some detail had changed and was comforted that it hadn't. Familiar surroundings reassured her weary soul in a way she hadn't expected.

Maybe it was a sign that she should stop traveling for a while. Only hers was the good life. The free life. No relatives to bother her. No friends to pull her down. No mortgage or things she had to do just because she was a part of a group. She'd noticed a long time ago that the more possessions someone has, the more they have to repair, or clean, or worry about them being stolen.

She was free to live, to explore, to pick her own adventure.

Shoving the wild thoughts aside, she continued on her walk. Some days just walking was all the excitement she needed.

Three doors down from the bed-and-breakfast, a little brown cottage had huge clay pots, each a different color, lining the long porch. Every pot was overflowing with colorful plastic flowers. The cottage reminded her of San Francisco. Only the flowers weren't real.

They almost looked as if they'd grown there, but the plants were fake. Make-believe pretty. The yard was only dirt with a few weeds scattered around as though to catch trash blowing by.

The scene didn't make sense. Such detail to the porch. Such neglect of the yard. An ugly frame surrounding a third grader's colorful painting.

She found herself wondering about the people inside the house. Before, she'd never cared who people were, or why houses looked as they did. Her surroundings were simply markers along her path and she was only passing through. What currently bothered her thoughts: Was she more balanced then, when she didn't care, or now?

As she turned on Main, the dull, damp grayness of the day seemed to settle, not just over her, but *into* her, as well, clouding her thoughts as the happenings of the weekend pirouetted around in her mind.

The school snapshot that had disappeared from her secret library box. The closeness she'd shared with Connor that had bonded them as friends, real friends. The feeling of not being alone in the old house even after she'd walked through every room except Mrs. K's private quarters.

Even the strange message left on her cell phone from Mrs. Kelly, saying she wouldn't be back for a few days, bothered Jillian. If she didn't think it impossible, she'd consider the option that the round little woman was holed up in her room having an affair.

Jillian smiled, realizing she'd always thought the only man in Mrs. K's life was old Willie Flancher. They old guy must have had something going for him if he found five women to marry him back in the 1800s.

Maybe the innkeeper was simply worried about leaving her tattered Tara in the care of a stranger. Maybe she'd asked someone to walk through the downstairs last night to simply check to see if the place was locked up. A neighbor would do that.

Maybe Mrs. K simply got out of the house for once and found herself in no hurry to come back.

The big old place was usually so quiet when no guests were there. No wonder Mrs. Kelly talked to the shy ghost. Another weekend like this one and Jillian decided she'd not only be seeing him, but talking to him, as well.

As she moved toward the quilt shop, all the stores appeared to be still sleeping. The flower shop called Pot Along. The coffee shop lined with bookshelves. The antiques store with a hundred dolls with porcelain eyes staring at her. She knew she was early, but she'd expected some life before eight in the morning.

Seven forty-five. She was really early. Mamma Bee's Pastries had lights on inside, but the Open sign hadn't been flipped.

Jillian unlocked A Stitch in Time's door. She glanced across the street and noticed the lights were also on in the *Laurel Springs Daily*. Connor must have not been able to sleep either. He was always there to meet Gram when she climbed off the Autumn Acres bus, but Jillian never thought that he'd already been at work for hours before.

Whatever his work was… He was a man who wore many hats, it seemed. Gram said he managed the family properties better than the past three Larady men. Sunnie claimed he wrote books that never sold. Joe Dunaway told her being mayor in this mess of a town was a full-time job.

Jillian swore she could feel Connor close. The need to talk to him again had kept her awake last night, but she'd be wise to take no action. Keep it polite and formal. She didn't want to leave sadness behind when she drove away. Connor deserved a friend who didn't count their time together in minutes.

Smiling, she thought of Joe Dunaway and his Jeanie. They'd been friends for decades and still had plenty to talk about. She'd never have that, but she'd seen it and guessed that was a rare thing to witness.

"Mornin', Jillian," a squeaky voice sounded from a few feet away.

Almost dropping her keys, Jillian turned, half expecting to see Minnie Mouse behind her. "Oh, Stella, I'm sorry I didn't see you there."

The nervous little quilter hiccuped a giggle. "I may be a little early, but it's quilting day and I never miss the bee. I got my bag full of 'fixing to-dos' to help me pass the time till the others get here."

"'Fixing to-dos'?"

"Yep. Every quilter has them. Projects we don't get finished before another one comes along." She tick-tocked her head from side to side, sending her gray curls bouncing. "The older I get, the earlier I am to everything. At the rate I'm going, I'll outrun dying and jump into heaven while I'm still alive."

Jillian pushed the door open. "No problem. We'll have time for tea before the others come in." An hour of time, since Gram's bus wouldn't be along until almost nine and the quilters tended to wander in after that.

She held the door as Stella stepped inside, muttering something about how it was hard to tell what time it was on foggy days.

"How long have you been quilting?" Jillian asked, just to make conversation.

"For as long as I can remember. When I was little, I'd take my naps under the quilting frame as I listened to the ladies talk."

Jillian made herbal green apple tea and brought it out to one of the tables by the huge front windows. This special spot was called the Someday Corner because it was framed on two sides by supplies. Organized squares of material were bunched together. Fat quarters, wild confetti, drab pieces, and splashed segments. All waiting their turn to be pieced into a quilt someday.

In truth, it was simply pure marketing. Gram served tea in the one spot in the shop stuffed with sales items. She made money on the bolts and pattern books, but here the profits were higher. Fancy scissors that just cut batting or tiny ones made small and sharp for embroidery. Rulers and marking pens that could be erased by water or heat.

Stella patted Jillian's camera on the table and asked questions about how the cataloging project was going.

Jillian explained, telling only the facts, as she carefully

stitched the two-inch blue ID onto the back of the quilt she was working on.

No. 19
Cherry Bostock's pinwheel quilt, 1992
A blend of material from her thirteen bridesmaid dresses
Entitled: You'll wear it again.

"I'm managing to finish up two or three quilts most days. I write up their stories at night and file the photos." More to distract Stella than out of interest, Jillian asked which one of the quilts in the shop Stella thought had the most interesting story.

The old woman laughed. "Eugenia's quilt, of course. She's been working on it since she opened the shop."

"Eugenia's quilt? I haven't seen it. Which one is hers?" She scanned the walls, where two stories of quilts hung in the shadows.

"Last time I saw it she had it stashed in a drawer beneath the cutting table. It's not finished. Maybe never will be. It's her crazy quilt. We all make one if we quilt long enough. Some start with it, some end with it. Most are made from the scraps of our lives."

Jillian fought the urge to jump up and run to find the quilt, but somehow it seemed like an invasion of privacy. Gram hadn't mentioned it in the weeks she'd been in the shop. Maybe she'd forgotten about it. "I'll ask her to show it to me sometime."

Stella nodded. "I made a funny quilt once. It was a dozen blocks of all the cats I've owned. Or lived with, since no one really owns a cat. I put hats on them just for fun and to add color to the quilt." She giggled. "They would have hated wearing hats. My Sassy, a big red Somali, would sit on any hat I left lying around. I put a pillbox hat on him in his block."

"I'd like to see that quilt," Jillian lied.

"I'll bring it sometime and you can take a picture of it."

They talked their way through three cups of tea and all the leftover cookies. Jillian spent most of her time making a mental list of what she needed to do. If she planned to finish in three months, she had to keep a schedule, even if no one else in the quilt shop seemed to follow one. Sunnie would be a big help on Saturdays, but the other five days she'd be helping Gram more often than working on her cataloging project for the county museum.

Jillian listened to Stella talk about her cats as she stared out the window, hoping Gram would come soon. The street was alive now. People moving past the window. Cars parking.

Connor Larady suddenly rushed out of his office and headed directly toward her. Head down, steps long. He marched like a man on a mission and truly had no idea how powerful he looked at that moment. For a man who worked behind a desk, he somehow still managed to look like he stayed in shape.

Before she could stand, he banged his way through the front door. "Have you seen Gram?"

"No." Jillian glanced at the clock. "But she should be here by now."

He took her words like a blow. His brown eyes darkened to coffee and his hands were knuckle-white fists. The mild-mannered mayor looked more like a warrior.

"What's wrong?" she whispered, as if saying it too loud might alarm him.

"We don't know where she is." Connor paced back and forth in the small space in front of the windows. "A main desk attendant from the Acres called. She thought maybe I'd dropped by and picked her up."

Raking his fingers through unruly hair, Connor seemed to age before her eyes as he struggled to piece together an answer.

His words finally came out like a news report. "When she didn't get on the bus, the driver went inside to check on her. The receptionist said she'd seen Gram dressed and walking toward the little cafeteria earlier that morning. One of the staff said she'd walked with her to the front door where she always waited for the bus." Connor took a breath, as if fighting down anger. "Somewhere between the front lobby and the bus parked ten feet outside, they lost her. At first they thought she might have gone back to her room, but she wasn't there."

"Maybe she went to someone else's room. You said she has a lot of friends there."

Stella nodded her agreement, as if Jillian could solve the problem so easily.

Even Connor relaxed a bit. "They searched once, but you're right. She could have decided to say hello to a friend, or gone back for another cup of coffee, or maybe she simply went to the restroom. There are a dozen places she might have thought she'd stop instead of just waiting by the door. The chapel, the one-chair beauty shop to make an appointment, the little post office to check her box."

Stella's head kept nodding. "One of the girls said your

gram likes to go out the side door of the Acres and watch the construction going on along the new wing."

"I'll call them back and tell them to keep checking." The muscle in his jaw was still tight. "Only the nurse who makes sure she takes her meds said Gram had commented once last week that she could walk to work. Gram said she'd done it for fifty years. But not from the Acres. She was mixed up. Gram always walked from her little place in town to the shop."

He met Jillian's gaze. His voice came low. "What if she decided to walk?"

Jillian had only been to Autumn Acres once, when Connor took Gram home because the bus was running late. It was far to the west of town. Too far for an elderly woman to walk. The apartments were small, with a tiny living area and a bedroom. Staff was around, but it wasn't a nursing home. Tenants were independent. If Gram had decided to walk, she could have easily left without anyone noticing.

"She wouldn't walk," Stella whispered. "Not today. It might rain."

Connor showed no sign of hearing the little quilter. "I'm driving that direction. If she's walking, she'll need help. I have to find her."

Jillian grabbed her jacket. "I'm going with you."

"No. If she is walking she's headed to the shop. If she catches a ride she'll end up here. Someone needs to stay."

Stella stood up as if she'd heard the call to arms. "I'll man the shop and start calling folks on my cell. I'll keep the shop phone open so you can call in with news. The more people looking for her, the faster we'll find her."

Connor didn't argue with the plan. He opened the door

as Jillian buttoned her coat. When she passed him, her shoulder brushed his and she stumbled slightly.

His hand shot out and rested against her back for just a moment.

Neither looked up.

They climbed into his truck and began slowly tracing the route between Autumn Acres and Main Street. There was one obvious route, along the highway. But Gram wouldn't take that way. She'd told Jillian she always avoided the state highway even when she could drive. Too many trucks, she'd complained. Too much noise.

The other routes weren't so direct. There were half a dozen roads that would all end up on Main.

Connor drove slowly as he dialed the retirement home, clicked it on speaker, then dropped the cell on the dash. "Any luck?"

"No, Mr. Larady."

"Did you search…"

"We've searched everywhere twice. Our staff is trained for this. Not one room, not one closet is skipped. She is not in the building, or the garden, or even the construction site next door."

"How do you know? The site is a big place."

"It's far enough along to be locked at night. The painters haven't gotten here yet."

"Okay." Connor seemed to be gulping down the lecture he'd planned to give the staff. "I'm driving the roads between your place and Main."

"It's only three miles." The woman on the phone seemed to think her words would calm him. "The bus driver is tracing his route. Maybe, if she's walking, she'd go the same way he drives."

"Call me if you find her. I'll do the same." He clicked off the phone.

Jillian didn't make a sound. The last thing she wanted to do was speculate on what might happen in three miles of road on a cloudy day.

They drove over the bridge and into the warehouse area of town. This old part would be directly in her path unless she took the highway road or followed the winding creek. Neither of those routes would be likely, though—too rough. The warehouse crossing was her safest way.

Jillian tried to think of something to say that would help. Gram might be forgetting little things—names, dates—but putting an extra round of sugar in her coffee didn't make her senile. Just last week, she'd explained the layout of a six-point Lone Star pattern and helped cut bias binding for a scalloped-edge quilt.

She kept glancing over at Connor. Gram had told her he was only thirty-seven, but he seemed older now. She'd said when he'd left college and returned home to run the business after his parents died, Gram wondered if he regretted it. He'd had no wild twenties to find himself.

"The boy doesn't know how to live," Gram admitted. "Too many brains, not enough wildness in his heart, I fear."

Jillian considered that Gram might be right. He seemed to carry a heavy load on his shoulders.

As they passed through the grain elevators and warehouses littered with the bones of equipment left behind, Jillian said, "Gram told me you own this land."

"I inherited it. Not sure if it was a blessing or a curse.

It'd cost a million to clear all this out and then I doubt I could sell the land. With all these aging buildings, no one would buy it. So I keep paying the taxes until I figure out what to do."

He seemed to relax a little. At least he looked like he was breathing. Earlier she wasn't so sure. Talking came easy while they were both watching the road and not facing each other.

"You grow up in a town like this?"

She saw his effort to remain calm, so she played along. "No. I grew up in the oil fields, from the Gulf of Mexico to Alaska. My dad liked to travel. He went wherever the jobs took him."

"What about you?"

"I'm the same way. No strings to anywhere. I wouldn't know where to call home."

His short laugh held little humor. "I envy you a little. When I was in college, I thought I'd graduate and see the world. Wash dishes for gas money. Write all night in a cheap hotel or sleep under the stars on warm nights."

"You ever do any of that?"

"No. Melissa, my wife, got pregnant a few months after we met. She came to college one semester with me, but it was too hard on her. Sunnie came along a few months before my folks died, so we moved back and I finished my degree online. She never got hers started. When we moved back, she stepped into running with her high school crowd and none of them were interested in college. Melissa was younger than me. I figured she had some growing up years to finish."

Jillian studied all the corners and shadows of the district

as she continued to talk low. "Gram said Melissa died in a plane crash a few years ago. I'm sorry."

"We married because she was pregnant. We both loved Sunnie, but I knew my wife never loved me." His voice was bland. Simply giving a report.

"Did you love her?" Jillian couldn't believe she was getting so personal, but for a change she wanted to know someone better. Now might not be the time for these questions, but talking would keep them calm.

"I tried. A man should love his wife. After the plane accident, I found the paperwork she'd done for a divorce. I guess I failed in the loving her department. I think she was planning to leave me and marry the guy with her in the plane. I found out they'd traveled together several times. Her 'weekends with the girls' were mostly weekends with him."

Jillian thought of telling him that it took two people to make a marriage work, but now wasn't the time and she didn't know enough about relationships to advise anyone. The longest one she'd ever had was three weeks.

Connor turned down a dusty street, and Jillian saw a truck parked in front of one of the barns.

She pointed but before she could ask, he answered her questions. "That's Joe Dunaway's truck. He's probably still working on that crazy idea of making Toe Tents."

Jillian couldn't stop a smile. The old man was nuts, but ever since he'd mentioned them, she'd wished she had a Toe Tent when she crawled into bed.

Connor pulled up beside the truck. "I'll tell him Gram's missing. He'll want to help."

Out of curiosity, Jillian climbed out of the pickup and

followed Connor. The bay area had been scrubbed clean and long tables were laid out in a square. The abandoned building Joe had made his factory seemed to be holding up well.

"Morning, Connor," Joe shouted. "Come to check on your investment?"

"I'm not invested, Joe. The barn is yours to use. When you hit it big, it's all your idea and your profit."

Joe took off his welding gloves. "That won't be long. I've about got the assembly line set up."

"You mean assembly square." Connor reached the man and lowered his voice. "We got a problem I need your help with, Joe. Gram is missing. We think she left the Acres and started walking to work."

Joe moved so fast he almost left Connor behind. "Where do I look?"

"Take the creek road." Connor followed him outside. "It's not the shortest, but she always liked the wildflowers there. I'll go down past the grain elevators and the tracks."

Jillian followed the men out without mentioning that it was winter. If Gram thought she could walk, she probably hadn't noticed the weather, but she might be disappointed that there were no wildflowers.

They got back in the pickup. Connor took a long breath. "I feel better with Joe looking, too. We'll cover the area in half the time." He swung the truck around and the search continued.

"How long have you known Joe?" She kept her eyes on the side of the road as she asked.

"All my life. He and my grandfather were best friends.

The three of them grew up together, but he's the only one who calls Gram Jeanie."

"She's still a girl to him."

Connor nodded. "I guess so. Sometimes, when they're just talking to each other, I get the feeling they're two young people dressed up in old folks' bodies. The way they talk, how they laugh at jokes no one else gets. Maybe once in a while time stops between friends."

Jillian fought back tears. She'd never known that kind of friendship.

Silence hung in the air as he drove. They reached Autumn Acres, but had no luck. For a moment, she thought Connor might insist on searching the place himself. Each minute Gram was gone deepened the worry lines across his forehead.

Jillian used her cell to call Stella. No word, but Stella had organized a search in town. The Sanderson sisters were combing Walmart. Toad sent both her sons to walk Main. Gram might have stopped in somewhere. Paulina called the sheriff's office and suggested they block the state highway just in case Gram was kidnapped.

"We'll find her," Stella's squeaky little voice pledged, "even if we have to comb every street and alley in this town."

Jillian thought maybe Stella had watched one too many crime shows. Every street wouldn't take twenty minutes on a bike.

As they began another loop through the back streets of the district, Connor's phone rang.

"Yes," he said as he clicked on the speaker.

"I've got her!" Joe shouted. "She took a fall on the un-

even ground by the creek. We're on our way to the hospital. Meet you there."

"Is she…"

Gram's voice came through the cell. "I'm fine, Connor.
Don't worry about me. Skinned both knees and Joe's worried I may have broken my leg. He's just fussing over me."

"I am not. We're going to the hospital, Jeanie, and that's
final."

Jillian could hear the old folks arguing, and then Gram
said, "Connor, you make Joe get his blood pressure checked
at the hospital. He's overreacting."

"We'll get your leg x-rayed first. If you can't put any
weight on it, you got a problem." Joe sounded worried.

Gram didn't argue. There was silence for a moment, then
Joe said low into the phone. "She's crying, son. She's hurting and just too stubborn to admit it. But I'll get her there
and they'll take care of her. I promise."

Gram's voice was barely audible in the background. "I'm
just fine. I've seen more blood cutting up a chicken than
I've got on me. Don't you worry, Danny."

Connor smiled at Jillian but yelled into the phone. "We'll
meet you at the hospital, Gram. Thanks, Joe. You found her
and if she's arguing, her injuries are probably not that bad."

The call ended.

While he drove, Jillian called Stella and filled her in.

"We'll get the word out," Stella announced. "All the
quilters are here with their cell phones. Except Dixie. She
forgot hers."

"I'll report back as soon as we're at the hospital."

"Send pictures of any injuries. Those emergency rooms
are chaos, and they might miss something. We'll check the

photos and probably notice something they missed. After all, we've had our share of broken bones."

When Connor pulled into the ten-car parking lot of the local hospital, Jillian almost laughed out loud. This wasn't exactly a chaos emergency room.

Connor explained as they walked in. "Most of the rooms were for long-term residents needing more help than the Acres offered. Two rooms at the front were reserved as delivery rooms or emergency rooms." He took her hand. A solid grip as if he needed her beside him. "This care facility is packed. That's why we're building on another unit at the Acres. It'll have all levels of care in a few months. Since we doubled our doctor's clinic and built Autumn Acres, a strange thing is happening. Retired folks, even those who moved away for jobs years ago, are moving back."

Jillian didn't want to talk. The worry about Gram was too great in her mind. She fought the urge to say that she was with him in this, no matter what they faced. But there was no time. Panic of what they might face with Gram made her heart pound double-time. Deep inside a thought formed. This must be what it feels like to care about someone.

Suddenly her grip was as tight around Connor's fingers as his was around hers.

The tiny waiting room, which looked like it was furnished with someone's leftover sixties furniture, was empty. Gram was in one of the birthing rooms being checked by a nurse practitioner who had a doctor looking on from a computer screen.

She looked up when they entered. "I have the doc on

screen. He's got one more patient at the clinic, then he'll head over here."

When Connor frowned, the nurse tagged Morrison, RN, added, "She's stable. I'll make her comfortable until he gets here."

"I'm fine, Connor." Gram smiled at them but no one missed the white-knuckle grip she held on Joe's hand.

"Just relax, Gram. The doctor will be here soon."

Gram shrugged. "I just saw him last week. Every time I go to that young man he puts me on another pill. I'll be good as ever after he gives me another pill and then I'll head over to the shop. I've got projects to finish."

The nurse let Gram talk about all the things she needed to do as she checked her vitals and silently put in an IV, making everyone, except Gram apparently, aware that this was not going to be a short visit.

As the hours passed Jillian was impressed at how Connor took charge. He calmed Gram, talked to the doctor, signed forms, and made Joe sit down long enough to have his blood pressure checked.

While they waited for results on Gram, the dear old lady slept and Joe dozed in the chair beside her bed.

Connor offered his hand to Jillian as easily as if he'd done it a thousand times. Even in the bedlam he was comforting her. Pulling her out of the room, he leaned close and said, "It's going to be a while."

They walked down the hallway to a little room lined with vending machines.

"Can I buy you lunch?"

He turned loose of her hand and dug into his pocket for change.

"A Coke, nothing more. I had cookies for breakfast."

He collected two Cokes and they went out on a winter patio, lined with vacant birdhouses. The sun was warm enough to almost make them believe it was comfortable outside, but Jillian barely noticed. She slowly realized that Gram was safe. They might be dealing with a broken leg, but she would recover.

Connor talked for a half hour about the town and Jillian realized how much he loved the place. He filled her in on all the people she'd met and their stories. Neither wanted to get into the what-ifs concerning Gram until they had the facts.

When the nurse came to get Connor, he was much more relaxed than when he'd hit the door.

Gram finally rested, no longer frightened. Both she and Joe looked like they'd been scrubbed free of mud. The staff made X-rays and ran several tests. While the waiting continued, the nurse named Morrison asked if she could speak with Connor in the hallway.

He tugged Jillian out of the room with him. Joe and Gram were busy arguing over what to watch on the tiny TV mounted so high up in the corner of the room no one could have seen any program well.

"Mr. Larady," the nurse said after a moment of silence. "The doctor wanted to make sure you understand that this accident will not affect your grandmother's condition, but that her condition likely caused it."

"What condition?" Connor's words were low, but they seemed to echo off the walls of the silent hallway.

"Her Alzheimer's. Dr. Latham his been treating her for a year now, but the medicine only slows the progress."

Jillian didn't have to look at Connor. She could feel the shock, the pain, coursing from his body.

"She's forgetful," he said slowly. "She gets mixed up. She forgets words. She forgets if she's eaten now and then."

Jillian didn't move, but she felt one tear slowly roll down her cheek.

"She walked away from a safe place," the nurse added. "She put herself in danger." The nurse's tired eyes filled with sadness. "You didn't know, did you, Connor?"

He didn't have to answer.

Nurse Morrison flipped open a file. "When we informed her last year, she asked us to call her grandson Danny. His name was listed along with yours in our files."

Connor leaned back against the wall as if all the energy had drained out of him all at once. "Gram gets our names mixed up sometimes."

One more piece of proof, Jillian thought.

"Didn't he call you to tell you? Didn't Gram tell you?"

"No," Connor answered without emotion. "He probably figured since I see her every day, I already knew. He's busy. We don't keep in touch."

The nurse looked like she'd faced this dilemma before. "And did you know, Connor?"

He nodded. "On some level I think I did. I guess I chose to ignore it. I thought if I didn't think about it, didn't ask questions, that things would go on as always. Every time she forgot to do something, I just took over. I wanted to ignore all the signs."

"That's what Gram is doing, but you've got to deal with it from now on. Joe can't handle it all."

Connor straightened. "Joe knew?"

She nodded. "He was with her the day we tested her. The Autumn Acres bus brought her in for her checkup, but Joe was there just like he usually is. When they left, he must have driven her back because I heard him say that they were stopping for malts on the way home like it was just an ordinary day and an ordinary checkup."

The nurse was called away by a beep on her phone.

Suddenly, Jillian was alone with Connor in a little hallway that smelled of antiseptic and old age. She had no idea what to say. Part of her wanted to yell that she was an alien and didn't want to experience this kind of human pain. She'd lived her whole life away from people. Her father had been right. Don't get involved. It hurts too much to watch, much less feel.

But she couldn't turn away. Not this time.

As she leaned into him, he pulled her close. Hugging her.

For a while, they just stood here. She felt his heart beating, his breath drawing in and out.

Slowly, his tight muscles relaxed and she knew this strong man, who cared about an entire town, was taking on one more problem, one more worry, one more job.

Finally, he kissed the top of her head and pulled away. "Thanks. That was a great hug."

She shoved a tear off her cheek. "You all right?"

"Yeah."

"Plan to call your brother?"

"No. He knows. What else could I add?"

"But he steps out of all responsibility. Shouldn't he help?"

Connor's smile didn't reach his eyes. "But don't you see? I'm the lucky one. I get to be here. I get to help her through this. I get to know, when she's gone, that I did all I could."

He looked at her and she could tell he believed every word he said. "I'm the lucky one. I'll walk with her through this. Maybe pay back an ounce of the ton of love she's given me all my life."

He pulled Jillian toward Gram's room. "We'd better get back. You still with me, Sundance?"

"Yep," she answered. Good or bad, she'd walk through this crisis with him.

As the afternoon aged, there were more tests. Connor left to go get Sunnie. Jillian stayed behind with Joe to watch Gram sleep. Hospitals, big or small, seem to have their own kind of time.

When Sunnie showed up, she crawled up beside Gram and asked one question after another until Joe said, "Now, Button, ease off. She's all right."

To everyone's surprise, she stopped with the questions but stayed close to her great-grandmother.

Jillian watched the odd little family. They might be years apart in age and very different people, but there was a bond between them that didn't seem to need words to convey their love.

Midafternoon the doctor arrived and banished the family to the tiny waiting room. After an hour he stepped out of Gram's room long enough to say that he'd decided to keep Gram in care overnight. She'd suffered a fall that broke her fibula just below her knee, plus she had cuts deep enough to require a few stitches. He wanted to ease her pain but not overmedicate.

When they all crowded back into the small room, Gram greeted each as if she hadn't seen them in days.

She kept telling everyone, including the doctor, to stop worrying about her, but he still wouldn't let her go home.

Jillian felt like she was in the way. When Connor said he needed to go back to the office and at least lock up, she jumped at the chance to catch a ride. She wasn't doing much good here, and Gram didn't need more company. She'd seen airports with fewer people walking the hallways once the word got out that Gram was in the hospital.

After Connor kissed his grandmother, they silently moved out to his pickup. His touch was light along her back when they stepped outside, and lingered a moment longer as he helped her into the truck. The hug they'd shared had erased any awkwardness between them.

Finally, as he climbed in, he said, "As soon as I lock up my office, I'll be back at the hospital if anyone is looking for me."

"I think I'll work a few hours cataloging quilts. I need to match my notes up with pictures." She smiled. "When Gram is able, she'll be back in the shop and wondering what I've been doing besides eating her stash of cookies." Before, the timetable to finish the cataloging job was hers, and now Jillian felt like it was also Gram's.

He nodded. "I'll call if there is any change, but I think all she needs now is rest."

She could hear the sadness in his voice. They both knew rest would not heal Gram, but it might mend her broken leg.

When he pulled up to the quilt shop, he asked, "How about I pick you up for dinner at seven? Where will you be, here or home?"

"You don't have to…"

His smile was easy. "I owe you a meal. Joe and Sunnie can watch over Gram for an hour."

"All right. I'll be here. Call me when you're on your way."

His gaze held hers. "I think I needed you all day. Thanks for being there."

She thought of saying that all she did was tag along, but maybe even Batman needed Robin on a bumpy ride.

She'd shown up to help and it felt good, even though they'd faced troubles.

14

Connor felt like his nerves had been scraped by a razor-sharp rake as he left Jillian on Main and headed back to the hospital. He knew Gram couldn't live forever. Her mind was slipping. He'd even thought that it might be dementia. Old folks sometimes got that. But it was more. He hated that she'd been hurt and frightened in a town where she'd always felt safe.

He should have seen what was happening. He should have called the doctor. He should have…

When the nurse in the emergency room said the word *Alzheimer's* she'd finally put a title to what he knew deep down was wrong. Connor felt his heart crack and reality flooded in. He'd talked about Gram's memory loss, her mixing up words, but hearing that word somehow made it real. Joe had told him all people in their eighties forget things. Sunnie claimed Gram just had a lot on her mind. But at his core, Connor was a man who never lied to himself, and refusing to say the word wouldn't make the truth disappear.

It was time he faced what lay ahead. For Gram. For Sunnie. And for him.

Taking the slow route through the district, he checked his office phone for messages. The silence of the forgotten area seemed to close in around him as he drove. The calm of the empty building offered him no peace. They reminded him of what Gram would be one day. Just a shell. Her rich memories would be gone.

Not all at once, but one piece at a time. A year from now or maybe five, he'd still be able to hug her, but she wouldn't remember who he was.

The most important person who'd always been in his life, always loved him, would one day look at him as if he were a stranger.

He needed to take a few minutes to breathe, so he pulled into an alleyway and cut the engine. Relaxing against the back of the bench seat, Connor let his orderly mind piece together a plan. He'd return a few calls. A normal day. Let the Acres know Gram wouldn't be coming back tonight. He'd make sure all was set at the hospital. He'd reassure Sunnie. He'd call the quilters. He'd take care of every detail in preparation for her to leave the hospital tomorrow.

With the last wing of Autumn Acres still not ready to move into, his only choice was to bring her to his house. They were not yet set up to handle round-the-clock nursing care. Between friends and family, they'd keep Gram company while he had to be gone, and the nurse had given him a number for in-home nursing.

Connor would make sure that when he wasn't with her someone else would be.

His heart slowed. He could handle this. She'd need a bed

delivered so she could recover in comfort at his house. He'd need a ramp built. Once they let her out, he'd have to arrange for nursing care immediately and the housekeeper to come more often. They'd have to close the quilt shop for a while unless Jillian took over. Maybe she could keep it open and still manage to complete the logging project. Only she'd have to bring the quilts to Gram now, at least until she could be mobile in a wheelchair.

After five minutes of listing every detail over in his mind, he texted Sunnie for an update. Gram was resting and Joe was shooing away visitors.

Time to step back into his life. Time to get back to the hospital.

While reaching for the ignition, Connor glanced up. The shadowy alley made the time seem later, almost dark instead of midafternoon. It looked like the road ended with a gap-toothed brick wall, closing the space in like a boxed canyon.

He watched a trapped dust devil whirl, dragging trash and dead weeds in a deformed dance.

Just as he turned away, Connor saw the form of a man dart through the circling wind and vanish into a crumbling opening in the wall.

Connor blinked. Maybe the man had been only a mixture of shadow and debris rolling around. No one would be back in the rubble. There was nothing to steal. Nothing to do back there.

But Connor knew what he'd seen.

Logic took over. Maybe it was a kid, just looking around. Maybe a man hoping to find something interesting. Hell, Connor grinned, it might be someone trying to steal Joe's Toe Tents.

Starting the pickup, he slowly backed out of the alley. Right now he had his hands full with Gram. He'd deal with a trespasser later. If someone was stealing any of this junk, he'd help them load the truck, but he didn't want kids playing here. It wasn't safe.

By the time he'd reached the hospital the man in the alley was forgotten and Connor turned all his attention to what had to be done.

At seven, he called the quilt shop and wasn't surprised Jillian was still there.

"Tell me all that's happened," she said the moment she knew it was him.

"How about I come pick you up? I'll fill you in while we run a few errands."

"When will you be here?"

"Turn off the lights, lock up and I'll be pulling up."

She hung up the phone and followed instructions. He was there waiting for her when she stepped outside. Even though it had only been a few hours he couldn't help smiling, and he realized he'd been working his way back to her since he'd left her.

"You all right?" Jillian asked, from what seemed like a mile away on the other side of his pickup.

"I'm fine." How could he tell her that he felt like he was crumbling? All his life he'd always been a rock. The one everyone depended on. He needed to hold it together now. The doctor had told Gram her leg would heal, but outside in the hallway, he'd explained to Connor that this might be simply the first of many breaks to come unless Gram was very careful.

Connor shoved the pile of worries aside for a moment. "Where would you like to go to eat?"

Jillian seemed to read his mind. "How about we get hamburgers and take them back to the hospital for Sunnie and Joe? I'm sure they've already fed Gram."

Connor grinned. "Good idea." His thoughts were still there anyway.

Half an hour later they were all huddled around the hospital bed, talking and laughing. Joe told them how his cousin shot him in the calf one night when they were out drinking so far out of town only the stars offered light. They'd taken their guns along so folks would think they were looking for coyotes.

"It was daylight before we made it to the doctor's office. My cousin was too drunk to carry me in so I had to hop on one foot all the way in from the parking lot."

Sunnie claimed she didn't believe him, so he pulled up his pants to the knee and they searched through his hairy leg for the scar.

When Connor finally stopped laughing, he sat back and wondered what reasonable people talk about in the hospital. When he glanced at Gram she was laughing also, even though Connor would bet she'd heard the story a dozen times.

Finally, the nurse came in and said all but two of them had to leave. Joe said he was staying and so did Sunnie. Connor didn't argue. He just offered his hand to Jillian and said, "Time to go. They're kicking us out."

She pouted. "I guess we have to go." She looked from Joe to Sunnie. "Call me if anything happens." Then she slipped her hand into Connor's.

At last, they were alone heading home. "Thanks for having dinner with me, even if it was a few bites of cold hamburgers around Gram's hospital bed. It's been a long day. Not much of a dinner date."

"I didn't mind," she answered. "No one but Joe ate." Then she laughed. "This was a date? Mayor, you've got some serious work to do."

"I thought it was a date, but I don't know." He needed this light conversation. He didn't want to think about all that had happened since dawn. "Maybe you could just consider I'm starting with a low bar so there will be no way to go but up." He turned onto the highway, deciding not to take the district road again. "By the way, I'm still hungry," he said more to himself than her.

"You want to come in? I could make you scrambled eggs. Mrs. Kelly's fridge and pantry are stocked, and she told me to make myself at home. She's out of town again."

Connor pressed on the gas, suddenly in a hurry. "Any idea when she'll be back?"

Jillian shook her dark hair. "Nope. Before the food runs out, I hope."

A few minutes later he pulled to the side of the bed-and-breakfast and they went in through the garden door. It seemed so quiet; the whole town must be asleep by now. He followed her to the kitchen, and they began to cook.

When he'd remodeled his own kitchen a few years ago, he and Sunnie had stayed here almost a week, so Connor knew his way around.

Jillian made tomato and cheese omelets while he warmed banana bread and microwaved thick bacon slices. The smells of good food, real food, drifted in the air, spicing the evening like scented candles. He'd felt his mind and body twirling in a hurricane all day, and finally, he'd fallen into a calm sea.

When they sat down at the bar, he passed her a glass of orange juice. "This looks great. It's the first meal I've had today."

"Me, too. The cookies for breakfast and the two bites of cold hamburger don't count."

She clanked her glass with his as their eyes met and he realized his calm sea was her. It was that simple.

As they ate, the day poured out in a running commentary about all that had happened. The frantic drive when they thought Gram was lost. The way Joe took care of her as if she were just a girl. The hospital treating Gram like a queen, because in a way, she was. Stella reporting in on everything that had happened at the quilt shop as though she were a dispatcher at a big city precinct. The way Sunnie refused to leave her gram.

Neither mentioned the hallway talk with the nurse. That conversation could wait for another day.

Connor stole a slice of Jillian's bacon. "I fear the power we've given Stella may go to her head. Stella thinks the whole plot of the cop series *Justified* was about her family. Claims they just moved it to another state to protect the guilty."

"I thought *Justified* was a Western."

Connor frowned. "You don't watch enough TV, Jillian."

At last their plates were empty, and he realized his muscles had finally relaxed. He'd felt like he'd been holding his breath all day.

"You want anything else?" Jillian picked up the plates and slipped off the stool.

"Yes," he said, more to himself than her. "I'd like to hold you for those six minutes we talked about last week."

With a clank, she set the dishes down and turned. "We weren't going to talk about that. The stolen minutes thing was just a crazy idea on a stormy night. It was never meant to happen."

He stared into her stormy eyes, more blue than gray tonight. All day, no matter what had happened, he'd been aware of her. A few times, he'd felt himself holding back, waiting, hoping for this moment, and he didn't intend to let it pass by. "You asked what I wanted. I want the six minutes you offered."

Leaning back against the counter, she folded her arms over her chest. Her head lowered and her beautiful midnight hair curtained her face. She wasn't what people would call beautiful, but she was pretty in her quiet way. Classic, he decided, and when she smiled, no one could help but smile in return.

He knew he'd stepped out of line, but it was too late to pull back the words. He stood, trying to think of some way to walk away. He wasn't sure he wanted to hear what she had to say. Her body language told him all he needed to know.

She wasn't interested anymore. Maybe they'd missed their one chance.

Maybe if he simply left, she'd forget about what he'd just said by tomorrow and they'd go back to being polite strangers. She probably hadn't noticed how often they'd touched today. He'd steadied her once when she'd tripped. He'd helped her out of the truck. She'd rested lightly against his shoulder once when she'd perched on the arm of his chair in the hospital. He'd held her hand as if it was his one lifeline to sanity.

He had to say goodbye before he made a fool of himself.

Her voice came so low he barely heard the words. "I don't want to hurt you when I leave. And I will leave, Connor. That's what I do."

He thought of saying that it was already too late to think about being hurt. She'd affected him far more than any woman had since his wife died. Maybe he should laugh it off, say *never mind, it was just a suggestion*, but then he'd be lying.

He hadn't been kidding. It was a need that had followed him around since he'd walked away a few nights ago. He wouldn't apologize for wanting to step into uncharted territory for a change.

Reaching for his jacket, Connor knew all that was left now was to go. Maybe in a few days she'd forget he'd asked.

He'd taken two steps toward the side door when he heard her whisper, "I want you to hold me, too."

Crossing the distance between them in two seconds, he pulled her into his arms.

She came to him without hesitation, wrapping her arms around his neck so tightly he could barely breathe, and he didn't care.

Her body pressed solidly against his, and he lifted her off the floor in a hug. He'd needed her hug earlier, but now he wanted it, and he didn't plan to let go.

"I...I..." She breathed against his ear, so close he could read her thoughts.

"I know," he answered. "Let's steal a few minutes off this long day."

He touched his lips to hers as his hand slid along her side. She leaned into him and opened to his kiss.

He took his time learning how she wanted to be kissed. They were both experimenting, testing, learning. This kind of closeness seemed as new to her as it was to him.

Finally, he circled her waist with his arm and pulled her tight against him, needing to feel her heartbeat against his own.

Both laughed, knowing the period for hesitation was over. He kissed her soundly, and this time when his hand moved up from her waist, his palm pressed lightly against the side of her breast.

"You said I could touch you anywhere in these few stolen moments."

He felt her laughter against his throat. "I did, didn't I?"

With each breath they were coming alive to the other.

"This feels so good," he said against her ear.

"I agree."

He kissed her cheek and nuzzled against her hair. She could feel, more than hear, the rumble of his laughter.

This wasn't foreplay, or aggression, or even flirting. This was simply pure enjoyment. After all the turmoil of the day, all the raw emotions, all the panic, it felt so grand to just hold someone close.

As he drank her in with deep kisses and bold strokes, she seemed to melt against him. She needed his touch as dearly as he needed her, and that knowledge made him feel half-drunk.

When he broke the kiss, he dug his fingers into her

silky hair and held her head in place as he kissed his way to her ear.

"You may leave me. You may hurt me when you go. But you will never forget me, Jillian. Just as I will never forget you. There is something between us and acting like it isn't there doesn't change a thing about how I feel inside."

Then, he held her tightly against him until their breathing slowed and blended. Every cell in his body seemed to absorb her, memorizing the way she felt so close to him, the way she smelled, the way she cried silently on his shoulder as all the tension of the day was melting from her.

Another time he'd ask why, but for tonight it was enough to just hold her and know that she wanted this as much as he did.

Neither of them counted the minutes. He had no idea if he held her for six minutes or an hour. She felt so good against him.

Over and over again he'd lean down a few inches and kiss her softly. When he reluctantly pulled away, she'd smile and whisper, "I've been waiting for that. Again, please."

He felt like he was learning to kiss. All the times in high school and college were just practice. This time he got it perfect. He wasn't just kissing a woman; he was kissing Jillian. She'd walked into his life on a gray day, and no matter how long she stayed, he knew from the start that she'd be someone who brightened his world.

Finally, she tugged free and took his hand. They moved to the sunroom where an overstuffed couch in the corner seemed to be made of dusty pillows. Gently, she pushed him down and cuddled beside him.

"I think my time is up," he admitted against her hair as he circled her shoulders.

"I haven't got my fill of being held." She laughed. "You think you could stay just a little longer?"

"I'll try." He moved his hand over her thigh and pulled one of her legs onto his lap. He could have gone further. Maybe even undressed her, but that wasn't what he wanted.

He wanted to discover this quiet woman slowly, learning every part of her, enjoying every step. When he'd been twenty he might have hurried into loving, but not now.

She rested her cheek against his heart. "We'd better not get too carried away. After all, Willie is watching."

"Willie?"

"The ghost."

Connor laughed. "Oh, him. After five wives, he's probably seen it all. I doubt we'll shock him."

They were silent for a while, then she said what he guessed had been on both their minds all day. "I know you wish you could have Gram forever. I've known her a month and wish she'd be in my life for years to come. But one day, she'll pass, and a whole town will have been blessed to have known her."

"I know. I'm no stranger to funerals in my life or as mayor, but I fear laying her to rest won't be easy. Only someday, way in the future, Gram's funeral will be a celebration of her life. I can handle that."

When Jillian seemed content against him, he added, "You know, I've probably attended half a dozen funerals just this year. I've started rating them on a one-to-ten scale. How many people come, how many flowers, whether people cry or just seem to wait for it to be over, does the preacher even know the deceased. You can tell a lot about a person's life by what kind of funeral he or she has."

"I've never been to a funeral."

"Really?"

"Nope. Not one. I've never thought about when I die. I guess the city takes care of bodies not claimed."

Connor pulled away. "Are you telling me you have no relative, no friend, no partner or neighbor who'll stand over your grave and say goodbye?"

She shook her head. "And before you ask, I'm not running away from anything or anyone. My father liked to travel and so do I. I always have and probably always will. It's just my way. I don't stay around long enough to get too close to people. It's easier that way."

Leaning nearer, he kissed her lightly, letting her damp lips feel his words. "I can't make you stay. It wouldn't be fair. But while you're here, you have someone. We'll start with being friends and I swear, if you die, which I hope you won't, I'll stand over your grave."

She kissed his cheek. "I'd like to be a little more than friends, Mayor, and I have no intention of dying."

He grinned. More than friends, not quite lovers. Sounded like a good place to be for now. "You may have traveled the world, but there is something about you, Jillian, that seems to be born yesterday."

Stretching his legs out, he leaned back into the pillows as he held her in his arms. "You tell me about the world you've seen, and I'll tell you about growing up in one place."

She lifted her head. "I have a feeling you've learned more than me. I see wisdom in those brown eyes."

"Don't mistake confusion for knowledge." In a low voice

meant only for her, he told her of all the places he wanted to see. The castles of Great Britain, the moors of Ireland. The battle that broke the back of the Clans. Culloden. Britain versus Jacobites. "I read so much about it as a kid I used to dream about being there. And Italy. I used to keep a list of all the places I had to see in Italy. And France. They say everyone should go to France before they die."

After a while, he heard her breathing slow and knew she was asleep. He thought about waking her and leaving. It was late, but it felt so good to have her against him. He tried to remember a time like this, when he'd held a woman so tenderly. When he'd been so happy.

Melissa and his marriage had been among the walking dead for years, and he'd never sought comfort elsewhere. Maybe because he saw the failure as his. He couldn't be what Melissa wanted. He wasn't enough for her.

But with Jillian, it was different. He knew she wouldn't stay. Maybe all she wanted was shelter in a storm. He could be that. He could be enough for Jillian, and no matter how many weeks they had together, that would have to be enough for him. When you get a slice of happiness, you can't expect the whole cake.

He closed his eyes and drifted off, thinking how lucky she had been to get to travel. He might never travel, but maybe she'd tell him about all the places and he'd see the world through her eyes.

15

In the recesses of his sleeping brain, Connor heard a door open and close, but he didn't move. Sunnie was coming in late, he thought. He'd talk to her in the morning.

Footsteps across a tiled floor pulled him more awake, and he felt something warm against his side. Warm and breathing. Reality washed over him like a tsunami as the first slice of dawn crept across the sunroom. Before he could move, he heard Mrs. Kelly's high voice. "If you're going to sleep here, Mayor, I'll have to charge you."

Dread stabbed him in the gut like a boxer's first blow. He opened one eye. Worse than the Grim Reaper, Mrs. Kelly stood smiling at him.

He could already hear her brain logging the order of who she'd call to tell all about what she'd found going on at her place. And in the sunroom, no less.

Shifting away from Jillian, he slowly stood, adjusting the pillows beneath her without waking her. "What time is it?" he asked, as he herded the little lady through the kitchen doorway.

Mrs. Kelly puffed up, looking quite proper in her mourner's dress he'd seen at every funeral for the last ten years. "A little after seven, I think, but that's not…"

Before she could continue with her interrogation, Connor said, "I've got to get back to the hospital."

It worked. She forgot about him sleeping over.

"The hospital! What's happened? I leave for a few days and something changes. That's the way it always is. You'd think I lived in the country, fifty miles from town. I'm the last to hear anything."

He made coffee as she continued to ask questions. When she finally slowed, he answered one. "Gram's had an accident."

"Oh, my." She plopped down on a stool. "Is she all right? How did it happen? Does anyone know?"

Connor couldn't hide his smile. Mrs. K wanted to be the first to know everything that transpired in town. He couldn't make that occur, but he could fill in details that probably hadn't made the rounds. "Half the town started looking when she went missing yesterday morning. She took a fall on the creek path trying to walk from the Acres to her shop."

"The creek path must be a mile or more from the Acres. Oh, poor dear."

"Joe Dunaway found her. Muddy and hurt. She spent the night under observation at the hospital. Lucky for her, only one bone in her leg was broken. She'll be coming home with me for a few days once they release her. I think it'll calm her nerves to be with Sunnie and me, and you know how she hates people making a fuss over her. The staff at the Acres said they'd do their best to watch over her, but I don't want her to be alone and hurting, not even for a minute."

Mrs. K nodded. "She won't like being babied, so you go easy on the bossing, mister. I remember we all tried to give her a birthday party a few years back, and she threatened to print all our ages in your paper. Those people at the Acres are good, but I can just see them pestering Eugenia right into an early grave."

Connor remembered the party plans. "It wasn't a threat. She said she'd pay me to print all the dates and names in bold type."

"We all feared that. But this time, if she's hurt and can't get around, she's going to need some help." Mrs. K popped off her stool and tied on an apron. "I got some thinking to do, and I do that best on my feet."

Her apron read *Some of us are born left-handed, and the rest of you will just have to cope as best you can.*

"You got to get organized, Mayor." She pulled a skillet from the rack. "I'd hate to think of her sitting alone at your place, wishing for a drink of water or ice cream or something. And pills. When you get out of the hospital, they stock you up with pills, and just to confuse you, they have you take each one at a different time."

"Stella can set up a volunteer schedule to cover all hours I'm not home, plus I'll get caregivers coming in to help her with medicines and baths. I'll have a phone pinned to her bed. No matter what happens, I can be home in five minutes."

He paused. "What no one knows is she will insist on keeping the shop open, so Jillian will probably be taking over until Gram is well enough to return. I did my best to fill her in on all the details last night, but it was late and we'd both had a long, stressful day."

Connor swore he saw a light bulb blink on inside Mrs. K's mind. "Now I understand. You and Jillian must have worked most of the night figuring out the details. You poor babies."

Mrs. K cracked two eggs on the edge of a bowl as she motioned him out of the kitchen with her head. "Go get washed up in that bedroom on the second floor. The one you stayed in during your remodel. You've got a full day, I'm guessing, and I'll have breakfast ready in no time. You two probably haven't had a meal since all this started."

Connor nodded as he noticed Jillian leaning against the sunroom door. Her clothes were wrinkled, and her hair wild as a tumbleweed. His words were for Mrs. K, but his gaze never left Jillian. "I love being bossed around by a woman who can cook."

Following orders, he did his best to clean up, even shaved with an expensive razor left in the samples basket by the sink. When he walked out of the second-floor bedroom, Jillian was coming down from her room upstairs.

"Morning." He wished he were brave enough to tell her how he'd liked sleeping with her last night. "I never would have taken you for a cuddler until last night."

"I was cold." She didn't look at him. That beautiful midnight hair concealed her face.

"I wasn't cold at all. You kept me warm." The need to touch her almost blocked out all other thoughts. He had no idea what people say to one another the morning after.

He could kid himself and say nothing happened. They hadn't removed a single piece of clothing. But he made a point of never lying to himself. They may not have put it in so many words, but they'd agreed that while she was in

town they'd be together. Last night wasn't just a few stolen moments. It was the start of something, and he had
no doubt that when it ended he'd be the one who walked
away hurting.

She slipped past him. "Smells like breakfast is ready."

He caught her hand in a loose grip.

She didn't try to pull away. Finally, she looked up at him
and he realized he had nothing to say. "I...I..."

She grinned. "I know. I feel the same way." Then she
was gone, dancing down the stairs.

Connor stood on the second-floor landing, watching her
disappear. She'd said all that needed to be said. No promises. No scene about what happened last night. No regrets.

16

High school should qualify as a lower level of hell when you've been up all night at the hospital, Sunnie decided as she tapped her forehead against the door of her locker. Most of her classes were barely tolerable when she'd slept the night before. Now, when she was exhausted, they were layers of torture mayonnaised with boredom.

She already hated everything about her sophomore year, so there was no downhill to slide to. She felt like a lifer the state had imprisoned for no reason at all.

She hadn't learned anything in school for years. Why did they need teachers anyway? She could find out any information she wanted to know on Google in one minute.

Like a drunk zombie, she moved down the hallway.

Half the kids in her class had already reached their mental heights and were just hanging around, hoping to have fun, so they could talk about the *good old days* on fifteen-minute work breaks for the rest of their lives.

She'd slept through two classes and no one noticed. Mayor's daughter or not, she'd given up responding when she was called on. It took a while, but the teachers had finally stopped asking her questions in class. She read the chapter, watched the films, plowed though the computer games designed to make learning fun. But she didn't talk in class. That would be like talking to the goldfish in the commons aquarium.

As long as she made passing grades, no one pestered her for class participation.

When lunch finally came, she wove around all the groups that were talking in clusters. Sunnie decided they really did look like the schools of fish in the huge tank that separated the cafeteria from the hallway.

"What did you get on the algebra test?" Brianna Baxter bounced into her line of sight. She was a head shorter and three bra sizes bigger than Sunnie. Life was so unfair.

"I made a hundred. My mom says if I keep it up, I can have a mani and a pedi every month, even if it's not sandals weather."

One of the fish was talking. Sunnie kept walking.

Brianna stayed beside her. "Unless it's like, snowing or something, I think it's okay to wear flip-flops, don't you? Of course your toes get dirty if it's muddy. I can't stand that."

Sunnie shrugged and went back to the first question. "I don't remember what I got on the test."

"You failed it, didn't you?" Brianna made a sad face cute enough to put on any text. "Don't worry. You'll catch on. I could even help you. Mrs. McDonald said I'm a good tutor. I taught Elbert Rhodes his sevens last year. Can you believe he made it to the ninth grade and didn't know all his multiplication tables?" She raised her way-too-thick eyebrows. "So, we could study together if you want to."

"No, thanks," Sunnie managed to say without cussing as she wondered how pretty, perky Brianna would look with her nose inverted.

"I got to go. Thanks for the offer." Sunnie backed away. Another sad state of high school. Double B was probably her best friend, and she hadn't even asked about how Gram was. The whole town seemed to know that Gram had taken a fall and was in the hospital. Honestly, Dad did not need to bother with a news blog.

She walked out to the atrium—or the green space, as they called it—which was walled in by an eight-foot-high brick wall. Dead leaves and smashed milk cartons circled in baby tornados across colorful concrete blocks that had been designed to give a modern look to a worthless corridor. No one ever came out here. It was too cold in winter, too hot in summer, too depressing year-round.

Sunnie's favorite place to eat lunch. Alone. Cold. Quiet.

Pulling out an apple she'd stolen off Gram's tray at the hospital, she sat down under a tree that offered no shelter and dialed Gram's cell.

One ring. Two. Three.

"Hi, Button." Joe Dunaway answered after he juggled the phone for a while.

Sunnie smiled. The man had been old all her life, and he'd always called her Button for no reason at all. "Hi, Joe. You still at the hospital with Gram? Shouldn't you go home and rest?"

"I'm not leaving until Jeanie does. Which might be later today. We've been watching *Golden Girls* reruns since breakfast and she just dozed off. I'm supposed to call your daddy to come get her when they're ready for her to check out of this place. Once he picks her up, I'm going home and sleeping the clock around."

"You're a good friend, Joe."

"Have been since we were your age. She started dating my best friend, and I just decided I'd better hang around and watch over them both."

"You still are."

"Jeanie's got many others keeping up with her. For one, you're the best great-granddaughter she's got. Best one she ever had."

"I'm the only one she ever had." Sunnie decided they should make a talking doll just like Joe. It would be downright huggable.

"Tell Gram I'll see her when I get home from school."

"I will. Bye, Button."

Sunnie shoved the phone back into her pocket and finished her apple. She'd hear the bell when it was time to go back. She'd somehow survive the next three classes. Then, she'd go home and spend time with Gram.

The glass door clicked open, but Sunnie didn't turn around. All she wanted was her quiet time, alone time.

"You all right, Shorty?" A familiar voice sounded from behind her.

"I'm fine." She didn't have to turn around to know who'd wandered out to bother her.

"How's your gram?" Derrick moved into her line of sight, and she tried to figure out why she'd ever thought he was good-looking.

"I'm only asking because everyone thinks we're together, and they're all asking me how you're doing and how that old lady is. My history teacher even asked and so did that crazy secretary in the office. You know the one that has wooden jewelry for every holiday, including Flag Day."

"Tell everyone we're not together, me and you. That's a good answer." They hadn't even had their first date, but they did have one hell of an argument.

"I was thinking about that. Maybe I should give you another chance. This is a rough time for you and you might need someone to lean on."

"Any chain-link fence will do, but thanks for the offer."

He shrugged. "I'll give you some time to think about it. You don't even drive, Shorty. I could take you wherever you need to go."

"Thanks." A gnat's life would be too long to ponder her option, but right now she just wanted him to leave.

When he didn't move, she stood and asked, "Would you tell the office I had to go home? My gram needs me."

"I could take you?"

Since the Autumn Acres bus gave her a lift this morning, she could use a ride home. If she called her dad, he'd just tell her to stay the day. Even when she claimed she was sick, he'd make her go to school so the nurse could offer a second opinion.

"All right, but you can't come in. Gram will need her rest." Hopefully he didn't know Gram was still in the hospital.

"Sure. I'll just tell the office I'm running you home and will be right back."

Ten minutes later when she thanked him for the ride, he said he'd check in later. Sunnie was too tired to argue. Between the machines last night, the nurses coming in every ten minutes and Joe's snoring, Sunnie wasn't sure she'd slept, period.

She made it four feet inside, collapsed on the couch, and was asleep before Derrick backed out of the drive.

What felt like moments later, someone was pounding on something out front.

Sunnie scrubbed her face and staggered to the door. The noise wasn't a knocking sound, but banging coming from the side of the porch.

"What's going on?" She yelled out into the yard when she didn't see anyone.

Reese Milton raised his head, removed his dirty hat and let his wild, rust-colored hair stand up in every direction. He stared at her through the white spokes on the porch railing. "Sorry, Sunnie. Didn't know you were home."

She walked out far enough to see the pile of boards and piping scattered in the grass like a huge Erector set. "Shouldn't you be in school, Reese?" He'd been in every other class she'd taken since she started school but they'd never been friends. Funny how some people are just around, but you never really bother talking to them.

"School was out an hour ago. The mayor called my dad and asked him to put up a ramp. Dad's busy on a remodel so he told me to get started."

"Do you know how?" She shoved hair out of her face.

"It's not rocket science, Sunnie. I've been helping my dad the past two summers, plus most weekends on remodels." He cocked his head, studying her. "Were you asleep? You got serious bed hair."

"You got hat hair," she answered back like a third grader.

Reese shoved his cap back on. "I'm not picking on you.

I understand if you want to nap. Your boyfriend told everyone in biology that you stayed up all night with your gram at the hospital. He said you held her hand while she suffered."

"I don't have a boyfriend and Gram didn't suffer. She slept." The hammering may have stopped on the porch, but it still seemed to be going on in her head.

"That's not what Derrick said." Reese grinned and shifted his hammer from one hand to the other.

Maybe he was lying about Derrick, or trying to irritate her because she was keeping him from working. She tried reason. It was that or all-out screaming. "What would Derrick be doing in your sophomore biology? He's a senior."

"I didn't ask. He sits behind me, though, and it's my guess, judging from his grades, the guy may have a third senior year, but he's good-looking. Just ask him. There is no mistaking Derrick for anyone else. Every day, like clockwork, he makes an entrance into class just as the bell sounds." Reese started back to work. "I don't know what girls see in the guy. He's got no brains. He passed me a picture of an amoeba last week and whispered, 'Do you think this is male or female?'"

She didn't argue. Maybe Reese was right. She sat down on the porch and watched him work. Until last year, he'd been shorter than her, but lately he'd shot up. He'd finally gotten over that awkward stage when boys look like colts. Working for his dad had put muscle on his thin frame.

After a while, she said, "Reese, how long have we known each other?"

He didn't look up from measuring. "I don't know. Forever, I guess. I saw you naked when we were five. That's my first memory of you."

"How'd I look?" Her cover girl smile was wasted on him.

"Skinny. Skin as white as chalk. You took off your clothes right here in this front yard and slid down the slip 'n slide."

She laughed. "I think I remember that, or maybe I just remember Dad lecturing me for years about how proper young ladies don't take off their clothes in the front yard. You'd think it was some major crime."

"I don't think so." He smiled. "You never did it again. I was sorry for that. I used to ride by on my bike just to make sure."

She watched Reese work. "Have I ever lied to you, Reese?"

"Nope," he answered. "You usually don't even bother talking to me."

"Then believe me now. I am not involved in any way with Derrick. He just offered to drive me home."

"Someone needs to tell him that. Everyone's asking him how you are. You'd think by the way he talks that he's nearly one of the family."

"I plan to correct him, if I ever see him again. Then I'm giving up even talking to guys altogether. It's a bother I don't need. I plan to be someone. They'll put a sign up at the edge of town someday. Sunnie Larady was Born Here. I don't see that happening if I talk to Derrick often."

"I believe you. I figured Derrick out the first week in biology." He grinned. "That sounds super about you wanting to make the town proud. If anyone can do it, it's you."

He went back to measuring, but at least he'd listened to her. Sunnie curled into one of the porch chairs. Since she was awake she might as well talk to someone. "What about you, Reese? What do you plan to do?"

"Dad says he'll bring me into the business at full salary after I graduate. If it works out, I could be a partner by the time I'm twenty-one. Doing odd jobs and remodels keeps us busy, but I'd like to build houses someday. I can already read the plans as good as my pop can."

"As well," she corrected, then felt bad about it. Not everyone's father was an editor. "Have you ever thought of being an architect and actually designing the homes you build?"

He shrugged and shook his head. "That would be something. I did design this ramp though, so I guess that's a start." Reese pulled out a scrap of paper from his back pocket. "It's kind of like a puzzle figuring out exactly how to put it together, how much supplies, how much incline. Funny, before I started helping Pop I didn't care much about math, but now it's my favorite subject."

He hadn't offered the paper to her, so she stepped off the porch and took it from his hand. It made little sense to her. The drawing looked like some kind of modern art sketch with numbers floating around it.

He bumped her shoulder with his. "I wanted the ramp long enough so your gram could roll herself up without too much effort and wide enough she wouldn't scrape her hands."

"This is great." Reese Milton had impressed her. "Could you use a little help?"

His eyebrows rose to the rim of his baseball hat. "Sure. If everything I've already cut is right, this should fit together pretty fast. Another pair of hands would really come in handy."

An hour later, the ramp was taking shape when she saw Derrick's car turn the corner.

"Reese, did you brush your teeth this morning?"

"Yeah, why?"

"Would you kiss me?"

While he thought about it, she leaned over and kissed him. Thankfully, he didn't pull away. Not until Derrick had driven by.

When she leaned back, Reese just stared at her. She couldn't tell if he liked the kiss or not. In truth, she really didn't care. The show was for Derrick's sake. Now maybe he'd get the hint that she wasn't his girl and never would be.

"Where'd you learn to kiss?" she snapped at Reese.

"You have to learn?"

She rolled her eyes. "Don't tell me this was your first kiss. No one makes it to sixteen without being kissed."

"I'm still fifteen. I don't turn sixteen for two more months."

"I guess you don't have a girlfriend, then?"

"No. I don't have time."

"Good. You mind if I'm your girlfriend until Derrick goes away? You wouldn't have to do anything and I'm not kissing you again, I promise." She frowned at him. "You're still fifteen. Somehow, kissing a fifteen-year-old just seems wrong."

"What happens when I turn sixteen?"

"We break up. Are you okay with helping me or not?"

"Let me get this right. I'm your boyfriend?"

"Right."

"Until Derrick gives up on his lie and goes away."

"Right. This isn't rocket science, Reese. All I'm asking is for a few weeks at the most."

"All right, I'll help you out. I'll be your new boyfriend, but you have to help me out on all that entails. Any chance, since you're my girlfriend, that I'd get to see you naked again?"

She caught his shoulder with one swing and sent him rolling over the ramp.

He bounced, landing on his feet and rubbing his arm. When he grinned at her, she knew he was kidding her. "I was just asking to see if you've changed. I was kind of hoping your chest might have popped out."

"It doesn't work that way and don't ask again."

"I think I'll remember." He rubbed his arm. "I'm guessing the answer's no anyway."

She thought of hitting him again.

Reese was smart enough to change the subject. "How about we get back to work before I'm too beat up to swing a hammer."

When she moved closer, he flinched. "I didn't know having a girlfriend would involve pain."

She felt sorry for him. Reese hadn't asked for this and he was being good-natured about the whole thing. "Tell you what I'll do." She patted his shoulder. "You be my boyfriend long enough to get rid of Derrick, and I'll teach you to kiss before we break up."

"Fair enough, but you have to promise to tell Brianna Baxter that I'm a great kisser."

She hit him again on the shoulder, but this time he absorbed the blow without moving. "Don't tell me you like Brianna because she's popped out?"

"No. I like the way she giggles at everything I say."

Sunnie shook her head. "You two were made for each other."

"So you'll tell her?"

"All right. I promise, if you'll be my boyfriend and swear you'll not tell anyone it's only a trick we're playing to get rid of Derrick."

As she helped him build the ramp, Sunnie decided it wasn't half-bad having Reese around. He wasn't popular and his clothes were nothing special, but he was nice and he made her laugh.

She could get used to that.

17

The hours flew by on Jillian's first day without Gram at the quilt shop. Most people just came in to ask about the accident, and they all wanted details.

She finally realized how important the shop was to the town...how important Gram was to them. It reminded her of a fairy tale where one old woman was the heart of the village. Gram kept the stories. Lived through all their lives with them.

Over and over she heard them say things like, "She was there when..." or, "It wouldn't be Christmas if Gram wasn't..."

Gram had walked through all their memories. At birthdays, weddings, christenings, funerals. She'd woven herself into the fabric of their lives simply by caring.

A few times, as people talked and reminisced, Jillian would ask if anyone remembered a Jefferson James or maybe his wife Marti James who might have lived here thirty years ago. Jefferson was tall, thin, and had Jillian's dark hair and eyes.

No one offered one clue. Jillian might have her papa's

logbook with this zip code penciled in, and Laurel Springs was within the circle around Oklahoma City that was close enough to drive to in one night, but if he ever stopped here, he didn't stay long enough to leave an impression.

The next zip code was in southern Kansas. Maybe in a few months, she'd try up there. Deep down she knew she was wasting her time looking for a ghost, but somehow, living in this town, among these people, made her long for something she'd never had. A home. A place she was from.

If her father had wanted to find her, all he'd had to do was read the letter she'd left him. But he hadn't opened it.

Closing her eyes, she forced back tears. If he didn't care about her, or think about her, why had he taken the picture? It had to be her father. Anyone else would have left the school snapshot and taken the money.

Sometime in the past few years he'd stopped by the library. Maybe he didn't take the time to read the letter. Maybe he didn't care enough to leave her a note. But he'd taken the picture. One memory of his daughter. The school picture was nothing special, only it was the one memory he'd ever taken away with him that she knew about.

It made no sense. Just one more mystery in her life packed with unanswered questions.

Connor called a few times while she worked, with updates on Gram. He reported them like news blasts. "The head nurse informed me Gram made it through the night in the hospital without problems. They'll be releasing her around five. The nurse also ordered a hospital bed delivered to my house. With the new wing at the Acres not ready, we all agreed, with a few adjustments, my place would be best. Gram's insisting Sunnie and I keep our schedules but she'll never be alone. I'll make sure of that."

"She comes with her own bed?" Jillian tried to lighten his mood.

He didn't take the hint. "It's going to have to be set up in the dining room of my place before I get her home. All my bedrooms are upstairs, but there's a bathroom off the kitchen that has a shower. We'll make her comfortable there."

Connor also conveyed that, since the shop opened today, Gram had asked him, at least once an hour, how Jillian was handling the quilters. "You'd better say great or she'll steal a wheelchair and come check on you."

"I'm fine. You're the one with your hands full."

Connor didn't argue. "I plan to keep the night nurse coming to the house until Gram is mobile again, then we'll switch to just having a caregiver come by during the day. Between Sunnie and me, we can handle the meals, and thanks to Stella, she'll have round-the-clock friends dropping in to keep her company or bring lunch."

"Is there anything I can do?" Jillian was surprised at just how much she meant the words.

"You're doing the most important job. You're taking care of her shop. Don't be surprised if she wants a full reporting each day." He hesitated. "Thanks for being by my side through all this."

She didn't know if he meant during the day at the hospital, or Monday night when they'd slept curled up on the couch.

The door chimed and she said a quick goodbye, then went to greet two ladies who were looking for OOP fab-

ric—out of print—by Tula Pink. They said they wanted
to finish a quilt started years ago.

Jillian had no idea what they were talking about, but she
said they were welcome to look.

Joe Dunaway stopped by the shop about noon with a bag
of donuts. He'd finally abandoned his post by Gram's hospital bed. He claimed there were too many people around
to really talk to her. "She ran me off, telling me I needed
to get some rest. You'd think all last night would have been
enough. I slept like a baby with all them machines hum-
ming away around me. But when Jeanie makes her mind
up, she's a hard woman to argue with. You'd think every
decade or so she'd let me win one argument."

Even in his grumbling, he seemed tickled that Gram
was fussing over him and Jillian did the same, offering him
coffee and trying to talk him into eating one of the salads
she'd stocked in the tiny fridge.

Jillian also suspected Joe was Gram's spy. When she con-
fronted the old man, he didn't bother to deny it. His assign-
ment from Gram was to check up on what was happening
at the shop at least once a day. "Course, I won't stay long.
I got a business to run."

He did, however, plant his old body at the counter stool
and answered questions like he was a newly installed information desk attendant.

Joe tried to play down his part in the rescue, but everyone knew he was Gram's hero. He'd found her in the tall
grass by the creek and carried her back to his truck. When
they arrived at the hospital the emergency staff claimed it
was hard to tell which one had the most mud caked on—
the patient or the rescuer.

He told the same story over and over to everyone who walked in.

"I knew her leg was broken, just by the angle of it, but I didn't want to scare her, so I told her it was just a sprain. I wrapped my jacket around her knee and tied it with the sleeves so I wouldn't bump it against anything and cause her more pain. Jeanie don't like to be lied to, but I figured she'd forgive me this one time." He laughed. "Course, I lied again this morning when I said she looked great. Truth is, she's got scratches on top of scratches and is as pale as the sheets. I'm just hoping she heals a bit before she gets near a mirror."

After he finished off most of the donuts, Joe left, claiming he needed to get over to Connor's house and make sure them boys from the delivery service had Gram's bed put together right.

"You staying there until Connor brings her home?" Jillian asked.

Joe shook his head. "I'll check on her later, after she's settled in. I need to get back to work. Those Toe Tents won't make themselves. I got to get a dozen ready. I got investors coming in later today."

No one believed him, but a few of the quilters offered to drop by his workshop and help him with the stretching of material over his frames.

Jillian couldn't help but feel that Joe was slowly drawing people into his crazy plan to get rich. He even offered her a half-price special on the first dozen made.

Joe stayed true to his word. The next morning he was back with his bag of donuts and a new report on how Gram was doing.

Jillian loved having him near. This way she could know everything that was going on with the Laradys without having to question Connor.

About five, Sunnie stopped by to collect a few things from the shop for Gram. Apparently she needed her sewing basket because the quilting club was bringing supper tonight, and she might feel like working on one of the projects she kept stuffed in the bottom of her huge bag.

Sunnie lifted the bag in one hand and the sewing basket in the other as if they were dumbbells. "Gram calls this her UFO bag. It's full of UnFinished Objects. I think all quilters have them."

The girl hesitated at the door, then added, "Dad said if the women do come over, I can go get a pizza with Reese. He's been hanging around helping get everything installed that Gram needs." Sunnie grinned. "The guy is kind of growing on me. And, face it, anything's better than sitting around that circle."

"Reese the new boyfriend Joe told me about?" Jillian winked as if silently agreeing to keep a secret.

Sunnie shook her head, making her sunshine hair fly. "No. Well, maybe. Yes, I guess. He's more just a friend. He can't even drive legally, but he does it anyway. He started hauling building material for his dad before he was fifteen. Our part-time sheriff, Thornton Daily, says as long as Reese doesn't have a wreck or go outside the city limits, he can help his dad out, but that's all. So, if we go for pizza, he'll probably be hauling toilets for the remodel."

She still looked confused. "So it's not a date. Or, if it is, it's a really strange one."

Jillian just nodded as she started logging in another quilt.

She guessed that the girl simply needed to talk, and she didn't mind listening while taking pictures of the next quilt. "The strange dates can be fun."

Sunnie helped Jillian as she rattled on. "Old Thornton has his own way of doing things. He's been a sheriff since the Stone Age. Every Fourth of July, when all the oil field workers for a hundred miles around come over for our rodeo and dance, Sheriff Daily sets up horse trailers in both directions leaving the rodeo grounds. When the drunks walk out looking for their cars, he walks them right into the trailers. Locks the gates. Lets them out in the morning.

"Dad says, come dawn, they're hungover and mad as hell, but when they find out there is no fine, they thank the sheriff and go home.

"If we go for pizza, that will leave Dad with Gram and the quilters." Sunnie seemed like she was finally getting to the point. "How about you talk to Dad and ask him out to eat? You'd be saving his life, trust me."

"So if this Reese is more friend than boyfriend, maybe your dad could just tag along with you guys and eat pizza."

Sunnie giggled. "Oh, no. If you ask him out, promise you'll take Dad somewhere else. It'll be embarrassing enough to be with a guy younger than me. The last thing I want is Dad watching, or worse, trying to talk to us."

"I'll think about it." Jillian watched Sunnie lug Gram's bags to the door. "Don't worry. I'm sure your father will find someplace to escape to besides the Pizza Place."

As Sunnie disappeared, other people were coming inside. To talk. To buy a few things. To look around. There would be no more logging quilts today.

By closing time Jillian realized one other fact. There was

no one in her life, not one person, like Gram. She'd never thought to ask her father what his mother's name had been or where his people had come from. He probably wouldn't have answered her anyway. All he'd ever told her about her mother was that she went by Marti.

They must have married, because she'd put Marti James on Jillian's birth certificate and left most of the other information blank. When she'd asked him to tell her about their marriage, Papa had said there wasn't much to it. They just said the words to each other one night.

Jillian could almost hear his sad words crossing twenty years of time in her mind. *Your mom said it counted because we meant it forever. But it turned out that kind of ceremony doesn't count. She was wrong about the forever part, too. I didn't see her much after her family found out she was pregnant, but she promised she'd call when the baby came. She said we'd run away as soon as she could leave the hospital and I promised I'd be there to raise the kid we made.*

When I got to the hospital she was gone and I knew there was never going to be a forever, but I swore I'd keep up my side of the bargain.

Her father probably never even told Marti that he loved her. He'd never told Jillian. Maybe her family talked her out of keeping the baby. Jillian didn't know, but she had a feeling her mother never planned to keep Jefferson James either.

When Jillian locked the door and circled the store, she felt alone, really alone, for the first time since she'd been a little girl, curled up as the wind blew against their trailer and monsters scratched at the door.

She hadn't followed Papa's rule: *Never get involved in other people's problems.*

She'd slipped. Let it happen. This was just a job like the dozens of others she'd had over the years. She was making good money, living cheap, staying under the radar. This should have been easy. In a couple of months, she'd move on. Somewhere like Atlanta, or Kansas, or even New York. Somewhere she'd just be one of the crowd. Invisible. Usually, after she left a place, no one even remembered her name. But here, they might.

She smiled. If Gram was in her right mind, she'd remember Jillian. Folks had commented several times that she never forgot a name. Joe even said once that she remembered every person she ever met. Someone might pass through town and stop in at the shop and five years later she'd call them by name when they returned.

Jillian told herself she'd never think of this little town or its people again once she walked away. Missing someone only brought pain, regret.

"Never. Never." She could hear the word echoing off the shop's walls, but that didn't make it sound any more true. She'd collected memories here. This time, the people would be hard to forget.

As she passed the cutting table, she remembered the quilt Stella told her Gram used to work on.

No one would notice if she looked now. The door was already locked. She was alone.

Hesitantly, she opened the almost invisible drawer beneath the table. Jillian had no idea what to expect, but what she saw was beyond any quilt she'd ever seen before. Bright colors mixed with embroidered names and numbers in a crazy pattern that had no beginning or end. No balance. No symmetry.

It didn't fit with any of the quilts in the room, not blocked or patterned in any order. It was like a piece of modern art among Renaissance paintings.

As if handling a treasure, she slowly spread it out on the table. It was so wide the unfinished quilt hung over the sides almost to the floor.

She stared at it, having no idea where to start the description. Pieces of color bright as shards of glass, writing and dates seemed to flow in a whirlpool, bumping into each other, interfering, almost as if crossing over one pattern to form another on top.

She didn't know if she was looking at a genius's or a fool's work.

A light tapping on the door made her jump.

As if she'd been spying into state secrets, Jillian quickly folded the quilt up and shoved it back into the drawer.

She was out of breath when she finally opened the door.

Connor had already retreated toward his pickup. He turned. "Sorry. Sunnie told me you were waiting for me. She said you wanted to take me to dinner."

Multiple-choice answers bounced across Jillian's brain. The truth was, she hadn't said yes; Sunnie had just made the suggestion. But if she admitted it, he'd know his daughter had lied to him.

"I was just folding up a quilt. Can't wait to go to dinner and hear all about how Gram is settling in at your place."

Connor's smile was all the proof she needed to know she'd picked the right answer.

He held the truck door for her, then circled around and climbed in. "Where to?"

"Somewhere quiet. I've been surrounded by people all day."

"I agree. The house has been full of friends since I got Gram home. I managed to run most of them off early last night so she could sleep and and again this afternoon to let Gram rest a few hours before the quilters swarmed in."

He drove through the Hamburger Hut, picked up malts and burgers, then crossed the bridge to the old part of town. The boards over the water were uneven, rattling her from side to side like a cheap, twirling carnival ride.

Jillian raised her eyebrows but didn't say a word. Where they were going didn't matter. She was with the one she wanted to be with. She needed to stop worrying about lingering memories and just relax.

He parked by a three-story building and climbed out.

She waited, not sure what to do. The malts and burgers were still on the seat beside her. Surely they weren't stopping here. This place was scary even in daylight. She didn't plan on staying around to see how it looked in less than an hour.

When he opened her door, he raised his arms to catch her. "Come with me." He encouraged as if offering far more than a lift down from the high seat.

Her legs were plenty long enough to take the step out, but she slid into his embrace. He lowered her to the ground. For a moment they were so close they touched as they breathed. She thought he might lean in slightly and kiss her, but he simply brushed his cheek against her hair. "Trust me, Jillian, you're going to like this restaurant."

He grabbed his raincoat from behind the seat, handed her the drinks and picked up their meal.

Following him into the building, she was surprised to see how sound the old factory seemed to be. The ceiling was tall, over twenty feet. Decaying ropes still hung from pulleys, and worktables stood dusty, silently waiting for craftsmen to arrive. The windows were high, ribboning the building with natural light.

Staying close, she whispered as though she might disturb ghosts, "What did they used to make in here?"

"I'm not sure. I think parts of oil rigs were shipped in and assembled here. I don't know much about it, but there's an old Christmas tree over there in the corner." He pointed to a six-foot structure that was formed from a mixture of valves, spools and fittings welded together. "They're used at oil or gas well sites. I see them in the oil fields around. I'm not really sure why they call them Christmas trees. A roughneck would have to be drunk to mistake this jumble of metal for a tree."

She turned in a complete circle. "Nice restaurant."

"Oh, we're not there yet." He pointed to a staircase along one wall. "We've got rooftop seating."

Suddenly excited, she climbed ahead of him, her shoes tapping a rhythm in double time. At the top, she waited impatiently with a malt in each hand.

He juggled the bag of burgers as he shoved the heavy door open. They stepped onto the rooftop with no one else around. She could see for miles in every direction. The trees, the fields. Oil rigs, scattered homes and barns, schools and churches.

"It's beautiful!" The sun's low glow gave everything a golden light.

He set the bag down and spread his raincoat out like a tablecloth on an air vent cover. "It's not yet, but it will be." He pulled up two empty five-gallon buckets to use as stools.

She sat the malts down. "You've been to this restaurant before."

"Guilty. But I've never brought anyone here. Only you."

While he unwrapped his burger, she looked around, pointing out everything as if he was also seeing it for the first time. "Look how winding the creek is.

"I had no idea there were so many trees.

"Oh, look at those horses running." She loved the way the evening clouds moved over the land, darkening the hues of the earth in shadow as they drifted.

"It's winter now, not near as pretty as it'll be come spring." He set his hamburger beside hers and came to join her near the roof's edge. "I lease that flatland out to a farmer who plants cotton every spring. That brown dirt will look like a green carpet in a few months."

"I won't be here in spring." She let the wind catch her words as she turned away from him and the view. The black tar roof beneath her feet was all she saw now, but she stared hard, willing not one tear to fall.

This time. This place she would miss. When she left, Jillian knew memories would be packed in her heart. A year from now, a decade, a lifetime, she'd still remember the beauty of this view in winter and wonder how it looked in spring.

Silent for a minute, his words came calm, questioning.

"Is there someone pulling you away? Are you running away from someone? Or to another?"

He'd asked before. She'd answered. But he must not have believed her.

"No one is waiting for me or looking for me." She walked to the edge of the roof and stared down at the alley in shadows. "No one cares about me, or for me, Connor."

Moving up behind her, he whispered, "I do, Jillian." He seemed to be dragging the words out. They didn't come easy. "I care. I think I have since the day you first walked into my office. There is something about you that draws me to you."

Pulling her gently against him, he kissed her as she fought back tears. Part of her wanted to run, like she always did, but this time she decided she'd stay long enough to feel just a bit. Connor was a kind man. He'd be easy to care about but she wasn't sure he'd be easy to leave.

She kissed him back, knowing she was gambling. Loving the way he held her as if she were a treasure. He kissed like a man thirsting for one drink and he'd suddenly found an ocean in her. Feeling every touch not just on her skin, but all the way to her bones. When they were close she swore she could hear his thoughts. No one had ever gotten so near.

"I've been wanting to hold you all day." His words blended with the evening wind.

"I know." How could she explain that she'd been sleep-walking all through the day and now, for the first time, she felt awake?

Without a word, he turned her to face the sunset. With his arms wrapped around her, they watched nature's grand show. "This is why I reserved the rooftop table. I wanted to show you this."

She didn't say a word. Couldn't. The calm beauty of this quiet place melted into her soul.

Just as the last bit of sun disappeared, she had to admit, "It's breathtaking!"

"Yes, it is," he answered against her ear. "I've been up here dozens of times, but it's never been as gorgeous as it is tonight.

"You know, Jillian, you affect me as no one ever has. Like a warm wind blowing away a kind of loneliness that settled over me years ago. I know it doesn't make sense. We barely know each other. But you make my world feel whole." He laughed, nervous at his admission. "When I look in those stormy-day eyes of yours, I feel like I've found a safe harbor."

A tear slowly slid down her cheek. She understood him. But he'd never understand why she had to leave.

And leave she would.

18

When the sun's last glow disappeared, Connor watched the town begin to sparkle with lights. Not bright like Las Vegas must be. Not breathtaking like New York City. But welcoming, like nowhere else but his town.

"It looks like a toy village set up on a velvet board." Jillian leaned her head on his shoulder. Something he was growing quite fond of her doing.

"It's beautiful at Christmas," he said, knowing she would be long gone before summer, much less December. "Ribbons of lights string across Main, and lots of people trim their homes in twinkling lights. From here it looks like the whole town is sparkling red and green."

"I won't..."

He ended the conversation with a quick, firm kiss, wanting to taste her before words came between them.

When he pulled away, he sounded harder than he meant to. "Let's not talk about your going. I know you'll leave. You told me from the start, but for now could we just pretend that you belong here? I think I'd rather take the jolt of your leaving all at once and not in tiny pricks."

"All right." Her voice sounded flat but her hands fisted around the material on the front of his shirt as if she didn't plan to let go of him.

Maybe she wanted to pretend, too, or for once she just didn't want to talk about it. He didn't care. He knew what he wanted. He wanted to imagine three months was a lifetime.

He touched her lips softly in apology, as his thoughts seemed to slip out. "You're here, with me, until you leave. You're here." His arm tightened around her waist, telling her the *here* was with him.

"I'm here," she answered as her mouth opened to his kiss.

He couldn't believe how completely he could lose himself in one woman. It had never happened before. She felt right in his arms. He didn't know when or where they'd make love, but he knew they would and whether they did it one time or every night while she was with him, Connor knew that he'd fall asleep for the rest of his life holding her in his dreams.

Knowing that every touch was both a beginning and an ending made the moment so much sweeter. She melted against him and still his hands moved over her, pressing her closer. He wanted to memorize every curve of her, the way she smelled and how she liked to be kissed, what made her laugh and the taste of her tears. He wanted to know it all so he'd remember.

The night darkened, traffic on the other side of the bridge slowed, the wind began to rage, but he barely noticed. She was here now. She was with him.

Maybe, as rational adults, they should talk about the way

they felt, but for now all he wanted was to feel. To live in the moment without the shadow of loss hanging over him.

When they finally climbed down from the roof, they had to move in total darkness through the old factory. Laughing. Touching. Bumping into one another.

Once in the truck, she slid over close to him, seeming to need him as near as possible.

After one kiss so hot he felt like it fried several brain cells, he grinned. "Did you ever do it in a pickup?"

"No. And we're not doing it now." She laughed, teasing him as she pressed against him. "How would it look? The mayor spotted making out in his pickup. Sheriff Daily would lock you up."

"I don't really care," he admitted.

"Well, I do. I don't go all the way on a first date."

"This is a date, then?"

"It almost was." She kissed his nose. "I almost asked you out. You almost fed me dinner. I think a crow carried off my hamburger while we were watching the sunset."

"Hungry?"

"Starving."

"Where to now?" She was threading her fingers through the back of his hair. He had trouble forming words, much less telling directions. Everyone in his house would probably be asleep by now. No one would notice when he came in.

She scraped her nails along his scalp, then curled her fingers in his hair and pulled him to her for one last kiss before she whispered, "We're going to your house. I'd like to check on Gram and then raid your fridge. We can't stay lost forever."

He groaned. She was right, of course. It was time he got

back, but part of him wished all clocks, all problems, all responsibility would stop for a few hours.

Slowly, she pulled a few inches away. He started the truck, then rested a hand on her leg, fearing she might slip farther away. They drove back across the bridge.

A few minutes later there were so many cars parked around his house Connor had to pull to the curb three houses down. As they walked slowly to the two-story home he'd owned since Sunnie was born, he finally felt in control of his emotions.

This time they had spent together, alone, had changed them. He knew it and more important, he knew she knew it. They were no longer polite strangers. No longer flirting. No longer guessing how the other felt.

In the shadows of evergreens on the edge of his property line, he stopped. Looking down at Jillian for a moment, he wished he could see her eyes as he admitted, "It wasn't enough tonight."

She stood so still he wasn't sure she heard him.

Then, she added, "I agree." Her hand reached out to stroke his arm as though she had to feel him near. "It was perfect, but it wasn't enough."

He fought to keep from closing the few inches separating her from him. "When we go inside, I won't touch you. I may not even look at you, but I'll be thinking about what happened on the roof. We're not two kids playing around. I think after thirty-seven years I've finally found my addiction. It's you, Jillian."

He wasn't courting her or seducing her. She wasn't flirting or manipulating him. This was no game they were playing.

Finally, she met his eyes. "When we go inside, stay a room away from me because if you don't I may shock the ladies of the quilting circle."

He laughed. "I'm tempted to test that theory."

She straightened, her hands locked together in front of her. "Thank you for the date, Connor. I had a nice time."

Slowly, they moved into the glow of the porch light. As they paused he said, keeping his voice neutral, "It was nice getting to know you better." In the shadows behind them, his hand slid along her thigh. "I love the feel of you so near, Jillian. It's like I've found something I'd missed all my life and didn't know it until the moment I touched you."

"Me, too," she answered as she stepped onto the side porch that led to a brightly lit kitchen window.

Every part of him wanted to remain in the shadows with her, near her, touching her, but their private evening was over. Reason told him the quilters had stayed too late and he needed to go in and break up the party.

Before he could tease her more with their well-bred conversation and bold brushes, Connor joined her on the porch. The newly constructed ramp made it necessary that they brushed shoulders while walking.

His gaze caught movement by the door. A shadowy figure almost like the one he'd seen in the alley of the district. Only this one was huddled, hiding between two wooden rockers.

For a moment, he stepped to shield her from danger. Then his eyes adjusted to the night enough to see. It wasn't a man curled and ready to strike, but a boy huddled in pain beside the kitchen door. Hiding. Or trying to.

Connor took a step backward, his logical mind trying to find reason.

Jillian spotted the crumpled form. A heartbeat later she was running forward.

"He's hurt," she cried as she lifted the boy's face in both her hands.

Connor knelt beside her. "Reese?" He turned a bloody face toward the light and recognized the kid whose father did all the handiwork around town. "Reese, what happened?"

19

Sunnie had enjoyed as much of the quilting group as she could stand. Her goal in life was to never put a needle in her hand. No knitting, no crochet, no sewing. The whole idea of quilting didn't make sense when all anyone had to do was go to the store and buy a blanket. They weren't pioneer women anymore. They didn't slaughter their own pigs or wash their clothes on rocks at the creek. Why piece together scraps for a quilt to keep warm in homes with central air and heat?

But, of course, she didn't express her opinion to this posse. The sweet old ladies would probably burn her at the stake. That's what undoubtedly really happened in the Salem witch trials. It was all about whether to quilt or not to quilt.

For the past two hours, she'd popped up every ten or fifteen minutes and gone back into the kitchen to stare out the window and hope to see Reese. He'd called at six and said he'd be a little late.

It was after eight and there was no *a little* left. He was

just late. Or, she had to reason, by now there was the possibility that he wasn't coming at all.

The guy was fifteen. Who knows, maybe the idea of
eating pizza with a girl made him sick. Or maybe he was
scared she'd kiss him again. He didn't act as if he liked it
much when she'd kissed him before. He obviously didn't
know how to be a boyfriend, even a short-term one.

This was the last time she would go out with a younger
man. Correction. She hadn't left the house. He hadn't
shown up. There was no *going out* this night. And he wasn't
a man, not like Derrick had been. But then, Derrick had
turned out to be a jerk. She was quickly moving from restless to annoyed. Maybe she'd been cursed by fairies at birth.
This dating thing was not working out.

"I'll get more sandwiches," she said, popping up again.
She'd look out the window one more time. If she didn't
see Reese's old pickup out front she'd tell everyone she had
homework.

She'd been up and down so many times none of the ladies paid any attention to her anyway. They were all talking
except Gram, who'd dozed off about an hour ago, without
anyone noticing.

The strange thing about women with needles flying in
their fingers—they don't tend to look up and make eye
contact.

Bumping into the swinging kitchen door with an empty
tray in each hand, she stopped abruptly and stared at the
bizarre scene before her.

Her father leaned over someone slumping in one of the
two kitchen chairs. The smell of blood hit her nostrils about

the same time the swinging door slammed against her back. With a thud, the squeaky door pushed her forward.

"What…"

"Keep the door closed and lower your voice," he ordered in that parent tone that might as well have added a screaming *NOW* to the request.

Sunnie dropped the trays on the counter, passed Jillian, who was dumping ice into a baggie, and rushed to her dad. She felt like someone had slowed a horror film down to one frame at a time.

Her father looked angry, worried. His sleeve and shoulder were covered in blood, but he didn't look hurt. Sunnie brushed her hand over his shoulder, making sure he was sound before she breathed.

Red drops spotted the white linoleum like crimson rain, and a bloody handprint ran along the side of the bar.

A tossed tea towel, more red than white, lay on the breakfast table.

"Dad?" She focused on his bloody hands holding the ice pack over someone's face.

A patient, or victim? She couldn't tell from the cussing mumbling out from behind the ice pack. He was tall, long legs. Thin. Worn jeans. Muddy tennis shoes. A jacket like the one Reese had on at school when he'd passed her in the hallway a few times.

"He's going to be all right, Sunnie." Dad's tone didn't convince her. "I've just got to stop his nose from bleeding." Her father slowly lifted the bag of ice.

Sunnie swallowed a scream. Reese!

He looked terrible. His left eye was swollen closed and rainbow-colored, leaving out any happy hues. His lip was double the size it should be on one side. His whole face was a patchwork of blood, bruises, and one-inch-wide cuts.

His nose still dripped as he looked up at her with his right eye and smiled.

He smiled! Well, with the left half of his mouth anyway.

"What happened?" She turned to her father, as if the victim couldn't answer for himself.

"I have no idea." Dad shook his head as he pressed the ice pack down again. "We found him like this. He was bleeding all over the porch. I don't think anything is broken, except maybe his nose."

Reese pushed away the ice bag.

Her dad didn't force it back. He just studied the mess of blood and bruises a moment, then wiped Reese's nose as if he were a three-year-old.

Sunnie had never had an ounce of patience. "What happened to you, Reese? Tell me right now." She caught herself doubling up her fist as if planning to add another bruise if he didn't answer fast.

"Look at the bright side, Sunnie." He laughed at his own words. "I still got all my teeth. It can't look that bad."

Dad put the pack back over his face. "Shut up, Reese. Trust me. You look terrible."

He mumbled a few cusswords and then settled, allowing them to care for him.

Sunnie just stood, watching Jillian switch ice packs and her father dab at the blood leaking out of several cuts.

The next time Dad pulled off the pack, the faucet that was Reese's nose had slowed. Dad reached for a clean tea towel. "It might be a good idea to get that one deep cut on your cheek stitched up. Otherwise it might leave a scar."

"It's fine." Reese's voice had hardened, more man than boy now. "I don't care if it scars."

Sunnie couldn't stand it. She fought down the urge to yell for someone to call 911, but the last thing she wanted in this bloody kitchen was half a dozen quilters. "What happened? And this time I'm not interested in your teeth."

She'd thought of punching Reese for standing her up. Maybe this was her fault. No. Wishing didn't blacken eyes. Maybe her dad thought he was a burglar and pounced. No. Dad wasn't the type. If he ever killed anyone, it would be by lecturing them to death.

Jillian put a hand on her shoulder. "We don't know anything, Sunnie. We found him curled up on the porch like this. He was either trying to get to you, or away from someone here."

Dad wiped a wet hand towel over Reese's face and all three spectators waited for blood to drip. When it didn't, Dad straightened. "It's stopped, Reese. Your nose doesn't appear to be broken. How about telling us what happened?"

"I was late picking Sunnie up for our date."

To her utter horror, her father stared at her in that questioning way he had. The look that silently shouted, *What have you done now?*

"Don't look at me," she snapped. "I haven't even seen him since school."

Dad rolled his eyes as though he was insulted that she even felt the need to explain. Maybe she'd guessed his expression wrong. Maybe it was more a *Can't believe you had a date* look.

New looks had been popping up on Dad since she got her period four years ago.

Reese didn't seem to notice their exchange. He just lifted the ice pack to his eye and continued, "When I started up the walk to pick up Sunnie so we could go get pizza, Derrick stepped out from the shadows. He told me he was dating her, and if I knew what was good for me I'd disappear."

Reese managed a lopsided smile. "I told him I guess I didn't know what was good for me. I said I was going to take Sunnie out for pizza whether he liked it or not.

"That was the first time he hit me. I wasn't prepared. When the stars in my vision finally cleared, he was still there snarling at me. He said I didn't know Sunnie like he did.

"I explained that I'd already seen her naked." Reese shrugged and moved the pack to his lip. "That's when he hit me again."

Sunnie didn't dare look at her father, but she was fighting back taking a slug at her one-eyed short-time boyfriend who was now talking way too much.

Reese wiped blood away from his swollen lip. "After that, I decided to fight. It's kind of a blur. Derrick cussed me out and walked away, but I think he was mad more than hurt."

"You want to call the sheriff?" Dad asked.

"No. My dad used to work with his dad. They're friends. This was between us. I probably shouldn't have even told you guys, but one look at Sunnie convinced me she probably wouldn't take silence for an answer."

He looked up at her and kept his promise. "Sunnie is my girlfriend, Mr. Larady. Derrick needs to get that through his head and back off. I'm dating her." He tried to grin. "I didn't expect it to be easy, but I didn't think it would be this hard on me."

Sunnie swore under her breath. She couldn't deny Reese's statement, not even to her father. The guy just got beat up because of her, and he was still holding up his end of the bargain. The guy had grit. She'd give him that.

Jillian asked if Dad would bring her a first aid kit. He nodded and reluctantly left the kitchen while Jillian moved the bloody towels to the sink.

Sunnie knelt down, her hands on Reese's knee. "I'm sorry," she whispered. "I thought he might get mad, or yell at us, but I never dreamed he'd fight you."

"It wasn't much of a fight." Reese hung his head. "Maybe you should have picked a senior to be your boyfriend for a few months. Some guy who knew how to box."

"No. I picked you, if you're still up for it. You're starting to grow on me. Of course, I plan to slug you, when you've recovered, for telling my dad you saw me naked."

"Fair enough. Sorry I was late. We had work to finish on the remodel. Every day we're still working, the family has to stay in a hotel." He carefully laid his hand over hers. "I'm starving for a pizza, and now I'll be lucky if I can close my jaw enough to eat. It hurts like hell."

She laced her fingers in his, noticing that his knuckles were scraped. "You know, Reese, I don't care if you are fifteen. When your lip heals, I plan on kissing you again."

"Really?"

"I swear."

He grinned, then winced. "Sunnie, I got to admit, being your boyfriend sure has its ups and downs." He tugged on a strand of her light hair. "But I think I could get used to it."

Dad was back, interrupting as usual. He acted as assistant while Jillian put a butterfly bandage on Reese's cheek.

"You sure collected a lot of cuts." Jillian doctored each one.

"Yeah, Derrick has a senior ring on both hands. That's what I felt, not the fist or the blow, but the rings pounding into me."

Reese never complained. When she finished, he still looked terrible, but he hadn't turned loose of Sunnie's hand for a moment.

Dad said they could go upstairs and watch TV in her room if Reese wanted to stay a while. He'd order them pizza and bring it up once it arrived.

"Leave the door open," he added as they headed up the back stairs. "And, Reese, let me know if you feel faint or dizzy."

Sunnie pulled Reese into her cluttered room and closed the door. The only light was the TV. It was easier to look at him that way. They leaned back on a dozen stuffed animals stacked on her bed. He used the buffalo as his pillow.

She sat beside him and flipped channels. Neither said a word. It occurred to her that no one in the room knew a thing about dating. They'd just have to make it up as they went along.

Finally, he lifted his hand and touched her arm, slowly sliding his finger along her skin from elbow to wrist, as if testing to see if she were real.

"You okay with this," he said. "Me being here? Me touching you?"

"Sure. You want to see me naked?" She had no idea why she'd said that. Words just dribbled out of her mouth sometimes. At this point in her life she rarely made it through a day without saying at least one terrible, dumb, stupid comment.

"No. I'll wait until I have two eyes." After a minute, he asked, "Can I touch your hair? You've got angel hair. I've always wondered what it would feel like."

She flashed him an impatient look. "How about you touch me where you like, and I'll let you know if you go too far."

His hand slid down over her hip.

"That's too far." *Making it up as they go* probably wouldn't work with Reese. He'd probably need boundaries, or a fence, or a brick wall. Maybe she could find a dating manual online.

He slowly crawled his fingers up to just below her breast. When he pushed an inch farther, she said, "Too far again."

"Just testing. You can touch me and test my boundaries, too."

"Do you have any?"

He shook his head. "I don't think so, but I don't mind if you run a test for them."

Dad banged his way into her room with sodas and a pizza. She was glad to see him for a change. She'd just had the strangest conversation with a guy she'd known forever and realized she didn't know him at all.

Dad set the pizza down between them and backed away. "Enjoy." He cleared his throat like he always did when he had something important he thought he had to say. "And, Sunnie, keep your clothes on."

She rolled her eyes. "Dad, I was five when he saw me playing in the water in the front yard."

"That's right, Mr. Larady. But I wouldn't mind seeing her again."

Dad tilted his head as if trying to see Reese more clearly. "You get beaten up often, son?"

"Why'd you ask?"

Dad shook his head. "I don't know. The thought of hitting you just crossed my mind, and I'm not prone to violence."

"I know how you feel, Dad." Sunnie added, for once understanding her dad. "He kind of brings the violent thoughts out, but don't worry, he's harmless. He's kind of like a pound puppy. The longer he stays around, the cuter he gets."

"Leave the door open." There was no negotiation in her father's tone.

"Why? Don't you trust me?"

"I do. I just have a feeling if you two talk much, I'll hear his screams for help better with the door open."

When Dad walked away, Reese slowly sat up and took a bite of pizza. She flipped channels until she found a *Harry Potter* movie they'd both seen when they were kids. They leaned back and watched it again, saying the lines at the same time the actors did.

Finally, when the drinks and pizza were gone, she took his hand in hers and they watched the end of the movie together.

Both were almost asleep when they heard the quilters leaving. They all seemed to be talking at once as they passed below her window.

"It's late." Reese stated the obvious.

"Yeah. We should do this again sometime."

"Yeah." He squeezed her fingers, which were still laced in his.

She walked him all the way out to his old truck loaded down with boards and smashed boxes. After two hours of healing, he didn't look any better, but the darkness made it easier to face him.

"You all right to drive?"

"Sure. I'm only going six blocks." He ran his fingers through her hair slowly, like it was something special. "Sunnie, is it too early to tell you I think I love you?"

"Yes," she answered with no emotion. "Definitely."

"Okay." He moved away and pulled the door open. "Let me know when it's time."

Laughter, the kind that tickles up all the way from your heart, suddenly shook Sunnie. "Give me about ten years to get used to you first, Reese. Then I'll think about letting you love me."

"Sounds good. We've got lots of time." He climbed into his truck. "See you at school. Any chance you'll eat lunch with me?"

"Nope. I always eat lunch alone. But I'll speak to you if I see you in the hall."

He nodded. "Definite improvement. Night, honey."

"Don't call me honey."

"Right."

The good side of his mouth rose slightly and she knew he was lying, but he raced the engine and was gone before she could answer.

When she walked back to the porch, Dad was waiting for her. "That boy needs work."

"Tell me about it. I'm starting a list."

"Does that mean he's coming back?"

"I'm afraid so."

"I'll stock more chips, cookies and frozen pizzas." Dad shrugged. "And bandages."

"I think I like him, Dad."

"Yeah, me, too."

20

As he had every evening since Gram's accident, Connor drove through the deserted district of town, though it wasn't on his way home from work. Even in the dying light, the shadows seemed longer on this side of the creek, but he explored the alleyways and peered between the buildings. Searching for a ghost. The outline of a man who'd disappeared amid the ruins.

When he'd been looking for Gram that morning over a week ago, he hadn't had time to confront the shadow in the alley, but now he had no intention of forgetting someone was there.

Maybe it was just a kid playing around. Maybe a druggie looking for a place to get high. Maybe a drifter hunting for something worth stealing. But somewhere, trouble was hiding out among the buildings he owned.

This place might not be worth much, but it was his land. His problem.

As before, he found nothing, but just to make sure, Connor circled by Joe's workshop and checked that the old guy had locked up for the night. Wouldn't want anyone stealing his worthless invention.

Connor drove down each dusty street one more time. No one had worked in these warehouses and workshops since he'd been alive, but many of the buildings were still standing tall, as if waiting for someone to blow off the dust.

The structures that had crumbled reminded him of ancient ruins. Forgotten churches from the Roman era, or piles of stones left when a castle fell to Vikings. When he'd been a boy, he'd dreamed of roaming down the Rhine River, seeing the castles and fortresses that survived and the ones that left only crumbling shells.

He'd kiss the Blarney Stone at Blarney Castle and walk the grounds around Marksburg Castle in Germany. He'd always said that he would go someday. Now, he feared someday would never come. It occurred to him that maybe people don't give up on their dreams—maybe dreams give up on them and simply fade away so slowly no one sees them go.

Connor turned toward home, hardly believing nine days had passed since Gram's accident. Funny how the world turns upside down then rights itself to a new normal. You settle into it as if life had always been that way. Within two days she'd been running both his house and her shop from her hospital bed in the dining room. Or at least thought she was. All those around her filled in the gaps she'd forgotten.

While still in dusk's shadow, he parked his pickup behind Gram's shop and crossed through the darkened rooms. He joined Jillian just as she locked the shop door for the night. She'd said she needed to work a little later to catch up on the quilt cataloging. Running the shop was not what she'd been hired on to do, but she was managing.

With his old pickup parked behind the shop and his Audi at home in case Gram needed to go somewhere, Connor still managed to have his favorite time of day. Twilight, when he walked home with Jillian. It might be only a few blocks, but they were almost alone. They could talk and tease and flirt.

"I'll work on Gram's books until you're ready."

"Thanks, I won't be long." Jillian smiled at him as she did so often lately. That shy little smile that seemed to say they shared a secret.

He stepped into the office, knowing that if he didn't put a wall between them neither would get any work done.

Half an hour later, she leaned her head in and said she was ready. He stood, leaving the books, knowing they'd still be there waiting tomorrow.

As she closed up A Stitch in Time, he stood close. It was night now and the shadow he'd seen in the district might have crossed the creek. There were a dozen dark hiding places someone could stand and watch the street without being seen.

"What's for dinner?" Connor kept his voice low. He wished they weren't standing in such a public place. The need to be closer to her grew with each day.

"No more hamburgers or pizza. Tonight we stop at the grocery store. I'm starving for real food." She handed him two empty shopping bags. "On our way home, we shop."

"But the grocery is a block in the wrong direction. I could go back and drive."

She laughed, as he knew she would. "When I lived in

New Jersey one winter, I had to walk a mile from the train to my apartment every night after dark. If it wasn't raining or snowing, I could cut through a back trail that was once used for coal deliveries. Every time I crossed that trail, I had visions of being mugged. It never happened. Maybe even the muggers felt sorry for me."

"There is a mystery writer in you, Jillian. What were you doing up north?"

She ignored his question. "No. I'm only a hungry article writer. Walk faster. When we finish dinner, I want to read you two new quilt stories. I'm thinking I'll have a folder full of photos of quilts made from other things. Grand-dad's ties, old T-shirts, overalls from a farmer. And today, I saw one made from all the drapes that were in a woman's childhood home. The lady said she felt like she was going home when she curled up in it."

"So you're telling me it's going to be all work tonight," he teased. "No time to just talk." In truth, he loved every minute they spent together. When she'd offered to help with dinner in the evening, he hadn't turned her down.

The only downside was they were never alone except on the way home. He liked talking to her, working beside her as they cooked dinner, visiting with Gram's hospital bed in between them, but the need to touch her was a slow ache inside him. How could a woman he'd never known existed become an addiction so fast?

If he were a different kind of man, he might have just pulled her into the shadows and kissed her, or slipped into her bedroom long after Mrs. K was asleep. If he were a different kind of man... No. He was who he was. He didn't want to step outside his skin and be someone he wasn't.

She moved in step with him, unaware of the argument he was busy having with himself.

"I can cook three things: spaghetti, meat loaf and BLTs." She smiled over at him. "And I can read, so I guess I could cook anything."

"Wow. You should write a cookbook." He acted like he was giving her choices some thought. "Meat loaf. It will be easier for Joe to eat."

"Did he eat every meal with you before the accident?"

Connor shook his head. "Sunday dinners sometimes. We would get together and all cook in Gram's little kitchen. Sunnie and Joe would compete for who could make the biggest mess. I think he often ate breakfast with Gram at the Acres after she moved in there. He really cares about her. I think he and Granddad both fell for her in school. Gram loved my grandfather, but Joe still loved her."

"You think it ever went physical?"

Laughter rumbled out no matter how hard he tried to hold it back. "I don't want to think about that one at all, but I'd bet the answer would be no. Only, I don't think it made the love any less."

He took Jillian's arm as they crossed the street and went into the market. "Since Gram got hurt, Joe seems to be afraid to leave her. The old guy knows she's with the nurse in the morning and at noon one or more of her friends always drops by with a meal, but after her nap, he thinks he's got to be there. It's his time to be with Gram."

"So when you get home, he's there and you have to feed him, right?"

"That's about it.

"Gram might be slow to heal, but her spirit remains up.

I think Joe can take credit for that. She enjoys having Sunnie or me sit by her bed at breakfast. When we leave, the day nurse is there to help her dress, and then there is her routine."

Connor grabbed a cart and pushed it behind Jillian as she shopped and he talked.

"According to the nurse, Gram is happy when Joe takes over. If the weather allows, he wheels her to the porch. If it's cold or windy, they play cards."

Ten minutes later, their argument over the grocery bill ended in Connor finally agreeing to split it. They left the store and walked the few blocks to his two-story white colonial house that Connor had told her he'd grown up in.

"Tell me about your house," she said as they neared.

He shrugged, never having introduced a house before. "My dad floored the attic as a playroom when my brother and I were little. I built the sunporch across the back so I could add a little study to write. It's nothing special. Three bedrooms upstairs, a basement no one would want to go in and two sets of stairs, both of which I've fallen down more times then I'd like to admit."

"Did Gram ever live here?"

"No. Gram, my dad's mother, had a place closer to Main until she checked into Autumn Acres. It was a cute garden home she designed herself when she moved to town after Grandpa died. She and my grandfather lived a few miles out of town when they first married. It is just a little farm his father had homesteaded."

When she didn't say anything, Connor continued, "Folks used to call it the 'newlywed farm' because every generation that came before me spent time there. They raised my father on that property. He and my mother stayed there until I was born, but my mom was sick after my brother came along a few years later. So they moved in to be closer to the doc.

"My mom and Gram liked living 'in the nest,' as they called living in town. Four generations of Laradys and not one farmer. Some claim even the first Larady made his living gambling while his crops died in the field."

As they banged their way through the kitchen door, Joe hollered from the dining room. "You guys need any help?"

"No, we're fine." Connor opened the swinging door. "You and Gram all right?"

"We're great." Gram laughed. "Joe talked me into playing poker."

"What kind?" Connor's expression made both the senior citizens laugh.

"Texas hold' em, and she's winning," Joe grumbled.

Connor backed into the kitchen, letting the door swing closed. "They don't need us. We might as well cook."

Jillian agreed. "I see what you mean about gamblers."

He winked. "Don't ever bet against a Larady."

"I'll remember that."

He liked that they talked and laughed as they cooked. Joe was now considered one of the family and never left before dessert was served, so Connor made s'mores while Jillian mixed up the meat loaf.

No one was surprised when Sunnie's new boyfriend popped over a few minutes before they sat down to dinner. He was skinny, ate everything in sight, had hair the color of the Red River, and never said the right thing at the right time. Add to that one eye was ringed in bruises and his face had more scabs than pimples.

To Connor's amazement, Gram and Jillian seemed to love Reese.

No accounting for taste. Must be the same reasons why people love ugly dogs.

When Connor complained to Sunnie about him, she simply shrugged and said, "He's got all his teeth." Which made no sense.

As he had every night since the accident, Connor left Sunnie with Gram and walked Jillian back to the bed-and-breakfast. This late the streets were dark between streetlights, offering them a kind of blinking privacy.

He'd put his arm around her shoulders or they'd lock arms and casually brush together as they walked. "Tell me something about when you were growing up. I know you moved around, but describe one place you lived."

"We lived along the coast of Florida once. A tiny house near a beach. I slept on the couch and remember being afraid of the waves."

He laughed. "How old were you?"

"Seven, maybe eight. I worried that the waves would wash up to the house one night and get me."

"Was there anything you liked about Florida?"

She smiled. "I learned to play the piano in the basement of a church there. After school, the church had a kind of day care I went to. I didn't know anyone, so one sweet lady used to let me sit with her on the piano bench while all the kids sang songs and listened to a mini-sermon every afternoon.

"When I showed some interest, she taught me a little and gave me a few beginner books. I played those simple songs so many times I memorized every one. I never wanted to go outside to play, so I practiced three hours a day. She always came down and told me she'd been listening and was proud of me."

"Did your dad play?"

"I don't know. I don't think so. My dad had the first finger of his right hand cut off about two inches."

"Rig or rodeo?"

"What do you mean?"

"Riggers working the oil field have been known to lose a finger in the chains. Calf ropers can lose part of a finger if they dally incorrectly."

"Dally?"

Connor grinned. "You know, a couple of wraps of the rope around the horn of a saddle. Ropers have lost fingers in rodeo events, even here in Laurel Springs."

"Really? Dad never mentioned how he lost the finger, but I'd bet rig over rope."

He could feel her stiffen, mentally pulling away even though her hand still rested on his arm. Connor kept his voice low, calm. "When I was a kid, first grade maybe, a guy lost a finger at our Pioneer Days Rodeo. He was calf roping, but I remember he wasn't a cowboy because I heard some of them say he'd have known better if he worked cattle regularly. Back then lots of the oil field workers would sign up for the rodeo just for something to do even if they hadn't been on a horse for a while."

Connor covered her hand with his. "You all right?"

She nodded. "It just sounds so scary. As a kid, I guess I never thought about how my father's finger got messed up. It was just his hand."

"He didn't talk about himself much, right?"

"Like, never." She tugged on his arm, and they moved onto the sidewalk of the bed-and-breakfast.

"It must run in the family," Connor added.

They reached the door. Mrs. Kelly had left the parlor light on, as always. Connor had the feeling he was stepping into the past when he entered the B and B. Jillian called the place Tattered Tara. She wasn't far off. Mrs. Kelly's place might not be as big as the *Gone With the Wind* Tara or surrounded with land, but he had a feeling some of the furnishings might be old enough to have survived the Civil War.

"You want some hot cocoa?"

He shook his head as he followed her into the Victorian parlor. It was dark except for firelight dancing across the draped walls.

With no sign of Mrs. Kelly, Connor pulled Jillian slowly to him. He'd been waiting hours for one moment alone.

Neither said a word. She just wrapped her arms around his neck and moved against him. They'd talked; now it was time to feel.

He kissed his way across her cheek and finally greeted her like he'd been wanting to all day. A slow, deep hello kiss as he felt her heart next to his.

When they were both out of breath, he straightened but didn't let go of her. "I never get enough of you. I want you to stay here, with me, forever." There was so much more he wanted to say but it was too early. He'd probably frighten her.

His forehead pressed against hers, guessing he'd said too much already.

"I can't stay. You know that. It's not my way. But I will

promise to not leave without saying goodbye. I won't disappear on you, Connor."

"Fair enough," he said, knowing that nothing about her leaving was fair. All his life he'd been without someone who fit, someone who matched just with him. She was like a half of him that had always been missing. He was only whole when she was with him. Caring for her wasn't like a cold he caught and would get over.

She tickled his ribs. "We can't stay like this. Mrs. Kelly is somewhere in the house. She'll see us. You have to leave."

Connor fought the urge to scream that he didn't care. He just wanted time with Jillian. A moment, an hour, a day, didn't matter because no matter how much, it would not be enough. "I'm not going tonight. Not if the shy ghost pops out from the cellar," he said. "I'm not leaving until you play for me. There is an old piano in the sunroom. Just one piece and I'll go."

"I've tried that old upright. It's out of tune. I haven't practiced in months. It would hurt your ears. Probably do permanent damage."

Connor laughed as he took her hand. "I don't care. I have to hear you play."

"What if I only know 'Zacchaeus Was a Wee Little Man'? That was very popular in the church basement."

"Then I'll sing along." He took her hand. "I'm not leaving until you play."

He was still tugging her behind him when they passed through the kitchen with Mrs. Kelly at the sink washing up. She turned, wiping her hands on an apron that read *It's hard to make a comeback when I haven't gone anywhere.*

"Evening, Mrs. K." Connor smiled. "Mind if we borrow your piano for a few minutes?"

"No," she answered, her eyebrows raised in shock. "Go ahead, Mayor."

Connor managed to yell thanks as they disappeared into the shadowy sunroom. He sat Jillian on the bench, opened the dusty piano and waited.

"Aren't you going to sit down?" she asked without touching the keys.

"And give you room to bolt? Not a chance."

He watched her fingers move over the keys as if finding their places. She started once, then twice. On the third try, she began to play. A gentle tune he hadn't heard in years. "Edelweiss."

The slow, whispering song seemed to circle the room. Warming all the shadows. Calming his world. He closed his eyes, taking in the music as if it were a pure gift.

When she finished, he lifted her up into his arms and kissed her, still hearing the melody in his head.

For one moment there was no place, no person, no world, but her in his arms.

21

When Connor finally left, Jillian felt his loss like a hollow ache deep inside her. She stood on the porch making herself list all the reasons he had to go, but it didn't help.

By the time she stepped inside, Mrs. Kelly had disappeared into her living quarters in the back. Jillian had no idea if she'd seen them kissing in the sunroom, but she didn't care. Maybe for once the little lady wouldn't tell what she saw, but it really didn't matter. Jillian would not deny how she felt and she knew Connor wouldn't either. In a few months she'd be gone and there would be nothing to gossip about.

"He listened to me play," she said softly. Something her dad had never done. Something no one had ever asked to do. Over the years she'd often found a piano in hidden-away places where she could play. Now and then, in big cities where anything can be delivered, she'd even rented a piano for a few months just to polish up. No one had ever stopped to listen.

Only Connor had known how important it was to her, and he'd wanted to share her music.

The old house creaked in the wind and Jillian swore she heard footsteps on the tiny landing of the second floor. The ghost was restless, rattling, moaning through the cracks.

Making one last cup of herbal tea, she rushed up the stairs and disappeared into her room. As she undressed she thought what Connor would do, would say, if he were with her now. He was a gentle man, a kind man, but there was deep passion in him, as well.

The thought that she'd probably never know made her cry. How many years did he have to be gone before she stopped missing her father? He could find her if he looked; she'd written how to contact her in the letter she'd left in Oklahoma City. But she had no way of finding him. He'd left no trail. No clue. No way.

She'd always believed he loved her even though he'd never said the words. But now, she considered the possibility that raising her had been no more than a responsibility he'd promised someone, maybe her mother, that he'd do.

Sleep seemed impossible tonight. When she closed her eyes, she could almost see her father's hand covering her little fingers. He rarely hugged her, but he'd pat her hand and tell her not to worry. With her eyes closed, she could still see his first finger shorter than all the others, the nail gone, the scar zigzagging across the tip.

For once she tried to remember every part of him. His hair was black as coal, with a touch of gray by the time she was in high school, and he always seemed sad. He was older than most kids' dads, and his eyes reminded her of rainy days. She never saw him read, and he rarely drank more than a few beers around her, but sometimes on weekends, he'd leave her on Saturday night. He'd be home when she woke up on Sunday, but he'd always say he didn't feel good.

She'd spend the day trying to be quiet and he spent it napping in front of the TV. Then Monday, he'd be well. He'd send her to school and he'd go to work. As far as she could remember, he never missed a day's work. He only had Sunday sickness now and then.

She lay on her bed, thinking of how different her dad was from Connor. Books say a woman looks for a man like her father, but Jillian didn't believe that. In her case, it was the opposite. If she were looking for a man, she'd want a man who cared.

Her dad hadn't cared for anyone. Not even her. Maybe he was born that way, or maybe it had been beat out of him early in life. His rules had taught her survival, but he hadn't taught her how to love.

She turned on the lamp by her bed and looked through one of his tiny logbooks. Dates, some smudged as if they'd melted off the page with time. Zip codes in one long single file with slash marks lining up beside them. Only not four up and one across, counting in fives—these tiny slashes were in groups of six with the seventh going sideways. He was counting weeks.

The covers of both books were water-spotted and oil-stained from a working man's hands. They weren't something he valued or treasured. Dates, when they were there, were in months and days, not any year.

She flipped to her laptop page where she kept her log. All by dates, including year. All days since she'd left college were logged and accounted for. All places she'd stopped even for a night were listed. Those first few years she'd traveled wherever she wanted, loving the places where music was in the air. Warm climates in the winter. The northern states in the summer. Then she migrated to the bigger cities where the money was better and she could always get lost in a crowd. Museums, art galleries and concerts filled her free time.

But the past few years she'd followed her father's trail. She doubted, at his age, he was still working the fields. He was over sixty now. But many of the early codes were small towns, telling her he must have been comfortable there. She picked the ones close to Oklahoma City. Who knows, maybe he'd finally settled somewhere and she'd just bump into him one day.

Not likely.

She wasn't even sure what she was looking for exactly. Her father? What would she say to him if she saw him? Her mother? The one who left her at the hospital the day after she was born? No great love there. Maybe all she was looking for was some link to the past. One place to say she came from. Not a person at all.

Belonging nowhere could slowly erode a person's soul.

22

Connor walked through the quiet rooms of his house. Sunnie was sound asleep with all her stuffed animals crowded around her. They'd been on the shelves in her closet for years, then her mother died and one by one they'd somehow found their way back to her bed.

He tugged a blanket over her shoulder, knowing it was long past the time when she needed tucking in.

Gram was downstairs sound asleep. The night nurse, with a book spread out over her ample belly, was snoring.

As he walked from room to room, he knew he would not be sleeping tonight. Too much on his mind.

Finally, he slipped out the back door and drove the silent streets in his old pickup. He knew who lived in almost every house. He knew their names and where they worked. With some of the people, he felt like he knew their life stories, and a few, their secrets.

He could name a hundred others who'd moved away. Kids who went to college and never came back. Couples who retired and moved out to a lake community or a few towns over to be with their grandchildren. He felt like he knew them all, except Jillian James. She'd shared more tonight than she ever had, but he didn't think she would again.

Turning down Main, he parked in front of his office. If he couldn't find out about her, maybe he could find the father she kept asking about. For some reason she must believe that he stopped in Laurel Springs thirty years ago.

Maybe he had.

Connor walked through his office to the stacks in the back. Births and deaths had been logged since the paper started and, thanks to his last assistant, they were on the computer. It wouldn't be that hard to find Jefferson James if he was here thirty years ago. He'd search the year before and the year after, as well.

First, birth records. No Jillian James. New homeowners, nothing. Lists of people who joined clubs, churches, the chamber of commerce, the historical society. All blank.

He tried deaths spanning her lifetime. There were several Jameses, but neither Jillian nor Jefferson were listed under survivors. He tried her mother's name. Marti, Margaret, Marguerite, Martha, and a dozen others that might be shortened to Marti. No marriage license. No deaths. No one by that name ever graduated from high school in Laurel Springs. Or been arrested. Or divorced.

Two hours passed. Three.

Finally, on a lark, he dug up the article on the rodeo when he was seven. Nothing.

He tried the year he was six. Bingo. His father had written a detailed account of the rodeo including a calf roper who'd lost the tip of his first finger. Jefferson James. Hometown unknown. Employee of Phillips Petroleum.

Connor grinned. He'd found her father. It wasn't much, but for at least one day before she was born, her father had been in Laurel Springs. Fighting the urge to go wake her up and tell her, he made two copies of the article and headed home.

As usual, he circled through the abandoned part of town. If anyone was there, he might see some sign. Even a flashlight would be easy to spot.

The place was dark and unwelcoming as always. No movement.

Connor drove, turning his headlights down every alley. Nothing. It occurred to him that he wasn't sure what he'd do if he did see someone. There was a chance any person living in the shadows might be armed, and Connor had never carried a weapon in his life.

Maybe he should talk to the sheriff and ask him to drive through. "No," Connor said aloud. This was his property. His problem. The way stories spread in a small town, within two weeks they'd have dozens of kids combing through the building looking for a ghost, and someone might get hurt.

He'd deal with this problem, if there really was a problem, on his own.

When he made it back to the house, he was so tired, he crashed on the couch where he could see Gram sleeping in the next room. He liked her here, but he knew as soon as she was mobile, she'd be back in her apartment at the retirement home. Gram was independent. Even when Melissa died, she'd go back to her place every night after Sunnie was asleep and be back in the kitchen cooking breakfast when Sunnie came down the stairs.

As Connor drifted into unconsciousness, he pulled Jillian into his arms. She was there with him in his dreams. He would hold her all night long.

A few hours later, laughter woke him up.

"Dad, you need to slow down. The wild life must be getting to you."

Connor rolled and almost tumbled off the couch. He groaned and opened one eye.

For a second he thought the devil's angel was staring down at him. Tall and lean, dressed in black and chains, fiery streaks of red in her hair, huge black circles around pale eyes.

He scrubbed his face. No devil, just his daughter. "Morning, Sunnie."

"Dad, you really have to start taking care of yourself, or you'll age so fast I'll have to quit college and move in to take care of you."

"I do live with you." He slowly stood. "How about skipping college and just taking on the job of taking care of your old man right now?"

"No, Dad, I live with you. I go to school. You go to work. I'm not ready to change roles."

"All right. I guess I'll shower and go to work. Any chance you'd cook me breakfast while I dress?"

She looked put out, but she nodded. "All right. But don't take too much time. You have to take me to school in half an hour."

Gram laughed from the dining room, then smiled when they turned and saw her standing. The nurse was right behind her, and Gram was leaning on a walker, but she was standing.

Connor and Sunnie both took a step toward her, but she

held up her hand. "I'm fine. I've been practicing all week. One step at a time. This morning I plan to help with breakfast, and then I'll probably nap the rest of the day."

She took one step toward the kitchen. "Now don't either of you tell Benjamin I can cook or he'll want pancakes for breakfast."

Sunnie just stood staring at her dad. Big tears rolled down her cheeks.

Connor moved to Gram and held the swinging door for her. "Gram, Benjamin died when I was a little kid."

She looked confused for a moment, then smiled. "Oh, that's right. I forgot for a moment. It seems like I just talked to him yesterday."

The nurse took over and Sunnie pulled it together enough to start asking questions about how to make an omelet.

Gram remembered every detail.

Connor climbed the stairs, feeling like a boulder had replaced his heart. For a moment last night, he'd thought he might pack up and leave with Jillian. He'd dreamed of seeing the world. He'd thought he might just travel with her. For a few weeks, a month, forever.

But that was just a fantasy. He couldn't leave his daughter, or his grandmother, or even the town. People depended on him.

He couldn't, wouldn't fly away. He hadn't when Melissa told him she was pregnant or when his parents died, leaving everything in a mess, and he wouldn't now. It didn't matter how much he wanted to. He would stay.

An hour later Sunnie had been dropped off at school, his gram was napping and Connor was in his office. Since the accident, he'd left things for the city undone. He had calls to make, letters to sign, and proposals to draw up.

The book he'd been working on would have to wait. Nothing new.

An hour later, the fire chief, a big guy named Bob Stevenson, marched into Connor's office, complaining that Joe Dunaway wanted all kinds of changes to the district—streetlights, new fire hydrants, road work.

When Jillian walked in Connor jumped up, hoping to be rescued. Once the chief started talking, it seemed like hours could drift by without Bob even taking time to breathe.

She hesitated, halfway to his city business desk, when she saw he had company. He found the shy way she lowered her head and let her midnight hair cover her face irresistible.

Connor stood politely and introduced her formally to the chief but made no effort to get close to her. Even looking at her made him feel like a diabetic staring at a chocolate layer cake.

She took her cue from him and said she didn't mean to bother him but wasn't sure what to do with an order that had been delivered. Gram must have placed the restocking order several weeks ago and now three huge boxes of new supplies for the shop were cluttering up the store.

Connor knew what she wasn't saying. *Why would they need an order of new fabric if the store was going to be closing?*

The police chief answered first. "I'll be glad to help you move them, little lady. Just as soon as I finish filling in the mayor on what's been going on."

Connor almost laughed out loud. Jillian had asked for direction, not help, and at her height no one would mistake her for a little lady.

Part of him wanted to say, "Send everything back," but he couldn't, not yet. "Just give me the bill, Jillian. I'll cover it. Thanks for letting me know, though. I'll call the company direct concerning future orders."

He'd been managing Gram's personal accounts since she'd moved into the Acres. He might as well start handling the shop's, as well. Although, from the looks of her ledgers for the past year, she'd stopped writing checks and started simply using her debit card. There had been weekly deposits made, as always, but she hadn't bothered to log any into the ledger.

Jillian said goodbye to the fire chief as she handed Connor the invoice. All very formal.

Connor didn't look into her eyes. He couldn't have watched her walk away if he'd stared into those eyes.

She was already back inside the shop by the time he remembered the rodeo article.

The fire chief jumped back into their conversation, but Connor was only halfway listening.

The day was going from bad to worse, he feared.

23

Sunnie swore if she walked into school with her head on fire no one would notice. Not one person had commented on the red stripes she'd spent an hour painting into her hair this morning. Not even Gram.

Maybe she'd gone wild so many times she'd established a new norm. If so, she might as well give up. She'd gone from being shocking to predictable.

Besides, Gram didn't count on the observation scale. She still thought her dead husband was alive and just forgot to come home. She probably thought Sunnie was born with candy cane hair.

But Dad should have at least complained. While eating the great omelet she made, he could have asked how she did the coloring job. Shown some interest. Sunnie grabbed a juice and a granola bar from the snack machine and headed for her usual place to eat lunch. If she was going to pout, she might as well be cold, too.

The day was as dreary as her mood. Damp and windy. She found an out-of-the-way bench in the atrium where no one, unless they were really searching, would find her.

Sunnie wanted to give some serious thought to dropping out of school while she ate. A nitwit in her English class said that at sixteen you could take a test called the GED and, if you passed, it would be just like a high school diploma.

Made sense to Sunnie. Why learn more in high school than was necessary? She could hang for a while and maybe give college a try in a year or so. Or maybe just travel. She'd talked to Jillian and considered that life on the road might just be perfect. No ties, no *have to* list, no one to judge you or depend on you. Just float around, wherever the wind takes you.

Another goal Sunnie had was never to work. That was boring. Nine-to-five, five days a week. That left, like, no time. She wanted to be free to do what she wanted, when she wanted. She'd mentioned her plan to Dad over break-fast, and he'd simply buttered his toast and said, "Good luck with that."

He obviously didn't understand freedom.

"There you are," a low voice said from behind her.

Sunnie almost tumbled off her bench. When she turned, Reese stood a foot away holding a tray full of food. He looked better, if going from a one to a two on a scale of ten could be considered improvement. His clothes were clean. His left eye was slightly open and blood didn't seem to be dripping from anywhere.

"Mind if I share your bench?"

She thought of saying yes, she did mind, but he looked so beat up. It was hard to keep from staring, much less turn him down. The whole student body probably voted to kick him outside of the cafeteria while they ate.

She was a sucker for the guy. "It's a free country. Sit

where you want to but we're not having lunch together, remember. We just happen to be sitting on the same bench. I always eat alone."

"Fair enough." He lowered slowly and put the tray between them.

"You all right?" she asked. "You're moving about as fast as Gram."

"I got bruises in places that don't show." When she didn't ask, he added, "You want to see?"

"No."

"Suit yourself, but a person could live their whole life without seeing bruises where I got bruises."

She didn't want to talk about it. "You always eat that much food?"

"Yeah. I work after school most days and don't get a chance to eat anything until after dark. Today I'm off, but I filled the tray out of habit. My dad says he can't stand to look at me, so no work."

After a moment, he added, "I could share, if you like. You can have anything on the tray but my cookie."

She pulled her legs up on the bench and looked at him over her knees. "I want that cookie."

"Nope." He offered her half his sandwich.

"I'll trade you my nut bar."

"Nope. That's a granola bar. I'd rather eat the box it comes in than one of those. It looks like something you'd hang in a birdcage, not eat."

"It's good for you."

"Then you eat it."

Sunnie fought down a scream. They were arguing about nothing. Maybe his mood was even darker than hers. She might as well step into the ring and get the fight over with. Today was as good a day to break up as any. "How do you like my hair, Reese?"

He ate half his sandwich while he studied her. Finally, he said, "I hate it, but I like you, Sunnie. You can paint your hair and eyes, your whole body if you want, and it doesn't change a thing. I still like you."

This wasn't ending like she thought it would. They were no longer arguing. She took the other half of his sandwich and ate it, then they shared the chips, banana, and cookie.

He sat the tray down on the ground and just stared at her. "There's something we should talk about, Sunnie."

"What?"

"I didn't want to just be your boyfriend because you're getting rid of another guy. I kind of like knowing we're dating kind of, even though we haven't gone anywhere. We could fix that this weekend. We could go fishing or something."

"All right about you continuing to be my boyfriend, but I'm not so sure about fishing," she answered, realizing she hadn't given Derrick a thought since he'd beat up Reese.

Reese looked surprised. "Really?"

"Sure. You're my boyfriend." When he looked too happy, she added, "Until we break up, of course."

"Of course."

"And try not to look fifteen, Reese. It's embarrassing dating a younger guy."

"I'll work on it. But you got to promise me if you break up with me you don't just kiss some other guy as a way of telling me."

"Sounds fair enough."

When they walked back into the commons, he carefully put his hand on her shoulder and she didn't knock it off.

"You want to come over for supper tonight? With Gram staying with us, someone's always cooking."

"Sure. My folks are not speaking to me. After I told them I couldn't remember how I got beat up, they got all mad. Mom thinks I might have brain damage. Dad thinks I'm on drugs."

"Why didn't you tell them the truth?"

Reese shrugged. "One, they'd never believe I was dating any girl, much less you, and two, I didn't want them to know it was Derrick. Our fathers are friends. His dad sends work my dad's way. I figure naming names won't help me heal any faster. If my dad finds out later he and Derrick's old man will probably laugh about how their boys fought over a girl. But, right now, looking at me like this, Pop would think he'd have to do something."

Sunnie focused on one comment. "Why wouldn't they believe you're with me?"

He stopped walking and stared at her. "Sunnie, you're beautiful, you're smart and your old man owns half the land around here. I'm dumb, have rust-colored hair, and no girl has ever looked at me except you, and that was by accident."

She groaned. How could she not like a guy who thought she was beautiful and smart? "I'm not all that smart, Reese. I'm thinking of dropping out of school, and you're not dumb. I saw the math on your ramp design."

He frowned at her, then said slowly, "You can't drop out. I just decided to go to college. You were right. I don't want to just build other people's designs. I want to design my own houses. Plus, college is where you're headed—everyone in town knows that—and I'll need to be there to keep an eye on you. So I've got to start bringing up my grades and you've got to help. No more *Harry Potter* movies on weeknights. We've got to study."

"You got it all figured out, don't you, Reese?"

"Yeah. Pretty much. But you'll have to stop striping your hair before our kids are born. It'd probably scare them right back into the womb."

"I don't even want to think past the next class and don't start talking about us having kids. I'm never having kids. I'm never getting married, and you being in my life past next week is still in question."

She couldn't tell if he looked hurt or confused. With one eye barely open and his swollen lip twisted into a permanent frown, it was hard to read him. She said, "How about we just make it through dinner tonight?"

He nodded as he stopped at the gym door.

"How'd you know I had gym this hour?"

"Lucky guess," he said as he walked away.

"Very funny." She watched him, wondering if she had a boyfriend or a stalker.

Her first real boyfriend. Derrick hadn't lasted long enough to be in the running. Gram always said there was somebody for everyone. Reese was bossy, telling her to eat and stay in school. He was downright scary with all those bruises. He was off any girl's radar as cute. But he'd agreed to be her boyfriend, so she might as well keep him for at least a few days, or even a month.

Who knows, maybe even years. When you're confused, having someone give you direction is kind of like having an oar in the water.

24

As afternoon clouds rolled in for the third day in a row, Connor picked up the phone and dialed the quilt shop. Any other time, he would have simply walked across the street, but not today.

Today, he was home with Gram. Exactly where he'd been for the past three days. Even with the night nurse and the day shift in the morning, taking care of Gram, keeping up with her medicine, answering the door and the phone seemed to be a full-time job.

"A Stitch in Time, how may I help you?" Jillian's question came through the line.

Connor breathed, relaxing at the sound of her voice.

"Morning, Jillian." Saying her name made him miss her.

"Morning, Mayor." He could hear caring in her tone. Maybe she was remembering their quick kiss on the B and B porch last night. He'd said good-night and turned to step off the porch. She'd leaned forward to kiss him and they'd both almost tumbled into Mrs. K's flower bed.

Connor was silent as he remembered, and she added, "Connor, is everything all right?"

"Yes," he answered too fast. "Everything is fine here. Gram's doing fine.

"I just forgot about a board meeting tonight until the fire chief called to remind me. Any chance you could drop by after work and bring supper for Gram?" Jillian had been helping every night, so he doubted he was asking too much. "She'll want to talk about the shop."

"Sure. No problem. I'll be there in time for you to make the meeting by seven."

He thought of asking how she knew about the time, but this was Laurel Springs; even the boring city council meeting was talked about.

"I'm sorry. It won't last long. I'll be home as soon as I can."

She laughed. "It's all right, Connor, I got this. Joe and Sunnie will help me with Gram. You do what you have to do. I'll even save you a plate."

"Thanks." He hung up, afraid if he said one word more he might say too much. Since the day he'd met her, he'd been holding back things he wanted to say, feelings he needed to tell her about. Only if he said one sentence, he feared an ocean of emotions might rush out.

He had his briefcase packed with city files when she arrived late afternoon. There was no opportunity to share a moment alone. Connor didn't even try. Logic told him this attraction had come on too fast. Things like this took time, and that was the one thing they didn't have.

He picked up his case. "Most of the time no one shows up to watch at these meetings, but tonight we are voting on putting up new tornado sirens. The fire chief and the sheriff will be there in support of the motion, and the same half-dozen people who always come to complain about the city spending too much money will all want to have their say. After that, I'm home." Rattling on didn't help. She didn't care about the meeting. He simply needed to leave.

Jillian patted his shoulder. "I got this, Connor. We'll be here when you get back, no matter how late. I brought pictures of several quilts I need Gram to tell me the stories about. That will keep us busy."

"You'll wait?" He said the words low, so no one else could have heard.

She nodded as she looked directly at him with those stormy-day eyes that had seen the world and had chosen tonight to be right here in his house.

Even if he wasn't.

Connor was surviving on two hours' sleep. Possibilities rolled over in his mind, but reality kept shoving the what-ifs aside. He already had his pockets full of responsibility. He needed to come to his senses and realize he'd only been dreaming of traveling…of meeting Jillian in faraway places where there was no town, no family, no one to interrupt them.

It was never going to happen. Not with Jillian. Not with anyone. He'd never step away and she'd never stay, not here.

So when he walked into the meeting room, he smiled and pretended everything was great. He did his duty. He listened. He stayed calm, and finally, he ended the meeting. No one saw how he felt inside. Any adventure he'd had in his soul had died before it could break ground and grow.

As everyone walked toward the front door, Connor shoved his briefcase under an empty desk in the hallway and slipped out the back. From the alley, he headed for the wild grass near the creek. He needed to escape, if only for a few minutes. He had to know, if only for a moment in time, he was in charge of his own life.

The sun was low. He'd have thirty minutes before it would be too dark to see the path along the creek. But for one slice of time, he'd be free.

He walked, letting the weight of the day melt off his shoulders. When he reached the creek, he found his favorite spot and sat, listening to nature. Usually the sound of the water calmed him, but it didn't work tonight. He must be an overachiever. He was going through a midlife crisis early. The pieces of his life no longer seemed to fit together. Sunnie would be grown soon. Gram was growing frail, needing him more. Any dream he'd ever had seemed to be slipping away into the stream of everyday life.

The trees surrounding him made a ticking sound as bare branches tapped against each other. A lonely sound, he thought. The dark warehouse district loomed before him, strangely beautiful, like the Georgia O'Keeffe painting of a darkened back street in New York. The artist had simply named it *A Street*.

Connor stared at the district, seeing only shadows tonight. The buildings, the roads, were all dwarfed by creeping darkness. He felt like it was moving over his mind, as well.

If Jillian hadn't come to town, he might have lived out his life in peace, but he couldn't wish for that. She had woken him up. He cared for her like a man cares for a woman—correction—like a man cares for *his* woman. Only she wasn't his to love. She never would be.

He'd felt responsible for his wife, Melissa. She was the

mother of his child, but in the thirteen years they'd been together he'd never felt about her as he did Jillian. To Melissa, he was just someone who made her life easier, an accessory. No more important at the wedding than the groom on the cake.

But Jillian could be more. If she'd let it happen. If she'd stay. She could quickly become as vital to him as a heartbeat.

Connor laughed suddenly. As always, he was being too serious. Thinking too much. Jillian didn't want him. Not for long anyway. Maybe a short fling. She'd made it plain she was leaving. The only comfort was that she'd promised to say goodbye.

He was dreaming about someday, and she was only thinking as far as the few weeks she had left to finish her job. Maybe Gram's accident had delayed her departure, but only by days, not years.

He looked up, realizing night had moved in completely, not only in his thoughts, but across the land. The district buildings loomed black and stoic on one side of the creek. The town twinkled on the other. The path that wound through the tall grass back to Main had vanished.

Connor followed his mood. Not caring that his four-hundred-dollar boots were getting wet, he stepped into the stream.

The tall Western boots he always wore kept his feet dry as he slowly tested each step. Mud and rocks shifted beneath him, but he didn't turn back. If he fell, he'd have to walk home covered in mud. If he made it across, he'd be on the dark side. Exactly where he wanted to escape to tonight.

Cold water bubbled at his knees and slowly dripped into his boots, but he kept walking.

Finally, grabbing a limb from a cypress tree, he pulled himself out of the water and onto dry land.

Connor smiled for the first time since he'd woken up on the couch with Sunnie laughing at him. Finally, his location and his mood matched. He took a minute to tug off his boots, wring out his socks, then put them back on.

He walked the muddy streets silently, knowing his way, familiar with every building. Joe's workshop lights were off tonight. The old man would be with Gram.

As Connor passed the place where he'd taken Jillian for their rooftop dinner, he shook his head. It had been a beautiful sunset, but he should have planned the meal, maybe set up a table. He should have made it more romantic.

Walking down the alley, he realized he'd pretty much handled everything wrong with her. He might be able to run a business, keep the paper going, raise an independent daughter, but he sucked at planning a date.

He should have planned a real evening that she'd remember forever. Within an hour's drive in any direction there were real, fancy restaurants where they could have had a quiet drink, then talked over a relaxing dinner. He could have driven home slowly, maybe stopped to look at the moon. Women like that kind of thing, he guessed. In truth, he had no idea.

With his luck, she'd leave early in hopes of saving him from embarrassing himself. His mood darkened, following him through the alleys of the district.

A tiny cry echoed off the canyon walls of brick on either

side of him. Connor conceded, mentally beating himself up and pulled every sense into focus.

The cry came again. Not quite animal. Not quite human.

Something wasn't right. Something or someone was in this jungle with him.

The cry came again. Short gulps, as if someone was holding back sobs.

Connor realized he had no weapon. Hell, he never had a weapon. If trouble found him, he might as well be made out of wood, because he was a sitting duck.

Pulling off his jacket, he wrapped it around his arm. He'd seen that in a movie once. With a wrapped arm he could block a knife or a blow. Of course, it wouldn't help much if the attacker had a gun.

What if he was shot in this alley? No one would find him for days. The town would panic because they wouldn't be able to find the city's budget. Sunnie would be mad at him because he never taught her to drive, and Gram would think he just didn't come home like Grandfather Benjamin. No one would figure out his accounting system or find his briefcase.

And he'd be dead, of course. Jillian would never know how he felt about her.

Another cry whispered in the air. Not an animal. Human.

He kept walking toward the back of the passage as the hundred-year-old brick walls seemed to close in on him. This was the alley where he'd seen movement.

No matter what lurked here in the shadows, he needed to know. This was his land. His district. His town.

Movement waved dirty white from the corner of a doorway.

Connor braced himself for anything and stepped closer.

It took a moment for the tiny figure to come into focus.

A child, not more than five, looked up at him with huge eyes. He didn't seem hurt, or afraid, but his cheeks glistened with tears.

Connor crouched down. "Are you all right?"

The little boy straightened as he swiped his cheek with a dirty sleeve. "I'm okay, sir, but it's scary out here."

"You know who I am?" Connor kept his voice low, non-threatening.

"Yep. You're the mayor. My dad said you're the most important man in town."

Connor shook his head. "No, son, you are right now, and I think you must have a problem. A mayor's job is to help folks with problems, so how about telling me what you're doing here all alone?"

"I'm cold, but I ain't alone. My daddy's inside working. I got wet and he told me to come out here until I dried off 'cause we can't go home yet. I want to go home. I said I wanted to come tonight, but now I want to go."

Unwrapping his wool armor, Connor shook the coat out before offering it to the boy. "Slip into this. It's been in my way all night. I'd appreciate you taking it off my hands for a while."

The boy hesitantly put his thin arms into the coat that hung almost to the ground.

"Better?"

"Yep." He smiled. Pushing the coat sleeve up to his elbow, he offered his hand. "I'm Jack Elliot. My momma calls me Jackie, but my dad says my grown-up name is Jack."

Again Connor was impressed by the boy's manners.

"Nice to meet you, Jack Elliot. That's a fine name. I'd like to meet your dad if you think he has a minute."

The boy nodded. "Follow me, but watch your head, Mayor. You're tall. I'll take you to my daddy."

Stepping over the threshold, Connor moved into one of the roofless warehouses. The walls still stood solid, but the ghost-gray night sky shone above offering little light.

The kid's hand circled around two of Connor's fingers and tugged him forward. "Duck when I say to or you'll whack your head."

Connor lifted his free hand, feeling long pipes running just above him. The place was cool and damp, but not cold. He had no idea what the building had once been used for, but now it had the smell of the earth. Not decay or rot, just rich, damp dirt.

They moved into a maze of wooden frames.

"What is this?" Connor asked, as they passed from one building to the next.

"My dad's garden. He says he don't feel right if his hands ain't in dirt. He's raising baby plants."

Connor's eyes adjusted to the night. He saw tiny plants two, three inches high in the open crates. A greenhouse? But why here? Why so early? It wouldn't be warm enough to grow anything in the fields for another month. It couldn't be marijuana. Connor had read once that those plants needed intense heat and light to thrive. These buildings didn't even have electricity.

A yellow light blinked in the distance. The Coleman lantern's uneven glow made a wide circle around a table that appeared to be made of railroad ties and abandoned lumber.

The feeling he'd stepped into another world made Connor hesitate. How could this place exist in his town, on his property?

"Daddy, the mayor came to visit," Jack said, as a man leaning over the table raised his head.

Connor doubted the man could see them in the shadows, but he saw the stranger clearly. His clothes marked him as an oil field worker. His hands, even in the dancing light, were calloused and caked with dirt.

Farmer's hands, Connor thought as he took a step closer and saw the panic in the stranger's eyes. The dad, in his late twenties, might have run if he hadn't glanced down and seen Jack still holding on to Connor.

Connor offered his free hand. "I'm Connor Larady. Nice to meet you, Mr. Elliot."

"Alton." The man's handshake was solid. When he pulled back, he rubbed his hand on his pant leg. "Sorry about the dirt."

Connor smiled. "I just waded across the creek. I'm walking with mud on and in my boots. A little more dirt won't matter."

Alton Elliot relaxed a bit. "I guess you're wondering what I'm doing here?"

Connor moved closer to the table where Alton appeared to be planting slices of leaves into what looked like paper cups. "I'm fascinated," he said, noticing the tools scattered over the table. If Alton Elliot had meant him any harm, he would be on the floor bleeding.

"I work the rigs over in Shelby County when there is work to find, but I got land a mile from here. Not much, but prime ground for a huge garden. Neither of the stores in town carry organic vegetables, just what's shipped in.

You know, one kind of tomato, two kinds of lettuce. Three kinds of apples if we're lucky."

"I'm the mayor, Mr. Elliot. I've heard this complaint before."

Alton nodded. "I grew up on a farm that had ten types of tomatoes and a dozen kinds of lettuce, not to mention different varieties of potatoes and carrots and beets and…"

"I get your point." Connor relaxed. Vegetables were great. He ate one now and then. But what did that have to do with this place and midnight? "Why are you here, Mr. Elliot? This part of town has been abandoned for many years."

Alton folded his arms. "My folks sent me the seeds, the clippings, the bulbs. All I need to grow great produce. But I needed a place to get them started. I'll triple my yield if I can start them in a greenhouse, and these old warehouses serve the purpose. The brick walls hold in the sun's heat. No one uses the old buildings on this side of town, so I figured no one would care. They shelter my future garden, cut the growing time come spring."

"Fascinating. Only you don't own this property."

Alton shrugged. "I figured no one did. It's just a dead place. Folks say it has been for fifty or more years."

He turned up the lamp and what Connor thought were a few crates of baby plants were really rows and rows.

"I got a little carried away. Every night I build a few more crates out of all the bad wood around here and plant a few more plants. I rigged barrels on the roof next door so I could drip rainwater down."

Connor looked around. "This place wouldn't pass any kind of city code."

"I'm not living here. Just planting. Me and the plants will be out of here in a month or so." Alton looked straight at Connor. "You going to evict me, Mayor? If I put the plants out now, they won't be protected from the wind or the cold, but I figure you have the legal right."

Alton was clearly a man who took any blow coming straight on. No excuses. No complaining.

"No. But you should know I do own this land. First thing tomorrow morning I'll have a crew out here to make sure these buildings do pass inspection as greenhouses. I want to make sure one of these walls doesn't tumble in on your nursery. I'll add anything that you think might make this operation run smoother, like electricity, for one. It'll be my job to make sure everything passes code, then I'll rent it to you."

"Fair enough." Alton's entire body seemed to relax and he met Connor's stare for the first time. "I'll have enough to feed the family and sell some. I'll give you half the profits from any sales."

Connor shook his head. "That's not fair. I own the buildings you're starting the whole process in." Alton stiffened again, but he didn't have any right to argue.

Connor continued, "But you own the product. I want one gallon-size basket of vegetables a week for my share. If this idea goes over like I think it will, you'll be renting the front of one of these buildings as a market and I'll make money from that. You could open once a week with all your surplus, and I'm betting you'll sell out by noon."

Organic vegetables, grown here, not shopped in. Connor's mind began to race. If this guy could rig it right, maybe the greenhouse could grow year-round. People would drive to Laurel Springs for their fresh vegetables.

"Mayor, I don't know if you're crazy or a fortune-teller, but you got yourself a deal." Alton offered his hand once more as he smiled for the first time. "If you have the money to do a few repairs, I could use the space in the next building that butts up on the left side of this one."

"Done." Connor never hesitated when he knew something was right. "I know a kid who can probably build you a proper door without damaging the structure. I need to keep him busy."

"Oh," Alton asked as if he might be taking on trouble.

"Yeah. He's dating my daughter. Maybe you can keep him so busy he's too tired to come over for supper every night."

Alton laughed. "I'll do my best, boss."

"Not boss. Partner." Connor could see the future and it was bright.

Alton nodded. "I've been waiting all my life for a shot like this. If we do this together, I promise, you won't be sorry."

Connor understood. "You know, Mr. Elliot, I think these old buildings have been waiting for you, too."

25

Without Connor at dinner, the hours seemed to move in slow motion. Jillian made a tuna casserole from one of Gram's old recipes. Joe claimed it was the best he ever had. Sunnie swore it was the first she'd ever had and Reese, who was late to dinner, simply said he didn't like tuna so he only ate two helpings. The guy could eat more than a family of six. His folks were probably doubling his college fund by sending him over to the Larady house to eat.

She'd saved Connor a plate, but when he finally made it home, he didn't seem interested in eating. He had something on his mind, and no one asked for fear of hearing every detail of the city's business.

When Reese had offered to drive Jillian home, Connor nodded, and for the first time seemed to become aware that she was there.

He stood and pointed Reese toward the kitchen. "While you say good night to Sunnie, Reese, I'll walk Jillian out."

Reese started to say he was ready, but Sunnie jerked him into the kitchen so fast, Reese looked like the world's largest rag doll trailing behind her.

Jillian wanted to roll her eyes at the whole group. From Joe to Sunnie, they were all trying to give Connor a chance to be alone with her. Like whatever was between them might last if they just had a few more minutes.

As always, Connor opened the door for her. She thought about telling him the kindness wasn't necessary, but she guessed he wasn't doing it because he had to, or needed to. The small gesture was done simply because he wanted to.

Once alone on the shadowy porch, he didn't move close to her like she hoped he would. He just stood looking out into the night, lost in his thoughts.

When she touched his arm, he turned toward her and smiled. "I'm sorry. I've got a lot on my mind tonight. A new business venture if I'm lucky. I'll tell you all about it tomorrow. Maybe we can have lunch together and talk. Just me and you for a change."

"I'd like that."

"But tonight I need to tell you a bit I learned after doing some research on the town about thirty years back." He brushed her shoulder with a gentle touch. "Something important maybe."

"Can it wait until tomorrow?" Anything that involved research could wait.

"It could, but…"

She ended the discussion by leaning in and boldly kissing him. He might want to talk, but she simply wanted to feel tonight. If they only had a moment of time, she wanted it to count and as far as she was concerned, any discussion was over.

Pressing close, she molded her body against his in invitation, hoping for a memory that she could hold on to all night. In the stillness, the sound of his heartbeat echoed against hers. She loved the lean strength of him against her. He fit like a glove, a match, as no one else ever had. The feel of him. The smell of him. The taste of him. All were like deep cell memories she'd known a hundred lifetimes ago. The one person, one mate that was just right.

He took her bold invitation without hesitation. As his kiss caught fire, his hands moved along her sides, not touching, not caressing, but feeling her through the cotton blouse she wore.

She wanted skin on skin, but this was as close as she could get, and he wasn't shy as he explored. The shadows blanketed them in a cocoon, and for a moment she could relax against his warmth and simply feel.

When he moved his lips away from her mouth and began tasting his way down her neck, she knew she'd won. "I've wanted to be this close all day." Her mouth brushed his ear. "I want to melt into you until for a moment there is no me, no you, just us. It feels so good when you're this close."

He threaded his fingers into her hair and pulled her mouth to his once more. With words brushing against her lips, he whispered, "I want this, too. I want you, Jillian, like I've never wanted another. All day. All night. I have this ache inside of me as if something's always been missing." He kissed her hard and added, "It's you, Jillian. It's you next to me that was absent. It's you against me."

His deep kiss brought every sense alive. She'd kissed men who were practiced. Men who were bold. But none were right. Connor's kisses, his touches, weren't dances or games he was playing; they were basic needs. Like food and water and air.

His hand covered her breast and she straightened, pushing softly against his palm. Neither moved for a moment, then he leaned slightly and kissed her so tenderly, she forgot to breathe.

The door opened behind them, and both took a step backward. Both gulping for air as they returned to the real world.

In the shadows his fingers laced with hers. Holding tight for one more moment. They both wanted the same thing and whether it was once or every night until she left, Jillian knew he'd be the lover she'd always remember, always dream of, always measure every other lover by. This gentle man had a passion in him that might drown her if she wasn't careful, but for this one time she had to drink her fill.

"I didn't mean to..." he started.

"I did." She smiled and he gave up apologizing.

He grinned. "If we're ever truly alone again, I don't know what will happen. I'm crazy about you."

"I know exactly what will happen. The question is, Mayor, are you ready for it?"

His words came out in a breath. "I think I've been waiting all my life for you to come along."

Sunnie and Reese bolted out the door like two wild colts. She was beating on him for calling her "honey," and he was laughing so hard he kept tripping over his own feet.

Finally, he locked Sunnie in a headlock, kissed the top of her striped hair, and said good-night.

She turned back to the porch, mumbling death threats.

Connor looked at Jillian and shrugged. "What can I say, love's complicated."

"It's not love," Sunnie screamed.

"Hell," Reese yelled back. "I'm not sure it's even like, honey."

He darted to his truck for self-preservation as Connor opened the passenger door for Jillian. "You sure you want to ride home with him? He doesn't even have a license, and I'm not sure he's got any brains since he's dating my daughter."

"I'll live dangerously for a few blocks." She winked at Connor, telling him what they'd shared in the porch shadows had fueled her spirit.

Connor was still standing at the curb when they disappeared around the corner. She was already feeling cold inside without him. What they'd just done would keep both of them awake, she guessed.

She could tell herself that it was only a kiss. Only a touch. But deep down she knew it was far more.

They'd crossed an invisible line. From "if something might happen" to "when" and both knew it.

26

The next morning, the warm sun brightened Jillian's day as she walked to work, but all night she'd felt the loss of not having Connor close. He'd said they'd have lunch, just the two of them, but she knew his invitation came with ifs. If Gram is doing fine. If the nurse shows up. If the city doesn't need him. If Sunnie didn't have something traumatic happen like breaking up with another boyfriend.

Mrs. Kelly had gone into Dallas for the third time in the weeks Jillian had been in town. Jillian thought of asking Connor to have lunch in her room, but somehow that didn't seem right. They weren't two kids looking for a hideout, and what she had was too unique to be treated like an affair.

Walking past the little house with its colorful pots and neglected yard, she saw the owner sitting on the porch. Her hair didn't look like it had seen a comb in days, and her housecoat was stained.

As Jillian neared, she waved. "Morning."

The disheveled lady waved back from her wheelchair.

The colorful pots. The trashy yard. The wheelchair. It all made sense now.

When Jillian reached Main, she noticed Connor's office was still dark. If the light had been on she might have gone over, only for a few minutes. But instead, she unlocked the shop door and stepped inside. The quilt-covered walls greeted her with their warm colors and stories hidden in the stitching.

May Roger's butterfly quilt made of flour sacks her grandmother had saved back in the days flour came in bags made from cloth. May had wanted to leave it in the shop when she moved in with her daughter so that everyone could enjoy it.

Evie McWeathers's pinwheel quilt hung next to May's butterflies. Her scalloped edges and circles were made only with Highland plaids her parents had brought with them from Scotland. It took her so long to make all the circles fit, she gave it to Gram, claiming she never wanted to see it again.

Next was the Robertson family quilt. Everyone said the sisters had fought over their mother's Wedding Ring quilt for years. The mother asked Gram to keep it till she died. She claimed she wouldn't give it to any one of her children who mentioned it in her presence. From last reports, the quilt would be going to the county museum because the Robertson daughters were not known to be quiet about anything.

Jillian stood in the center of the shop and twirled around, loving all the colors and designs flying by.

All were treasures. All were unique. All were part of the history of this place.

Finally, Jillian went to put the coffee on. She decided to write a few of her quilt articles before the day got busy. But before she had the pot scrubbed, the front doorbell started ringing, stuttering as if a herd was coming in.

She leaned out from the tiny kitchen and saw half a dozen ladies, dressed in their Sunday clothes, carrying their big purses and their bigger sewing bags.

"Was there a meeting today?" she asked, as two more bumped their way inside.

Stella took charge. "There is no meeting. We're going to FART today."

All the others giggled. Two more crowded in, shoving the ones at the front farther into the shop. CNN should report this as a bag lady war.

Mass insanity, Jillian thought. They were making no sense, and worse, they seemed to have put Stella in charge.

Jillian glanced out the window, hoping to see Connor's light on across the street. No such luck. She was outnumbered and on her own.

Stella faced her troops. "Now did everyone bring their cell phones?"

The crowd of twelve nodded.

Stella stood on her tiptoes. "Now, remember, we all have to take pictures to send to Gram. She's going with us in spirit. No selfies. These shots are for Gram to see what's going on."

"What's a selfie?" one lady asked from the back.

Another added, "Don't you need a stick to do that?"

No one answered her.

Two women said they didn't know how to take pictures with their phones, and three more said they didn't know how to send anything. Stella mumbled something about how anyone can learn to use a phone, just find a kid over four and he'll show you. Then she yelled again, "Who brought snacks?"

Three ladies raised paper grocery bags.

"Who brought chocolate?"

Two waved smaller bags.

"We'll eat the chocolate first. Don't want it melting in the bus." Stella raised her voice once more. The Sanderson sisters weren't listening. "I've got a cooler of water and Diet Cokes. Everybody can have two drinks, so pace yourselves. We don't want to be stopping at every Toot'n Totum for a potty break."

Jillian saw the little Autumn Acres bus pull up out front as if Gram was arriving. All the crazies in the shop grew restless.

"Ladies, saddle up, we're going to FART. Five stops in six hours." Stella waved for them to start moving, but a dozen ladies with at least two bags each don't change currents easily. "Head 'em up! Move 'em out! We'll be back before dark."

Jillian followed them, fascinated. When she finally managed to get close to Stella, she asked, "What's happening?"

Stella smiled with pride. "I rented the bus, just like Gram usually does. She might not get to go this year, but she won't want the girls to miss all the fun. Every year we make our annual FART to five other quilt shops around the area. We visit and see what the others are doing. It's our Fabric Acquisition Road Trip." She moved closer to the bus. "Now hurry up, ladies. We got donuts waiting for us at Sisters Sewing Sensations and moon pies will be our afternoon snack at Around the Block. The Fabric Explosion over in Bowie has offered to feed us lunch if a few of you will agree to judge their quilt competition."

Stella looked serious when she lowered her voice and added, for Jillian's benefit, "They can't depend on locals to judge. Death threats, you know."

Jillian finally got it. "You ladies are going shopping for fabric and apparently eating your way from town to town?"

"Not just that. We're picking up new ideas." Stella patted her arm like she suspected Jillian might be a little dense. "Plus we have hours to talk between towns. Really talk, you know."

One of the Sanderson sisters wiggled between Jillian and Stella. "What's said on the bus, stays on the bus," she whispered, as if letting Jillian in on a secret.

Stella nodded. "That's right. I'm making a list of topics."

The other Sanderson sister passed by and leaned toward Jillian, her bags hitting against both her knees. "And you're on the list, Jillian. Just wanted you to know. Don't believe in talking behind someone's back."

Jillian smiled and whispered, "You'll fill me in?"

The sister straightened to her full five foot nothing. "Not a chance." She shoved through the door without another word.

The driver already looked terminally bored as he boarded.

"Have fun, ladies." Jillian waved as the bus pulled away, then she turned back into the shop. Whoever said small towns weren't any fun hadn't met the quilters.

The morning passed quietly. Jillian actually got some writing done. Half the quilts had been logged and photographed, and their stories were written. Today she'd add another three or four to the list, but she wouldn't touch

Gram's quilt. That would have to wait until she knew the story. Why had she made it? Why had she never finished it?

At noon, Connor stepped back into her world. For once he was all dressed up, his hair combed, his boots polished. He was handsome when he didn't look worried.

"Morning," he said formally. "I've come to take you to lunch, if you don't mind making a quick stop first."

"Are you sure? Shouldn't we go home and check on Gram?" Jillian forced the words out. "I'm sure we could make sandwiches and keep her company."

"No, she's fine. The day nurse linked her phone to my computer this morning. She's following every step of the quilting trip. Gram's feeling great today. In fact, she was walking around this morning with crutches. Said it won't be long before she's back to work."

"Really?" Jillian was surprised.

"I didn't argue with her, but I did talk her into starting with two hours only on quilting days. That way she can visit with her friends and be sitting down."

"Sounds like a plan. I can handle the store the other days until she's ready to come back."

His sad eyes met hers. "I'm afraid Gram won't be coming back here. Not alone anyway. I didn't think her memory was so bad until I spent so much time with her."

Jillian nodded. Gram was a smart woman. She'd hidden the small things by just claiming she was forgetful. But it was more than that. Much more.

He moved closer to her. "You've been great during this, Jillian."

"It was the right thing to do." She'd heard him say those

words a dozen times over the past month. "Besides, I enjoyed helping out. It was like being part of a family."

He grinned suddenly. "That reminds me. I've got something for you. I planned to give it to you last night, but you
were set on having your way with me."

"I don't remember hearing you complain."

"No, not at all. I welcome any attack you want to make."
He pulled a paper from his coat pocket. "But you'll want
to see this." As he unfolded the article he'd copied, a man
stepped into the shop asking for directions. Connor turned
to help him as Jillian smoothed the paper open.

She read the article slowly, wondering why he'd brought
it. The publication date was over thirty years ago. An account of a rodeo the town had sponsored for seventy years.
Lists of events. Lists of riders.

Her breath caught as she read about an accident. A calf
roper had lost part of his finger. The last line stood out
like a blinking sign. Jefferson James, hometown unknown.

She heard the door chime sound as the stranger left.
Connor's hand brushed her shoulder. But she only stared
at the paper.

"He was here," Connor said. "Your father was here.
Gram told me your birthday is in January. That means, if he
was in Laurel Springs in May, you may have been conceived
here the same month of the rodeo. Maybe your mother and
father met right here in town. Folks come from all around
for the celebrations and barbecue."

It was crazy, but tears bubbled in her eyes. He was right.
If her father had been in town, her mother must have been
here, too. Maybe she wasn't from here. Maybe she'd come

in for the rodeo, like him. Or maybe they'd come together for the rodeo?

Jillian moved to the window as Connor read the article out loud. The writing was solid, telling every detail. She felt almost like she was there that night. Closing her eyes, she could visualize how it must have looked. The crowd. The horses. The dust. The smells.

Her gaze moved along the street just beyond the shop's window. It was almost as if she could look thirty years back in time and see her mother walking the street. She'd been twenty-one when Jillian was born. Her father was thirty-four. What had drawn them together? And more important, what had torn them apart?

When she noticed Connor had finished reading, she asked, "Why would my father sign up for the rodeo? He wasn't a kid, and he never mentioned being a cowboy."

"The money, I guess," Connor answered. "A few minutes' ride could have won him a thousand dollars. I'm guessing he knew how to ride and rope. Probably borrowed a horse. Thought he had a chance. I saw a carload of guys from Denton come over one rodeo. They'd seen the rodeos on TV and decided to give it a try. They paid their money and signed up for every event. I heard they were all bleeding and headed home before the rodeo was half over."

She kept staring out the window. "He was raised on a farm. Told me once he hated it. He said there was nothing there or no one he wanted to go back to. When he walked away from that life, he didn't bother taking a single memento."

Connor moved behind her. She could feel his warmth. When she leaned back slightly, he pulled her against his chest. For a while he just held her, then finally he said, quietly, as if not wanting to startle her, "I called the county library. They have a record of Phillips Petroleum employees. Jefferson James was on the payroll from March to December that year. No forwarding address."

Jillian closed her eyes. "He quit just before I was born."

"Maybe he had to go. The job might have been over."

Too many unanswered questions. Why would he leave her mother pregnant? Why would her mother leave her at the hospital?

As naturally as if she'd done it all her life, she turned to Connor. He held her in strong, steady arms. She didn't cry. She wouldn't cry.

"Thank you for bringing me this," she finally said, pulling away.

"You are welcome," he answered. "We'll keep looking. Do you have any idea where he went next?"

"Yes. Oklahoma City. He worked there when I was very small. He told me once that he took me to work with him. He was a janitor who worked alone. Only my mother wasn't with him. She disappeared the morning after I was born."

"You think he might have relatives in the city?"

"No. To my knowledge he had no relatives anywhere."

Deep down she knew that her parents didn't want her to find them. Whatever bargain they'd made thirty years ago was between them. They'd never planned for her to find out anything.

"If they lived here together from the time of the rodeo to January, surely someone would remember them."

"I didn't know. I'll probably never know." The memory of her grade school picture came to mind. Her dad might have taken it to remember her, but he still didn't want her finding him. Or, she reasoned, he might have tossed it in the trash when he left the library, like he did everything else she'd tried to pack as a child that wasn't a necessity.

Connor seemed to read her mood. "How about we go to Mamma Bee's? It's noisy, and we'll be surrounded by people we know."

"I think I'd like that." If she never found her parents, maybe she'd find the places and the people they might have known. That would be enough.

As soon as they ordered, they were surrounded with folks, many of whom Jillian knew. They all asked about Gram, and as soon as they knew she was doing well, the conversation turned to guessing what was happening across the creek.

"Trucks are moving in," one man announced. "Can't imagine what's going on over there."

Before Jillian got her chicken salad sandwich, the majority opinion seemed to be that the mayor should go over and check things out. After all, if it was drug dealers, or outlaws opening a modern-day hole-in-the-wall, they'd listen to a mayor.

She saw the town clearly then. Connor was their hero, their warrior. If something was wrong, he'd make it right. He didn't see it. All Connor saw was the details of running a small town, but he was so much more.

Jillian leaned back and enjoyed the show.

Mamma Bee herself walked by, saying she thought it was probably one of those human trafficking outfits. They'd probably kidnapped young girls and were housing them right across the river.

Jillian had a feeling that Mamma Bee just liked to keep the conversation going. She'd also suggested that the truck drivers might be ivory smugglers.

"Maybe we should call the sheriff?" someone suggested.

While the group was taking a vote, Connor slowly stood. "I'll go check it out. No reason to worry." He winked at Jillian. "I'll take Jillian with me for protection."

Everyone laughed as if suddenly realizing they might be overreacting.

Connor took Jillian's hand in front of everyone. His grip was solid as they walked out of the store.

She had the feeling that the minute they were outside the conversation would shift from the district to the mayor's new girlfriend.

"You shouldn't have taken my hand. People will think there is something going on between us."

"There is." He tightened his grip. "Do you mind people knowing?"

"Not at all."

He walked toward his Audi. "It's only fair they know, after all, that there is something going on between us. You *were* on the porch last night with me, weren't you? That was you? Man, I'd hate it if I was kissing the night nurse by mistake."

She laughed, remembering how he'd kissed her. How she'd almost attacked him. "That was me. I can still feel your hand covering my breast."

He slowed and lowered his voice as they climbed into his car. "So can I. When we are alone again, it won't be for a few minutes and I don't want to worry about being interrupted."

Sitting very properly on the opposite side of the car, she asked, "And what will happen when we are alone again?"

His honest brown eyes looked directly at her. No shyness. No doubt. "I'll make love to you, Jillian."

When she didn't speak or move, he added, "If that's okay with you?"

She knew this was not flirting. This would be no light affair. "Yes," she managed as she stared straight ahead. "And, Connor, I plan to make love to you right back."

He started the car, put it in gear, then took her hand. Neither said a word. They didn't need to. They'd said all that needed to be said.

Now all they had to do was wait for the right time.

Driving across the creek, he turned toward Alton Elliot's greenhouses, which had spread into a third building thanks to Connor adding electricity and water.

Jillian climbed out ready to explore. "It's wonderful."

"It really is. Alton said he's been fighting to make ends meet. In a few months I think that problem will be solved and the whole town will have fresh vegetables."

"You did this, Connor."

He shook his head. "I only helped a little."

"No. You believed in him. You invested in his dream."

"He's going to start paying me rent once he's in the black. I was happy to help." Connor patted a brick wall. "Reese designed this passage between the buildings. Built it in two days. The kid's got more brains than I gave him credit for."

Connor took her hand as they walked back up the alley and turned onto the street where Joe Dunaway's shop was located. Three huge trucks blocked the front of his store.

Joe moved from talking to the drivers to greet Connor.

"Morning, Connor, Jillian. How can I help you?" the old man said.

"I'm just seeing what's going on." Connor put his arm around Jillian's shoulders as if it was the natural thing to do, the caring gesture he'd done forever when she was near. "I sent a few men over to survey some of the buildings a few streets over but they wouldn't be driving trucks."

Joe waved his hands as if erasing Connor's words. "Oh, no, no, these aren't your guys. I seen those fellows this morning. They said they'd have a report and an estimate for you in a day or two."

The old man glanced back at the three trucks. "These men are hauling my equipment and supplies. Had them shipped all the way from Dallas."

Connor stilled. "This must have cost you thousands."

"It did, but I need it if I'm going to get my Toe Tents out there. My niece told me I needed to step up production if she was going to help me get the word out online. I even gave her a few hundred to buy ads. She says we may need more to grease the wheel and get things going."

"How much more?"

"Maybe a thousand...or two. I thought I'd send her a little extra for her to buy another computer."

Jillian saw how Connor took Joe's mistakes onto his own shoulders. The old guy couldn't have much money on a teacher's retirement. He'd probably spent every dime of his savings.

Connor's voice stayed calm. "Do you know how many of those tents you'd have to sell to pay for this?"

"About twenty thousand, I figure, if all the profit went to pay for the equipment."

"That's a lot."

"Yeah, but we got orders for close to a hundred and my niece says we ain't really tapped the foreign markets yet."

"A hundred sold won't make a dent in what you owe."

Joe laughed. "Not a hundred tents, a hundred thousand are already ordered. My niece says her family's been living on pizza delivery for three days while she's trying to keep up with the orders. She put four of her kids to work and I told her that would come out of her ten percent." When Connor just stood staring, the old man added, "Maybe you should think about charging me rent, Connor?"

27

Three days after Joe's big news broke, Sunnie walked through the front door and heard the old guy telling Gram one of his wild days' stories. Running a million-dollar Toe Tent business might be important, but so were his daily visits with Gram.

They'd both grown up in Laurel Springs, but he'd left for college, then the army. Even after he came back, he spent most of his weekends for a few years following the rodeo circuit. Then, one day, he claimed middle age hit him and he finally settled down to teach. By then Gram and Benjamin were married and had a son almost grown.

"I was riding broncs one summer in Utah. Man, it seemed a mile to the ground when he bucked. I remember counting the seconds off in promises. If I lived through that ride, I swore off smokes, hard liquor and women."

Sunnie heard Gram laugh. "How'd you do on that promise, Joe?"

"Two out of three ain't bad."

They both laughed. Sunnie didn't want to think about which promise he didn't keep. She'd never seen Joe drink anything but coffee, and as far as she knew, he didn't smoke. That only left the promise she didn't even want to think about, much less picture.

Sunnie guessed Joe felt like folks around town had missed all the exciting parts of his life, so he never tired of telling them. He had college stories about going out and milking the ag boys' cows early just to mess with their research. He had army stories about being a paratrooper for one day. And he had rodeo stories about being crazy through his early thirties.

He'd taught school for over thirty years after he settled down, but most of his school stories weren't about him. They were about his students...his kids.

Stepping into their line of sight, Sunnie said louder than necessary, "Hi, Joe. How're the Toe Tents coming?"

"Fine. I've hired some good men this morning. Most I taught when they were in high school. They all know this kind of business won't last forever, but they'll make good money while it does. A few are talking about opening their own shops when the Tent business plays out. Your dad's saving the buildings he can and helping those not safe to tumble. He'll be ready when the men want to open their own businesses."

"My Connor always said those buildings were sleeping." Gram laughed. "Suddenly he doesn't have time to worry about me. He's working night and day. Which is fine with me. I don't need him hanging over me."

"Tell me about it," Sunnie added. "Good news is he's finally stopped calling me five times a day. Bad news is I had to chase him down to get my allowance."

Gram held her arms up for her daily hug. "I'm getting

stronger every day. Soon you won't have to rush home to take care of me. I'll be back with the girls at the shop."

Joe puffed up a bit as if he were part of the cure. "You are doing better, Jeanie—just great, actually. Another month and I'll take you two-stepping. Remember when we used to dance in the sixties?"

"I remember. Benjamin was always too tall to be a good dancer, but he'd watch, laughing at us as we tried every dance that came along."

"Right." Sunnie fought down a giggle. Even if Gram's leg healed, Joe and she were still over eighty. She wouldn't be dancing again in this lifetime.

He slowly stood and leaned over to give Gram a kiss on the cheek. "See you later, Jeanie. I've work to get back to and you need time to help Button with her homework."

"Don't have any, Joe, it's Friday."

Gram patted Joe's arm. "You coming for dinner later?"

"Not tonight, but I'll be here tomorrow, same time. I got a meeting to go to. All of a sudden, folks want my advice, like it's not the same I've been giving them for years."

Sunnie watched him shuffle away. When he closed the front door behind him, she crawled up on Gram's bed to cuddle. No matter how old she got, Sunnie knew she'd always love being close. Gram smelled of lavender and starch.

"How was school?" Gram patted Sunnie's cheek, then wiped the bit of black mascara she'd encountered on the sheet.

"The same."

"Did you break up with that nice boy, Reese?"

"Nope. I thought about it, but he said he'd bring the fixings for tacos and the two of us could cook dinner for everyone tonight. So I decided to keep him around."

"I'm glad." Gram sounded sleepy.

"Yeah, he's all right, I guess." Sunnie had to admit it. Reese was growing on her. She liked the way he never took touching her for granted. Even if just holding her hand, he'd touch lightly first and pull back as though he was testing a stove to see if it would burn him before he committed.

Sunnie rested her head on Gram's shoulder. "But I don't know if I want a nice boy. I kind of want a wild one. Adventure. Excitement. Maybe I'm one of those girls who likes the bad boys."

Gram squeezed Sunnie's fingers. "Like that other boy who came by the shop that day. He was good-looking, but the *like* wore off of him pretty fast."

"Derrick? No, I promise I'm not going anywhere with him. I think all the adventure and excitement around him was probably in my dreams. He had the look, but nothing else going for him. Kind of like you want your neighbors to be quiet, but not a living-next-to-a-cemetery kind of quiet."

"I understand. Life is a hand-sewn quilt, Sunnie. Sometimes you got to think about whether you want someone to be a piece of fabric that fits into your life or not. As you sew the strips in, they become a part of what you do, how you think, how you end up. Good or bad, that's something you can never rip out and remake."

While Sunnie thought about what Gram said, she watched the old woman drift into sleep. Just before she completely relaxed, her great-grandmother said, "Tell Chloe to put her shoes by the fire if she wants them to get dry."

Sunnie put her arm around Gram's thin shoulders and held her close, knowing that she was slipping away a little more each day. Chloe, Gram's younger sister, had been dead for years. Gram's mind was time traveling again. With them one minute and in another world the next.

In the silence of the house, they both slept as they had years ago when Gram would keep Sunnie on afternoons when her mother was shopping. As she did all those years ago, Gram hummed in her sleep, as if her dreams came with their very own score.

A few hours later, Sunnie heard a tapping on the kitchen door and slipped from the hospital bed.

Gram slept on as she pulled the blanket over her shoulder and Sunnie noticed she was smiling. Maybe she was dancing in her sleep.

Tiptoeing to the door, Sunnie wasn't surprised to see Reese waiting, all six feet of him. She swore he was so skinny his folks must stretch him on a rack every night. He was so thin, even skinny jeans wouldn't look good on him.

"Shhhh. We were sleeping," she whispered as she let him in.

He nodded and thumped his way into the kitchen. After he set the groceries on the counter, he looked down at her, both eyes finally open. "Sunnie, you think we're ever gonna sleep together?"

She smiled, thinking of what Gram said about letting people be part of the fabric of your life's quilt. "I don't know. Maybe someday, if you want to?"

"No. Not yet. I don't think I want to get in that race right now, though my body argues with my brain most of the time. Way I see it, if you start early, you play out early.

I don't want to turn thirty and realize I've used up all my sex life. What would I do for the next forty or so years?"

"I don't think it works like that." She wondered if Reese got his sex education from bathroom walls. "What does your dad say?"

"He says to be careful. In some cases beauty is only a flip of the light switch away, and come dawn, ugly lasts all day long."

Sunnie had no idea what that meant. "You know, Reese, half the time I don't have a clue what you're talking about. But if we ever do sleep together, you have to wear pajamas."

"I don't wear pajamas now. Do you?"

"Of course. Everyone does, except the people at your house apparently."

"Why? Just seems like more laundry you'd have to do every week."

Sunnie didn't answer. How was it possible to always argue with him over nothing? "Never mind. I don't even know what we were talking about."

Reese started pulling ingredients out of the bags. "That makes two of us, but I do know how to make tacos. After we eat, I thought, since it's Friday night, I'd take you out driving around town. We could stop for a malt."

"In that junker truck of yours?"

"Yeah."

"You don't have a license, remember? I'm not going any-where with you."

"I could teach you to drive. You're old enough to get a license. Then you could drive me around."

"Not happening. I don't even want to think about tell-ing Dad we're in a car alone together."

He nodded, almost as if he hadn't expected any other answer. He just started chopping tomatoes, not looking at her.

She couldn't stand that she always seemed to be turning the guy down. If nothing else, he had "trying" going for him. "How about we watch a movie? I need to stay around here anyway. Dad might be working late tonight. If Joe has a meeting, my dad will probably be there. I don't think he's missed any town meeting for fifteen years."

Reese looked up without a smile. "So…we watch a movie in your room? With the door closed?"

"If we watch the movie in my room, it would have to be with the door open. I'd need to hear Gram or the nurse if they needed me."

He slowly smiled. "Any chance you'll start those kissing lessons? I've been patiently waiting for a while, you know."

"No, not tonight. We'll probably be downstairs tonight watching a movie with Gram and the night nurse. They already invited me to watch *Gone With the Wind*, and I really want to see it."

"That's a movie?"

"Of course it's a movie. How could you not know about *Gone With the Wind*?" She caught the hint of a smile and knew he was teasing her. "And we're catching every minute of it. We're even sitting through the intermission."

"Will there be popcorn?"

"Sure. The night nurse will insist on it. The last movie she popped a bag for each of us."

"Then I'm in. No long drive. No making out in the dark. No wild exploring. Just me and you and *Gone With the Wind*. And the night nurse. And your great-grandmother who keeps calling me Danny. And probably your dad who thinks we're really in deep conversation when he asks me a math question." He shrugged as if facing reality. "You've got more people watching a movie here than at the Paramount. But it will be dark. Sounds like heaven." He leaned over and kissed her cheek.

She slapped his shoulder, but he didn't stop smiling. "I'm growing on you, honey."

"Don't bet on it. I'm thinking of breaking up with you if these tacos don't turn out great." He didn't look worried, and she realized that Reese might not be so bad to have around. He put up with her wild moods and seemed to like being tortured. The perfect guy for her.

Her cell rang, and she moved to the hallway to answer. It was Dad telling her he'd be late, but to call him if she needed anything.

"I'm fine," she answered. "I'll make sure Gram eats, and Reese is here to help with the dishes. The night nurse should be here at eight to get Gram ready for bed, then Reese is going to stay and watch a movie."

When she hung up, she realized her father had not mentioned the meeting everyone in town was talking about. The old district was coming alive. She had no idea how involved her father was in the planning stage and didn't intend on asking.

It didn't really matter anyway. Her father never did anything interesting. No one over twenty ever did.

28

Connor walked through his dark office, realizing he hadn't spent any time on this side of town for days. Between Joe setting up equipment and building inspectors telling him all that needed to be done on the warehouses to get them functional, he'd been too busy to write his online paper or spend a few hours writing his stories for weeks.

He tried not to be disappointed that no one in town had mentioned the absence of the online paper. He had to admit he loved all that was going on in the district. It might just be baby steps, but Connor felt like his town was learning to walk, growing, coming alive.

Yet, with all the excitement, when he tumbled into bed every night after midnight, he still couldn't sleep for thinking of Jillian. They'd had lunch every day, talking about the quilts and the happenings in the district and Gram's recovery and Joe's success.

They'd eaten at almost every place in town, and she didn't seem to mind that he put his arm around her waist when they walked out. They were a couple, something he hadn't been a part of in years, and he didn't care if everyone knew it.

Connor and Jillian talked about everything but them. Both ignored the future, as if by doing so, it might never come.

He loved talking other things over with her. Planning what they needed to do next. Dreaming about what the district might look like in a year and how the new factories and stores might bring in enough money to improve the town, and the schools, and the library.

But neither of them ever brought up the question of what would be next with them, or even if there could ever be a *them*.

He wanted to run away with her. Live out of suitcases. Go where the wind blew them. See the world with her.

He didn't want to think of what the days would be like without her. How dark his world would be once she was gone.

But with each passing day, there was less time. The county museum was clearing space for the quilt display. When it was finished, she'd be driving out of his life.

He couldn't hold her back. She'd never lied to him. From the beginning, she'd said she'd leave. She'd told him how she followed her father's logs, hoping to find pieces of him, or at least a reason why her mother disappeared and he never settled down.

The fire chief, Bob Stevenson, still called her Little Lady, and she'd started calling him Big Chief. They had spent an hour one morning talking about the rodeo thirty years ago. Bob had been a bit younger than her father but he'd never missed a Pioneer Days Rodeo in his life.

The chief had been a volunteer fireman the night her father had been hurt. He described every detail he could remember about wrapping the wound. How it looked. How her father never cried out or said a cussword. He just stood there taking the pain, turning it inward.

Jillian had asked questions, but Stevenson didn't remember any other people around or anything her father said. "We didn't have an ambulance then, so I'm guessing one of his buddies or maybe one of the rodeo organizers took him somewhere to get sewn up. I never saw him after that night, but I remember being surprised when one of the oil field workers told me James had gone back to work that following Monday."

She'd thanked him, then Connor, for helping her find this one thread that linked to her father, but Connor had the feeling it wasn't enough for her to stay longer.

Reality finally rolled over him like a boulder. He could not leave Laurel Springs. No matter how much his heart wanted to. If Jillian left, she'd leave without him.

So they played a game. Not talking of the ending. Acting like nothing was about to change.

He lived for the good-night kisses when, if only for a moment, she was his and the world stood still.

As he walked across the street, he looked up and saw her staring out at him from the shop's window. For a moment, before she realized he saw her, he read the heartbreak in her face and knew it was time for the pretending to end. They needed to talk.

He forced a smile and stepped into the shop. "Did you have a good morning?" he asked, almost managing to pull off cheeriness.

She moved out from behind the counter. Both were very much aware that the quilters were in the back, probably listening. "I finished a few more of the quilt stories and talked to the county museum. The curator told me I could start moving them over anytime I was ready. I thought I'd do a few at a time. Setting each one up before bringing more in."

Connor took a deep breath. "Wait until Gram says she's ready. I promised I'd bring her in for a few hours next week. If you show her what you've done, she'll see how grand this display is going to be."

Jillian nodded her understanding. It was Gram's decision.

He lowered his voice. "I just stopped by to say I can't go to lunch today. Meeting a crew across the creek. If trucks are going to be moving in over there, the roads should measure up."

Jillian's lip came out in a teasing pout. It took all his control not to pull her close and kiss her.

"How about dinner tonight?"

She laughed. "Let me guess? Your house. Two old people. Two teenagers."

"No. Just you and me. Joe told us to get lost for a while, that he was cooking tonight."

"Can he cook?"

"Who cares?" Connor laughed. "If not, they can eat one of the dozen frozen casseroles people have delivered. If Gram doesn't recover soon, I may have to buy another fridge. As for tonight, they'll manage while we're getting lost."

"I'd like that." Her fingers found his and she whispered, "I miss the feel of your hand."

He smiled down at her. "I miss the feel of you." He wasn't

a man who knew how to flirt, and she probably knew it. But he wasn't sure if she knew just how much he meant what he said.

A few minutes later, when he walked away from the shop, he knew he'd spend the day working his way back to her. There might be budget meetings and contracts to sign and people who wanted to talk to him, but at the end of the day, Jillian would be waiting.

It was almost seven by the time he made it back to Main. The closed sign was on the A Stitch in Time window, but the office lights were still on. Connor let himself in and moved silently through the shop.

He found Jillian at her laptop in the cluttered little office. "Evening," he said as he moved into her line of sight.

She smiled. "Evening."

He didn't miss the tear she brushed away. "You all right?"

"Yes. I was just reading over all the quilt stories. Happy ones, sad ones. They all weave together to showcase the life of a town."

He moved to her side. "I figured they would, but I never believed they'd be so rich. This is just a poor town in the middle of Texas. No famous people live here. Nothing ever happened that the world will remember Laurel Springs for."

"But the quilts tell a rich story."

He smiled and repeated, "'But the quilts tell a rich story.'" He took her hand. "Come with me. I've got one more story to tell you before it gets dark."

She followed him out of the store. For once silence rested between them. They had a few hours and neither seemed to want to waste a moment.

He drove outside of town until the buildings of Laurel

Springs disappeared. The sun was almost touching the horizon when he turned off onto a gravel road. The first hint of spring showed in wild sunflowers growing near the fence.

"See that line of trees?" He pointed to a windbreak that seemed to run a quarter mile. "My great-granddad planted them when he came here in 1900. Gram told me once that folks used to say he was wild as the West Texas wind. Sunnie must have inherited those genes."

Connor pulled up to a house built low to the earth with a wide porch running its length. "The first Larady built this house. My grandpa and gram lived here after he died. My father and mother were living here when I was born, then moved to town to run the paper."

He parked the car in front of the place and they climbed out. A windmill behind the house clanked a steady beat as the last bit of sun flickered off the blades.

"My great-grandmother planted those roses in 1904 and they still climb the east side of the house to the roof every year."

Jillian moved close. "What are you trying to tell me, Connor?"

He closed his eyes for a moment, knowing he was taking as big a gamble as his great-grandfather ever had. "I know you're a drifter, Jillian James. I know you travel light and have all your life. But I've got roots. Deep roots. I have to stay were my family has been planted."

He looked into her stormy-day eyes and knew the answer before he could even get out the question he'd come here to ask. She didn't need to say anything. He didn't need to ask her to stay. He knew she wouldn't, couldn't.

"I understand," she finally said.

Then she came to him as she had so many times before, easily into his arms as if she belonged there, even though they both knew she never would.

Neither said much as they watched the last light of day melt into the earth. The land, the air, even the sky was silent tonight. The whole world was waiting, holding its breath, waiting for an answer that would never come.

He drove her back to the bed-and-breakfast.

She didn't mention dinner and he didn't think about it until he'd already parked at the side door where his car was camouflaged by honeysuckle bushes that were now showing bits of green while still prickly with winter.

He told himself he'd kiss her one more time, and then somehow, he'd find the strength to walk away. Tomorrow they'd go back to being friends.

It was good plan, the only logical answer, until she whispered, "Come up with me."

Without a word, he took her hand and led her upstairs to her tiny third-floor room in a big empty house.

In the silence, he made love to her. For the first time. For the last time. Forever.

29

As the night aged, Jillian didn't move or fall asleep. She was wrapped in Connor's arms. She was safe and warm. For the first time in her life, she felt loved. But she couldn't stop the tears from silently falling onto her pillow.

All the times she'd been with a man drifted through her thoughts. Her senior year of high school, an awkward encounter in a car. Her freshman year in college when she'd had too much to drink. Then, she'd been twenty-five and didn't want to spend the Christmas holidays alone. A year later, when she'd thought she might be falling in love, only to find out he loved his wife more. One hurried affair in the office. One night when she went home with a total stranger and he passed out before he even tried to remove her clothes.

Not much of a love life, she thought.

Until tonight. For once someone had truly made love to her. So much more than sex. So much more frightening. She wouldn't walk away this time without leaving her heart behind. He'd made love with a passion that surprised her, but it was the way he held her after passion stilled that made Connor perfect.

He moved in his sleep, instinctively brushing her arm as if making sure she was still close.

"I'm here," she whispered.

He rubbed his scratchy chin against her shoulder. "I should go. If Mrs. Kelly finds me here she'll charge me for the night."

Jillian giggled. "Yeah, but she'll cook you breakfast while she speed-dials all her friends."

"I couldn't care less. I'm guessing half the town already knows how much you mean to me. I've never been any good at hiding anything from anyone. No sense in starting now."

Somewhere below, in the silent house, a door opened and closed. Connor sat up. "I thought Mrs. K was out of town again."

"She was."

Footsteps started up the stairs.

"Did you lock your door?" Connor asked, leaning low against her ear.

"I think so. I had other things on my mind." She laughed softly. "And your hands on my body, if I remember right."

His fingers slid over her hip. "I remember that."

They waited silently for another sound.

The steps stopped on the second-floor landing. Laughter rumbled through the stairwell, then one of the second-floor bedroom doors opened. One man's laughter, and one woman's, sounding very much like the short, chubby Mrs. Kelly.

"We're not alone." Connor leaned over her, suddenly more interested in tasting her throat than the fact intruders were one floor below. "It appears Mrs. K has a guest," he murmured, as his mouth moved down her throat. "Maybe we should be very quiet and try to do something to take our minds off the intruders."

"But that's not her room." Jillian understood he'd pressed close so they could talk, but she quickly became fully aware neither of them had any clothes on.

That unmistakable full laugh of Mrs. Kelly's came again, finally pulling Connor away from his exploring mission.

His low voice brushed Jillian's ear. "Maybe they're just trying out the room."

Jillian nodded and listened. It sounded like someone jumping on the bed below her room. She couldn't make out any words, but two people were talking or moaning, definitely laughing.

Connor kissed her lightly, distracted once more from what was going on twelve feet below. His hand slowly moved along her back from neck to hip as if learning every curve.

She sighed. "There is something to be said for a man with a slow hand," she whispered, then cried out with joy as he began kissing his way down the same path.

They settled back into the nearness of each other, both forgetting anything happening outside her tiny room.

Finally, Jillian heard the door below open and two sets of footsteps hushed down the stairs.

One word was loud enough to understand. "Pancakes."

Connor pulled away with a groan and stood. He began putting on his clothes.

"What are you doing?" she whispered.

"If Mrs. Kelly is making pancakes, I'm joining them."

Jillian grabbed the sheet when she realized she'd stood without thinking about where her clothes were. "You're kidding."

"No. We slip out the side door, come in through the front and act like we've just stumbled upon them."

Jillian giggled. "It won't work."

"Bet you dinner it will." He buttoned his shirt.

"Wait a minute. You already owe me dinner. We had a date tonight, remember? Just me and you alone. Dinner." She grabbed a sweatshirt from her desk chair. "We forgot dinner."

"That's probably why I'm willing to risk it all for pancakes." He pulled on his boots without bothering with the socks. In the milky glow from the streetlight, she saw him smile. "At least I got the *just me and you alone* right for a while."

She slipped into her jeans and tennis shoes.

"Ready, Sundance?" He took a step toward the door.

"Ready, Butch."

Connor took her hand in his, pausing just a moment to smile at her, before he pulled her out the unlocked door. In that one glance she saw how young he was. Not the mayor, the head of the family, the father, the one everyone turned to, but just Connor, the dreamer, the adventurer, the lover.

Two minutes later, the two outlaws looked quite proper as they walked through the foyer, crossed the parlor and stepped into the kitchen.

Mrs. Kelly's cheeks turned apple red, but the ghost sitting comfortably at the counter, who must have been haunting her house for years, just smiled. She introduced Mr. Murry as a fellow bed-and-breakfast owner from Dallas and said they were checking out each other's establishments for ideas.

Jillian noticed they were both dressed, except for shoes, but Mrs. Kelly's apron read *I break for wine, ice cream, and green-eyed men.*

The man in her kitchen had green eyes that seemed to twinkle with laughter.

When the two men shook hands, Jillian caught Mr. Murry winking at Connor and to her shock, Connor winked back. They didn't say a word but she swore she could read their minds. Both were thinking, *let the women play their roles, but we both know what's going on here.*

So Jillian acted out her part, asking Mr. Murry all about his B an B and Mrs. Kelly invited them to join Mr. Murry in a taste test of her famous pancakes. No one seemed to notice that the tasting could have waited until morning. No one asked why the mayor was there so late, or why Mr. Murry was visiting so early.

An hour later, when Jillian and Connor walked out on the porch, they hugged as they fought down laughter.

"You know what's going on between those two?" She giggled. "They're having a wild time and the affair comes with pancakes. From the sounds coming from below my room, they must have been trying out the beds."

"I know, but I don't care what they do." He kissed her lightly. "I had a wonderful night with you. Best of my life."

"Me, too," she added, and kissed him again. "We'd better get some sleep. I'm guessing you'll have a full day tomorrow."

"I will. I'm thinking of hiring someone just to take calls

in my office." He didn't let her go. "But I'd give up sleep forever for more time with you."

She felt the same. What they'd shared wasn't some fairy tale from a movie. It was real. Something they could build on if she'd stay. A perfect night they'd both remember the rest of their lives if she left.

"I'll see you soon. We're due at the museum at nine. By the time I get ready, it will be almost time." The kiss she gave him was gentle, a promise of others to come.

Finally, he straightened, his arms still refusing to let her go. He looked down at her and she saw sorrow cross his face for a moment before he hid his feelings. "Stay, Jillian. Stay forever." He'd said his thoughts aloud.

She gulped for air as though she'd been slammed too quickly into reality. "I can't. Please don't ask me again. It will only make it harder when the time comes to leave."

He kissed her forehead and stepped away. She knew his heart was breaking, but he was fighting so hard to make it easier for her. What kind of man does that?

Deep down she knew the answer.

The kind of man who loves without boundaries.

30

Jillian worked the next week finishing up the photos and facts about two more quilts. Only a few remained before her job would be finished. She hadn't seen Connor or Gram except at hurried dinners with usually half a dozen guests.

The town was changing, growing and everyone wanted just an hour or two of Connor's time.

The store had been busy, too. Half the new supplies had already flown off the shelves. She wasn't sure if there was a renewed interest in quilting, or people just wanted to stop by to talk.

Sunnie popped in and out every afternoon to see if she needed help, disappearing as soon as Jillian said no.

Once, she'd told Jillian that lights were going up all over the district. Apparently, everyone in town had driven to the other side. "They got a traffic jam over there." Sunnie laughed. "Our first ever."

As the weekend neared, Jillian turned down Saturday dinner and Sunday lunch at the Laradys' home. If weekends lasted twice as long, she still knew she'd barely finish with the quilts. She had to hurry. It was time to move on.

Connor called every morning and said that he didn't have time to walk over for coffee. He said Gram was having a hard time remembering where she'd put things, but her leg was healing. He realized she wanted to go back to where all her things surrounded her. She also needed to come back to the shop before all the quilts were moved to the museum.

Jillian asked for a few days to get everything organized and turned down his offer for dinner. She feared that if she joined the little family, it would only be one more distraction for Gram, and if Connor left his gram, the dear lady might be upset. Plus Jillian needed time and distance from Connor. She had to get ready to leave; only this time, like it or not, memories would be packed with her.

As the weekend ended Sunday night in the quiet shop, she almost wished she'd said yes to at least one of Connor's invitations. She wanted to see Gram and Sunnie and Reese. She ached to be near Connor. Just a few more times.

The work, Gram's illness, and the excitement in the town all seemed to be smothering the little time she had left to be with him. But maybe love doesn't always come as a whole cake—sometimes it only comes as a bite.

Her grade school picture floated through her thoughts. When her father had taken the picture from its hiding place in the library, maybe all he wanted as a taste of the memories of her. He was a man who settled for thin slices of life. If she continued to travel, would she whither until she'd be just like him?

It occurred to her that Connor might need a little space away from her to prepare for what would come. All day Saturday, every time she'd seen him out the window on

Main, he was walking with a group and seemed deep in discussion. Now it was Sunday, and the lights were up in the district. Maybe he was resting.

Jillian remembered she'd seen Reese right beside Connor several times, carrying tubes of what might be blueprints. The kid couldn't have looked happier if he'd been waiting for a ride at Disneyland.

Only today, there was no movement across the street. No movement anywhere. As dark clouds rolled in, Jillian felt like she was totally alone in the world. Strange how a town could be so alive one day and so dead the next.

Mrs. Kelly called midafternoon to tell Jillian she'd put on a stew. "Be sure and get back here before the rain moves in."

"I will," Jillian promised as she hung up and started photographing her last project: Gram's beautiful, crazy, busy quilt.

She spread it out carefully, as if she were handling a great treasure. The colors were rich and twirled in designs that made no sense when she studied each section, but when she stood on the ladder to get the shot, she saw the beauty of patterns on patterns swirling. Names, dates, and events seemed sewn into the stitches between the pieces. The earliest date was 1934, Gram's birthday, stitched in pink on sky blue cotton. The fabric intersected another date the same year, and another color ribboned the first. Benjamin's birthday in a darker blue, Jillian guessed. Then came the wedding date, layered in lavenders and pearl grays. Like a vine, the dates of Gram's life wove across the quilt.

Other colors, more names crossed the vine. Some births, some deaths.

Jillian couldn't stop studying the history of the town

written in stitches. Embroidered in flower bouquets and black shadows draped over headstones. Pink roses of births, black ivy for deaths. Fourth of July fireworks and Christmas trees. The stitching was so fine no one would notice all the details if they only glanced at the quilt.

Two lines shot off of the main vine. Gram's two sons, maybe. One line was short and ended in black ivy. The other, longer line intercepted a second line with roses. One gray line drifted near Gram's at times, never touching, but traveling the same path. There was no ivy at the end of either line, which told Jillian that Gram and whoever shadowed her were still alive.

Jillian had a feeling she'd never see another quilt like this one. It must have taken hundreds of hours to construct.

Jillian jumped when she heard a tapping on the glass door. She'd been so absorbed in the quilt, she hadn't noticed the time.

When she unlocked the shop, she was surprised to see Connor. He looked even taller than usual in his Stetson and boots. A man comfortable in his clothes, she thought, whether it be cowboy or businessman.

He only stepped over the threshold and stopped, hat in his hand. "I thought I'd give you a ride home. Storm is coming in. I had to drive past here to check that everything was locked down across the creek."

"Thanks," was all she could manage to say.

While she went to get her things, he moved to the cutting table where the quilt was spread out. "I've seen this quilt from time to time. Never realized how beautiful it was. Gram never put it on display."

"It's not finished," Jillian said as she pulled on her jacket.

As he always did, Connor opened her door, but he didn't put his arm around her in that easy, light way she'd become used to.

They'd be alone for only a few blocks. Maybe he didn't want to start something he couldn't finish.

He did drive slowly. For once, neither seemed to know how to start talking.

"How is Gram?" She finally broke the silence.

"She's moody. Restless. That's not like her. She couldn't remember if she'd eaten breakfast this morning. Swore she hadn't. So the nurse made her a bowl of oatmeal and after two bites Gram swore she was too full to eat another bite."

His voice was so low it blended with the wind's low howl. "She's slipping, Jillian. A little more each day. She wants her things around her and they are all at the Acres."

Silence fell again as they neared the bed-and-breakfast.

His tone became more conversational, like he needed to talk about something, anything else. "This little house, down from Mrs. Kelly's place, looks better somehow."

She turned to the cottage with the colorful pots on the porch. The one with the lady in a wheelchair who waved at her now and then. "I pick up one bag of trash on the way into work every morning. It only takes me a few minutes, but it's starting to make a difference."

"Why? Do you know the old lady who lives there? I've heard she turns away anyone who tries to be friendly."

"I didn't talk to her. I didn't ask. I just did it because it needed to be done."

He pulled in front of the B and B and looked at her then, really looked at her.

"You want to come in? Mrs. Kelly made a stew tonight. I'm sure she wouldn't mind you joining us."

"No. I need to get back. Gram had a rough day. She's ready to be over her broken leg. Thinks she's spent enough time taking it easy."

He put the car in Park but simply stared out at the empty street. "I just wanted to make sure you were safe." He took a deep breath. "I also wanted to say something and I don't want you to comment. It's just something I've got to get out before I explode." He stared ahead, still not looking at her. "I'm in love with you, Jillian, and whether you stay or go won't change that fact, not ever."

She fought back tears as thunder rattled over the sky. A storm was coming across the land and in her life. She could feel both rolling in.

Connor stepped from the car and pulled her into the wind. With his arm around her, protecting her, they ran for the porch as the rain started. It pounded hard and fast in huge drops as though nature was suddenly furious.

They took the steps at a run and instantly were out of the downpour. He held her close until her breathing slowed. "It's going to be all right, Jillian. It's only a storm. You'll survive. I'll survive."

She couldn't answer. They both knew he was talking about far more than the storm.

A moment later she was in Mrs. Kelly's kitchen, cuddled in an afghan.

While Mrs. Kelly fussed over her, Connor disappeared back into the storm without saying another word.

He'd said what he came to say. He'd seen her safely home.

The rest was up to her.

31

Sunnie decided her whole family had been taken over by aliens. Her dad, who always carried a book and quoted dead people, was now working like he really had a job. Gram was upset that she couldn't go back to work, and Reese barely had time to speak to her because he seemed to be addicted to work like it was a drug.

"Dad, pay attention," Sunnie yelled across the tiny kitchen table. "Reese is MY boyfriend. Get it? He is not your assistant. He's mine."

"Got it," he answered without looking away from the papers now spread out next to his cereal bowl.

"You're not listening to me. Reese is ignoring me. I might as well be invisible. Maybe I'll move to the Rockies and join a cult."

"Fine," her father answered. "Let me know if you need money."

Sunnie stormed out of the house. Why couldn't Dad be overprotective like everyone else's father? At least they'd have to face each other to argue. She wasn't sure her dad had looked at her in days. He'd made no comment that her hair was back to being light blond.

Even Gram was acting strange. Every day that passed, more people came over to the house to sit with her, but she talked less and less. The bars in town were probably quieter than the dining room with a dozen ladies having afternoon tea, but Gram barely noticed. Even Joe had disappeared, though he did call hourly as if he didn't want Gram to miss something happening in his new Toe Tent business.

Looking toward the street, Sunnie noticed Reese as he pulled up in his old pickup full of tools and junk and rolled out of the seat at a run, as always.

Sunnie met him at the kitchen door. "I haven't seen you all week."

He smiled and she realized his face had almost healed. "Sorry, Button. I've been busy."

Sunnie blocked his path. "Don't you dare call me Button. Joe's called me that since I was born and I've hated it."

He grinned. "I kind of like it. The nickname is so not you." He tried to step around her. "Can we argue about this later? Joe wanted me to bring these blueprints to your dad as soon as possible."

"I'm not invisible, Reese. I will not be ignored."

He lifted the tubes and added, "Five minutes, then we'll talk, I promise."

"Sure." She gave up. "If I'm still around. I don't plan to wait for your next available appointment."

He nodded and ran inside, probably knowing she'd change her mind if he blinked.

Ten minutes later, he found her on the back porch, pouting. She'd told herself she didn't care if he took time out of his busy schedule to talk to her or not. She didn't have time to be down the list of people he cared about.

But he didn't start explaining or apologizing; he simply walked up behind her and waited for the explosion.

When she felt his hand brush her hair, she turned toward him, nose to nose, just in case he didn't pay attention. "Look, Reese, if you're going to be my boyfriend you got to..."

He smiled and straightened. "So I'm still your boyfriend? After not seeing you since Thursday, I wasn't sure."

"Of course you are. Where have you been at lunch?"

"Doing homework mostly. I've been working in the district most nights this week."

"But you're my boyfriend. You're supposed to be around now and then."

"Then kiss me, Sunnie. Kiss me like you mean it."

She opened her mouth to argue, but gave up. She kissed him hard, right on the mouth.

"Again," he said. "This time really kiss me. Not so hard."

She kissed him again. Longer, softer.

His hand rested on her waist and the kiss continued. Reese wasn't a good or bad kisser, but he was learning. In fact, by the time she finally leaned into him, he wasn't bad.

When he eventually pulled away, she asked, "Why'd you want to do that?"

"Because if I'm your boyfriend, I'm your boyfriend for real. Not because you're using me to get rid of Derrick or just think it might be interesting, or want to bug your dad. Understand?"

"All right," she answered. In truth Derrick had fallen out

of her thoughts a long time ago, and she could be dating King Kong and her dad probably wouldn't notice.

"And if you're my girlfriend that means we kiss now and then."

"All right." After a little practice, she decided the idea wasn't half-bad.

He smiled. "And you don't have to tell Brianna Baxter I'm a good kisser. She doesn't need to know."

"Why not?"

"Because I don't plan on ever kissing her. I've got the girlfriend I want right here."

Sunnie smiled. Darn if he wasn't cute. "You could still use some practice. Don't go thinking you're any good at it yet."

He jumped off the porch and headed for the corner of the house. "I'll be back later, Button."

Then he was gone before she could cuss him out for calling her that again.

"Hell," she mumbled. "My name doesn't fit me—why should my nickname?"

32

One week from the day he'd told Jillian he loved her, Connor brought Gram to the shop. He wanted his grandmother to see the place one more time in its glory, just like it had looked for all his life. Tomorrow the last of the quilts would be moved to the museum.

But today, all the colorful quilts were still on the walls. The Singer Featherweight machines lining up as if waiting to be called in to duty. The dark mahogany counter waited, solid and warm.

Jillian had finished all the logging, all the photos, all the stories. Tomorrow, they'd be in a new home, but he wanted Gram to take it all in one last time. Jillian would shoot pictures: of the shop, of Gram, of the people who visited this last day so no one would forget A Stitch in Time.

It was early, only a little after seven, but Connor planned to get Gram all in and settled before anyone arrived. Her crutches were behind her chair so she could use them if she had to go to the restroom. Her sewing basket was within reach. Jillian made her favorite tea and put it in a special cup that fit in a holder attached to her wheelchair.

Joe Dunaway followed them in with two bags of donut holes. Sunnie and Reese stopped in to wish her a great day on their way to school.

Gram was beaming, happy to start the day. She even rolled a few feet to one of the supply racks and refilled a spot. Connor kissed her cheek and reminded her he'd be just across the street.

The hours passed as one long party. Everyone in town seemed to know this was the last day the shop would be open, and then next week they'd have the opening of Gram's exhibit and she'd be the guest of honor.

Jillian would be working with the curator to get everything right.

While Connor moved to the door, his gaze scanned the shop for one more glance at Jillian. She hadn't really spoken to him about anything but the store or Gram since the stormy night he'd told her he loved her.

All week the evenings had been clear, warming into spring, but for Connor, twilight each day was the time he dreaded. He knew he couldn't sleep. He couldn't think. All he saw was the expanse of forever without Jillian. Every time he tried to block out the nightmares, stormy eyes were crying in his dreams. Beautiful, almost-blue, almost-gray eyes.

How could he let her walk away when he knew she'd have those dark times when storms came and there would be no one to hold her? When she left, she'd be alone, all alone.

"You want a cup of coffee for the road? I made a pot for Joe," she asked, as if they were little more than strangers.

"No," he managed to say, just as politely. "I'm headed

over to the office to try to get a little work done. There are a few meetings scattered throughout my day. Mostly people wanting to rent one of the warehouses. But, Jillian, call me if you need me."

She nodded, but didn't meet his gaze. He stepped out the door and made himself walk away. There was nothing more to say between them.

He spent the morning working, but his mind was still across the street. He called a few times, and Joe told him to stop worrying. He called back half an hour later to see if Gram was ready to go home, but he could hear her saying no even though Joe was holding the phone.

Today, they'd all agreed, she would stay as long as she wanted to. The last day.

At lunch, Connor had chicken salad sandwiches brought over on a tray for all the ladies who were sitting around, not quilting today, but telling stories of all the great times they'd had in the shop.

Midafternoon, Joe called Connor, saying he needed help with a mission that had to be done today.

Connor walked across the street and asked Gram three times if she'd be all right until he or Joe got back.

She shooed him away. "I'll be fine. Jillian is doing all the work. I'm just relaxing. Besides, the girls at the Acres are planning a big dinner for me. When we leave here, I want to go back there. It's time. I miss seeing them and I'd like to get out of your dining room and into my own bedroom. All my things are there. I swear you're wasting your life worrying about me."

"She'll be fine." Jillian touched his arm.

Connor's muscles tensed and she moved away. All he

wanted to do was pull her close, but this wasn't the time or the place. Part of him wanted to demand that they spend one more night together, but he knew if they did, he'd never be able to watch Jillian James drive out of his life.

Joe drew Jillian's attention before Connor could say too much. If they parted now, without another word, maybe she'd have mostly good memories. Maybe he wouldn't make a fool of himself. Maybe, one day, she'd walk back into his life.

It could happen, he reassured himself. Even if he didn't know where to find her, she'd always know where he was.

Connor stepped out of the shop, telling Joe he'd be waiting in the truck.

He had to be alone. He had to start getting used to not seeing Jillian.

33

Jillian was thankful for Joe Dunaway. He seemed to know the right times to step close. Being near Connor and not touching him was hard on her. She wanted him so badly in every way. Somehow, Joe saw through their polite manners. He didn't say anything, but in little ways he offered comfort.

"Look at this, Jillian." Joe pointed to Gram's quilt, pulling her from the window where she'd been staring across the street for several minutes. "See this light gray line that follows along beside Jeanie's lifeline?" He lifted a corner of Gram's quilt.

"I see it." She'd notice the line before.

"It's me. My lifeline is parallel to hers."

Jillian was amazed. Through growing up, marriage, and deaths, the one line moved with Gram's life. Side by side. Never touching. "You've always been there, haven't you, Joe?"

He nodded. "I hope I always will."

Gram patted his wrinkled hand. "We used to dance in the sixties."

"That we did, Jeanie. Remember how Benjamin used to laugh at us every time we'd try one of the new dances. He made fun of us for weeks when we learned the *twist*, but the *bump* made him laugh so hard I feared he'd have a stroke."

Jillian swore she saw a fog in Gram's eyes, but somehow Joe was still clear in her sight. When she focused on him, she came back. She was time traveling, just like Sunnie said Gram did sometimes.

Joe kept talking. Gram settled, smiling, as her fingers moved over her quilt.

"I better get going. Connor's waiting." Joe nodded at Jillian, silently asking her to watch over Gram.

He left with the last of the lunch crowd.

For the first time all day, it was quiet in the shop. Bits of dust danced in the sunshine slicing through the front windows. The sudden stillness seemed strange, like the pause between a dying man's breaths.

Jillian moved close to Gram, wondering if she felt it, too.

Gram smiled at her. "I remember Jefferson James," she said, as simply as if they were talking about the weather.

Her thin, withered finger pointed to an embroidered lasso on her quilt. "Jefferson James got hurt. The girl with him got blood all over her pretty white blouse."

Jillian knew Gram's memories were fragile now. She sat down carefully beside her as if the movement of the air might shatter her mind.

"You saw my mother? You knew my dad?"

Gram shook her head. "No, not him. I just thought his name was nice, but I heard folks talk about her."

Jillian knew she was walking on thin ice, but she had to ask. "What did folks say about her?"

Gram leaned back as her fingers pulled at a thread. "She was visiting relatives that summer on a farm not far from where we used to live. She was younger than Jefferson James, much younger. Folks said she made such a show when he was hurt that she must care a great deal about him. She couldn't stop crying that night at the rodeo after he got hurt." Gram spread her hand over the material laced so beautifully together. "She liked the attention, that one."

Jillian was afraid to breathe. Gram was time traveling back thirty years. If someone came in? If the phone rang? This thread of conversation would snap.

"What else did folks say?"

"Some said she got pregnant and gave the baby away, but no one knew for sure. After that summer, she kept to herself on the farm, and then sometime after Christmas she was gone. I remember someone saying Jefferson James just walked away from his job about the same time."

The baby, Jillian almost shouted. Me.

"Do you know why she left?" Jillian kept her words low. "Maybe she followed Jefferson?"

Gram was busy, hand pressing the tiny wrinkles across her quilt. "No."

"She might have." Jillian knew she was trying to rewrite a story...her story. "Why didn't she follow him?"

"Probably because she was already married. A neighbor told me her husband was off at med school up north somewhere. They said Jefferson was a drifter. Oil field trash. Some folks whispered that she would have divorced her husband and married Jefferson anyway, but her family made her see the light."

"Is she still alive? Did she ever come back to Laurel Springs?"

Gram shook her head. "No. Her relatives said she went to live with her husband and that wasn't Jefferson even if folks claimed they acted like they were married for a while."

"Do you remember where the husband lived? His name?"

"Someplace up north. She went by a funny first name. I don't recall her husband's name, if I ever knew it. The family she'd stayed with moved away soon after that."

Jillian wanted to run out of the shop. She needed to be alone. She needed to think. After all the years of wondering, of asking, or looking, she'd finally found a scrap of information. Her mother hadn't wanted her. Not enough to stay with Jefferson. But her dad kept the baby—her, Jillian. Her dad, who never said he loved her, had cared enough to keep her.

She couldn't run outside. She needed to be here with Gram. No one else was in the store. Connor and Joe had already left for some mission Joe seemed to think had to happen today.

"What did the girl look like?" she asked Gram.

"Who?"

"The woman who was with Jefferson James. The one with blood on her shirt."

Gram looked blank. "I'm sorry, dear, I don't remember what we were talking about. Is it time to go home? I want to go back to the Acres and watch a movie. My friends are waiting for me."

"It won't be long." Jillian answered as she fought back tears. The time traveling was over. Gram might never go back again.

An hour later when she asked a few of Gram's friends if they remembered the rodeo, they both shook their heads and Gram looked blank again. Her mind was traveling somewhere else.

Jillian tried to comfort her as the afternoon aged, but Gram was tired. She'd be polite and distant one moment and upset the next. The third time Jillian asked about the woman with blood on her shirt, Gram grew frustrated.

As the last hour passed Jillian wished she hadn't walked to work. She didn't have a car to take Gram home, even if she wanted to.

She tried calling Connor. No answer.

People came in, distracting Gram. For a while, everything would be fine. But as the sky grew cloudy, fewer people dropped by.

Jillian tried Sunnie's cell as soon as school was out. No answer. Connor's cell and office. No answer.

She watched as Gram withdrew. She moved her hands, as if washing them with invisible soap.

When she began to cry softly, Jillian knelt down in front of her chair. "It's all right, Gram. They'll be back soon. Do you want me to try to call Connor again?"

Gram shook her head.

"Do you want to go home?" Maybe she could call the Acres and they'd bring the bus.

"No," Gram whispered. "I can't remember." She spread her hands over the quilt. "I can't remember."

Jillian wanted to pull her in her arms and hold Gram tight until the fear passed, but she knew with the broken leg it would only hurt her.

"What can't you remember?"

Gram shook her head and whispered, "Everything. It's all leaking out of my head like sand does in an hourglass. All the memories are leaving."

She was shivering now and Jillian couldn't leave her side even to call someone. "It's going to be all right, Gram. You're fine. Connor will be back soon."

She wasn't listening. Tears worked their way past wrinkles down her face as she whispered, "I've lost them."

Jillian started shaking as she tried to think of some way to help this wonderful woman who was the heart of an entire town. Telling her it was going to be fine didn't seem to help. Gram appeared to be curling into the chair, shrinking before her eyes. She'd had a rich, full life collecting memories, and now they were slipping away.

And Gram knew it. The saddest part of all was that Gram knew.

Jillian felt panic climbing up her spine, but she had to keep calm. She had to help. She had to be there to help.

She glanced around the shop, hoping, praying for something that might help calm Gram's fears.

The beautiful quilt caught her eye. She picked it up and wrapped it around Gram like a huge tent, covering the chair and Gram from her shoulders down to the floor.

"Here are your memories," Jillian said as she forced a smile. "They've been right here all along. They'll never go away. They're all around you."

Gram stopped shaking as she patted the quilt. In a weak voice, she whispered, "I was born in thirty-six. The same year as my Benjamin."

"That's right. You lived on a farm right outside of town. Wild roses grew up to the roof in summer." Jillian could see Gram coming back. "Connor took me there. It was so quiet. The only sound was of the windmill ticking in the wind, almost like a clock."

Gram nodded. "I remember. That windmill kept me awake on windy nights."

As they talked, Gram slowly began to calm. She talked about opening the shop and how she loved it when Connor's parents worked at the paper just across the street. "They were always busy, so Connor would come over here after school. One day I wasn't paying attention to him, and he took apart one of my Featherweights. I never did get that machine to sew right after that."

Jillian laughed in relief.

When Connor and Joe finally came through the door, she and Gram were laughing about the time Stella thought she was in labor during the quilting bee. All the ladies were breathing with her through the contractions because she wanted to finish quilting before she headed to the hospital.

Jillian stood, giving Joe her chair beside Gram.

He took Gram's hand. "You ready to go, Jeanie? It's almost suppertime and your friends will be waiting for you."

"I'm ready, Joe."

He gave a Christmas morning smile. "I got a surprise for you. Connor and the kids helped me move into Autumn Acres this afternoon. I figure since I'm rich now, I can afford to have folks cook my meals and clean up after me. And the best part is I'll be able to keep watch over you."

Gram smiled. "Just like always."

He nodded. "Just like always."

Connor lifted Gram and carried her to Joe's pickup while Jillian folded up the wonderful memory quilt.

"Now don't you worry about missing your quilting, Jeanie," Joe said as he followed along. "I bought the apartment between yours and mine. We're knocking out a few walls and turning it into a crafts room and Reese and me figured out how to build a quilting frame that'll come down from the ceiling with the push of a button."

"I think I'd like that," Gram said as Connor tucked her quilt around her. "Only you don't have to worry about me, Joe Dunaway. I'll be watching over you. Now we're eating meals together—no more bags of donut holes for breakfast."

"Now, Jeanie. I'm too old to be a-changing."

Connor closed the door on their argument and turned to Jillian. "I saw the calls I missed. Everything all right?"

They stepped back into the shop as Joe drove away. "I know you have to go with…"

He followed her in. "I don't have to go anywhere. Sunnie and Reese are waiting for Gram. They've been with Joe and me for two hours getting him all settled in." He seemed to be trying to read what she wasn't saying. "The old guy didn't have much to move."

Connor stopped rambling and asked, "What is it? What's wrong, Jillian?"

She turned to him. "Would it be too much to ask you to hold me one last time?"

Jillian was in his arms before she could let out a breath.

34

Jillian stayed one last day to help put up the quilts. The curator claimed it was the finest exhibit they'd ever had in the county. Each quilt had its own story printed and framed beside it, and pictures of the shop lined the backdrop like wallpaper.

As people walked into the exhibit, they'd have the feeling they were stepping into the shop on Main.

Jillian stood back in the shadows, watching the opening begin. Everything was perfect and folks came dressed up for the special occasion.

She thought she saw a white-haired woman reach out to touch Helen Harmon's quilt. Maybe, just maybe, the old lady's hair had once been red and she'd made the quilt as a wedding present that was never given.

A man about the same age as the lady brushed her arm and they smiled at each other as if the worst day of Helen's life had turned out to be a blessing.

Two middle-aged women hugged in front of the cheerleader quilt, and Jillian wondered if they'd once been part of the squad. No one would probably know why the names disappeared.

Jillian guessed one of the cheerleaders did it. Or maybe each wandered into the shop over the years and simply pulled the thread that marked their name.

An entire family laughed and pointed at the going to Florida quilt, which showed a childhood memory of traveling across country every summer.

Sometimes five generations posed in front of one of the pioneer quilts and a little girl stood before the butterfly quilt in a dress made of material that looked just like one of the flour bag prints.

The quilts were blankets, heirlooms, memory keepers, and works of art. Connor had been right. They were also the story of the town.

Jillian circled the displays again and again as if saying farewell to the quilts. She saw Connor and Gram and Joe and Sunnie, but they were always surrounded by people.

All but Connor hugged her and said they wished her well on her journey. Several of the quilting ladies were being treated like stars, and gave impromptu lectures during the show on the art of quilting.

Reese finally found her in a corner and stood next to her. "Quite a show."

"It is." Jillian fought down a grin. The kid was tall, almost a man. In a few years he'd be a heartbreaker if Sunnie wasn't careful. "How are you and Sunnie getting on?"

"Fine. Trying to hold on to her is like grabbing a stripped live wire. I know I'm going to get burned, but it's a hell of a jolt."

Jillian laughed. "You thinking of backing away?"

"No. I'm full into this. I'd rather die shaking than live without feeling like I do when she's around."

Jillian envied the boy. She watched it all, knowing that she couldn't leave her memories behind this time. There were too many.

Connor treated her politely, almost like a stranger, but the memory of him holding her that last night in the shop would be with her forever. He hadn't said a word, but she'd read his heart with every beat.

He'd held to their agreement. He hadn't asked her to stay again. When she left the museum, he walked her to her car, opened her door as always, and said good-night as if it were just an ordinary night.

Not the last night she'd see him. Not her last night in town.

Jillian couldn't sleep when she got back to the bed-and-breakfast. For a while she simply stood at her window and looked out over the sleeping town. When she went back to bed, she didn't even bother closing her eyes.

She'd finally gotten up and packed at dawn. Her car was loaded by the time she sat down to her last breakfast with Mrs. Kelly.

The sweet owner must have been dreading this day, too. She had to have been up cooking since five. She made all her recipes.

They sat before the feast and both tried to make small talk, but it was choppy.

Finally, Jillian hugged the dear lady whose apron read *I'll fry if I want to.* "I'll miss you."

Mrs. K patted a tear away with the corner of her apron. "You'll stop by when you pass near here?"

"I will," Jillian lied.

They walked to the door, arm in arm. Jillian kissed the innkeeper's rosy cheek and stepped out of the house for the last time.

To her surprise two cars were blocking her in. Reese's old pickup and Connor's Audi.

She walked to the end of the porch. "What's going on?"

Connor climbed out of his car and walked toward her wearing hiking boots and a fishing jacket that had at least a dozen pockets. He looked like he'd ordered one of everything from the travel catalog. A compass even hung off his belt and a huge hunting knife was on his side.

Sunnie and Reese sat in the old pickup, windows down, looking like they thought they were at a drive-in movie.

Connor stopped in front of her and looked up at her three feet above him on the porch. "I figured if you won't stay with me, I'm going with you. I bought all these clothes and another bag full so I'll be ready for any climate."

"No, you're not going with me," she said calmly.

"Then I'll follow you. It's a free country. I can drive behind you."

"You can't do that. It's called stalking." Before her words were out, the only police car in town pulled up on the grass of the bed-and-breakfast's front yard. A few other cars parked at the curb.

Connor didn't seem to notice anyone but her. "I asked the sheriff. He didn't seem to think there was a problem. Even offered to lock us both up in the horse trailer so we could talk out our problem."

"He can't do that. It's illegal."

Connor said, "You could call the judge and a lawyer. I

talked to them, as well. The lawyer said the sheriff's got a right to hold us for a short time, and the judge said he'd marry us so we wouldn't be living in a horse trailer in sin."

She smiled. "You can't make me stay, Connor."

"You're right. I'm packed and going with you, because I've figured out something. I don't want to go through this life without you, Jillian James. I want you by my side. One way or the other, here in Laurel Springs or on the road, I'm with you."

"What about Sunnie?"

"I told Reese he could finish raising her. Kid's got a lot of sense. They'll be fine."

Jillian laughed. "You're crazy, Connor." This kind, even-tempered, logical man had lost his mind, and she knew she was the cause.

"I love you, Jillian. I think I have since the day you walked into my office. I want to be with you for the rest of my life. If I didn't know you loved me, too, I'd walk away, but you do love me."

"What makes you think that?"

"Because I'm the one memory you packed with you. I'm the one you'll never forget. I'm the one you run to when you're afraid or you need a hug. I'm the one and only man you've ever loved and you know it."

She stood her ground. "I don't want you loving me just because I need loving."

Connor smiled. "I don't. I love you because I need loving and you're the only one who can do the job."

Several more cars had pulled up by the time he finished his speech. A dozen cars and pickups were blocking her in both directions.

"You're right. I do love you." She wanted to add that he was the only one who ever needed her so badly he couldn't, wouldn't let her go. Why had she wasted time looking for the people who'd thrown her away when a man was standing right in front of her, ready to give up everything to keep her?

"But, Connor, you're not going with me. I'm staying right here. There are too many things I have to do here. The district's just getting started and we've got to rent Gram's shop, and you haven't put out a paper in weeks, and..." She stopped and smiled, knowing the list could go on the rest of their lives. "We don't have time to go traveling around the country."

He ran up the steps and folded her into his arms. "All right, I'll stay with you, but you've got to promise we take a month of vacation every year. I want to see the world before we check into the Acres and no matter what country we're in, I want you sleeping beside me every night."

She smiled. "You drive a hard bargain."

He kissed her while fifty onlookers cheered. One long kiss that promised a lifetime of loving.

As he pulled away to look at her, Jillian swore she could see her forever in his eyes.

Then, Mrs. Kelly invited everyone in for breakfast, just as she'd planned to do all along.

★ ★ ★ ★ ★

Questions for Discussion

1. Jillian finds the life of a nomad comforting. Why do you think this is? Is there anything that appeals to you about this lifestyle? Why or why not?

2. Why do you think Jillian's father takes her photo from the lockbox in the library?

3. Connor was never close with his first wife, Sunnie's mother. Do you think he regrets that?

4. Alzheimer's disease affects our memories. Eugenia Larady—Gram—lived a good life and was loved in Laurel Springs. How would you deal with someone who had treated you poorly, but couldn't remember doing so?

5. How does Jillian's arrival in Laurel Springs affect Connor's personality?

6. How do you decide what becomes part of your story?

Which memories are important to the fabric of your life, and why?

7. How do you think people—specifically, women—can benefit from intergenerational friendship, like the one that Jillian forges with Eugenia?

8. Does Sunnie grow and change as a character throughout the story? If so, how?

9. What if Jillian had decided to leave Laurel Springs after all? How would her decision have affected the Larady family?

10. How does quilting form a source of community for the older women of Laurel Springs?

11. Jillian's project is to log and archive A Stitch in Time's quilt collection for a local museum. Is quilting itself a form of archiving, of preserving collective history in tangible form? How?

A Conversation with Jodi Thomas

What inspired you to write a story about quilting? Are you a quilter, or was one of your family members a quilter? How has the tradition been passed down through generations?

My mother quilted all her life, as did her mother and her mother. I have a room in my house we call the quilt room where colorful quilts cover the walls. But I don't quilt. I remember being small and lying under the frame watching shadows above quilting around a square. But it wasn't the quilting that fascinated me—it was the stories the women told. Every quilt carries a story for me.

In my books I love putting together pieces of peoples' stories and showing how we all affect the lives of those around us. Due to the onset of Alzheimer's, my mother was only able to read my first few books. Even as her mind was slipping, she'd often quilt on a little round frame while I typed away on my books. One day she looked up from her work and said simply, "Jodi, I think you quilt with words."

Eugenia and her circle are kind of like Laurel Springs's unofficial historians. Do you think it's significant that quilting—traditionally considered "women's work"—forms a sort of alternative historical account?

Quilts, even those we don't know much about, tell a story. Tom, my husband, and I took a few family quilts to an historian speaking at the college one night. She told me things I didn't know about quilts that had been in my family for a hundred years—one was made with the pattern popular in the Civil War. One old family quilt, well-worn, was a flour-sack quilt and the stitches were different in places, telling us it had been a group project.

She looked at one quilt and commented that it was an example of how not all people had a sense of color. But all quilts tell a story. Pretty or worn, they show a history or love, and talent, and sometimes survival when times were hard.

Texas history is a big part of your work, and southwest Texas Hill Country, specifically, is the backdrop for *Mornings on Main*. What should the reader know about this part of Texas? What makes it unique?

Like many Texans, for my family the Hill Country of

Texas is a favorite spot to get away. It's a beautiful drive with small towns like Fredericksburg and New Braunfels. Wineries, flowers, honey and peaches. And, of course, rich in Texas history.

When I was writing *Mornings on Main*, I used Fredericksburg's wide street 'big enough to turn a wagon pulled by oxen around in.' In late spring we walked the back path to town along a stream, and the scenes in my story came alive.

Is there any part of the story—characters, town, buildings—that are inspired by people or places you've encountered in your life?

When you grow up in a small town you're very aware of how much the people around you shape your life. No matter how old I get, I'll still be Cliff and Sally's daughter.

I've always loved wandering the main streets in small towns. Stepping into the shops. Talking to the people. Sometimes all you have to say is "How are things going?" and an hour later you're still listening.

What do you most want readers to take away from reading this story?

I hope they'll think about how they store their memories. Whether in quilts or scrapbooking, a diary or pictures. Our lives are stored in pieces, in memories that shape our beliefs and actions.

I hope that readers will smile when they finish my story and maybe pull out a few of their favorite memories to enjoy.

You're best known for your Ransom Canyon series. How did you change your approach to write *Mornings on Main*? What was the most challenging thing about writing this novel?

I wanted to write a story that didn't just entertain but that encouraged the reader to think about her life, as well. I wanted to go deeper into the core of who my characters were and how it affected how they lived.

I asked a friend of mine, Robyn Carr, for advice. She answered, "Your stories always *turn out*, Jodi, rich in action and sense of place. This time, for *Mornings on Main, turn in*."

What advice do you have for aspiring writers?

Of course, write from your heart and write the story you would love to read. I've never followed a formula or tried to make a book fit into a line. The story has to fit the people in it.

For me every story begins with a walk. Watch "Walking the Land" at www.youtube.com/watch?v=sG4IeXueJDA.

I create the place and meet the characters, then the story takes off. Some nights I write later just to see what is going to happen next. ☺